BLIZZARD OF MONEY

BLIZZARD OF MONEY

Max Isaacman

Good Luck
Max Isaacman

CREATIVE ARTS BOOK COMPANY
Berkeley • California

Copyright ©2002 by Max Isaacman

No part of this book may be reproduced in any manner
without written permission from the publisher,
except in brief quotations used in article reviews.

For information contact:
Creative Arts Book Company
833 Bancroft Way
Berkeley, California 94710
1-800-848-7789
Fax: 1-510-848-4844
www.creativeartsbooks.com

Although some settings actually exist,
any similarity to persons
living or dead is purely coincidental.

ISBN 0-88739-468-x
Library of Congress Catalog Number 2002110710

Printed in the United States of America

To Joyce.

BLIZZARD OF MONEY

One

A taxi raced by, its lights glowing dimly through heavy, early morning fog. Nick crossed the street while lights above in the offices of the Bank of America building shined down. A cable car bell clanged loudly, the car barely visible.

He walked by the Pacific Union building, a square, stone structure at the top of Nob Hill. A man sat in the reading room in a thick leather chair, his face buried in a newspaper. Across from him, a man wearing glasses sipped coffee. Nick remembered when he had paid a few grand a month to sip coffee in that club. He recalled the plush carpeting under his feet and tables covered with thick, white linen tablecloths. That's all over, he thought, dropping his eyes from the window and stepping faster.

Walking on down California Street, he passed the Fairmont Hotel, a sand-colored building covering an entire block. Flags just under its roof snapped and swirled in the breeze. He nodded to the porter, dressed in a sharply creased, blue uniform and matching blue cap. The porter nodded back. He had parked cars at Nick's wedding party many years ago, when his house had been crammed with hundreds of people. Nick and Julie's picture had been in newspapers in San Francisco, New York, Buenos Aires, Madrid, Paris, and other places around the world.

Oh, come on, can't you forget that? he thought. Arriving at his office, he opened the glass door, which stuck, and flicked the light switch. He sat down behind a battered desk smelling of faintly rotted wood, and started flipping through cards with names of people. He stared at the phone, but instead of picking it up he looked out the window. *I just can't call*, he thought, watching sunlight flood into the room.

A man was outside of the door. The door stuck and the glass rattled as he opened it. The man was short, and his balding head reflected the overhead light as he walked in. He stood behind a chair facing Nick's desk, his lips tight. "Nick Larson?" he asked.

"That's me."

"May I sit down?" He gestured to the chair, which had Nick's suit coat draped over it.

"Sure." Nick removed his suit coat and laid it on his desk. It was black, Armani, and expensive, and worn at the sleeves. *I need a new suit*, he thought again. *Oh, the hell with it. I'm over fifty. What do I care about clothes? But I do care*, he thought.

"I'll bother you for just a moment," the man said. "This isn't very pleasant but... " The man coughed nervously and handed over some papers. The top paper was entitled *Rental Lease*. "You're two months behind in your rent. Three months and you vacate. All rather simple. You can find it on page three."

"Isn't there any—"

"Or be evicted." The man rose and started toward the door. "Sorry. You've been a good tenant, but rents are high and we can use the space." The man thrust himself out of the chair and left; the glass door rattled as it closed behind him.

Nick stood up. He looked at his ring finger. It was bare, and he still missed wearing the ring. *How long has it been*? he wondered. *About seven years already. Ah, whatever. Past is dead. The way it goes.*

Pulling his pants higher upon his bony hips, he went over and looked out of the window to the steel and glass buildings in the San Francisco financial district. The blue sparkling waters in the Bay could just barely be seen far off. In the distance was Fisherman's Wharf. Flocks of tourists, some pushing strollers or with babies strapped onto their backs, were wandering, smiling, slurping sodas and eating pizza; cheese stretched from the pizza as bites were taken. People strolled past art galleries, bins and bins of crabs, oysters, and fresh fish.

His office was spare: a desk with a couple computers and a small lamp atop it, an old chair covered in cracking leather behind the desk; a fax machine, a plant, a metal filing cabinet. There were two paintings hanging on the wall, both bearing the initials *nl*, having been painted by Nick: a gondola in the choppy, green waters of Venice; a man and woman dancing on a cobblestone street, the woman wearing a black dress.

What the hell do I do? he wondered. *Get a cell phone and operate out of my apartment? But if I can't pay the rent there, where do I go to work or sleep*? Rows of seedy hotels in the Tenderloin district, with homeless and crazy people roaming the streets at all hours, flashed through Nick's mind. *Me, in the Tenderloin? I just can't. I gotta find… anything.*

He thought for a while, decided he just couldn't call, then shrugged his shoulders. After flicking a switch on the computer, he watched as the screen faded to black. He left. Out in the hall the stale odor of the aged building was a powerful mixture of cigarette smoke and cleaning chemicals.

***

"Haven't seen you for a while. Thinkin' you run off again."

Nick laughed and got up into the chair. Dexter set his shoes just right in the stirrups. Its bell clanging, a cable car rolled by.

Through his wire-rimmed glasses, Dexter studied Nick's shoes, then went to work, the white rag a blur in his black hands. "They still all still talkin' about you, the brokers, traders, all of 'em. Remember Spain, when you went there? They all said, why Spain? Fool. He can't make no money there."

Nick smiled. "I remember, me and my wife, remember Julie? We got off the plane and the sun was bright all over Madrid. Yeah. Europe was booming and the market was taking off. Nobody saw it back then; but I did. The Madrid Stock Exchange, like shooting fish in a barrel. I bought stocks, they went up. I made a bunch of money, Julie and he were happy. We laughed a lot, drank Rioja, times were good."

He sighed. Blue lights on the front of a café across the street glowed through the dark night. Julie loved Madrid, he remembered. He imagined her short brown hair, how her inky-dark eyes brightened when she smiled. He looked for her walking by now while Dexter shined his shoes.

Dexter popped his rag, and thoughts of her vanished. "Man, you ready for the street."

The shine was five bucks, and in the old days Nick gave him a ten. Lately he'd been giving Dexter a five. *But damn it, I used to be somebody*, he thought. He peeled off a ten and started walking.

Another night on Broadway in North Beach in San Francisco. Music blaring out of bars and restaurants and onto the packed sidewalks, streets jammed with honking cars. Signs in bright red lights: Live Naked Women, Sex Acts, Private Rooms.

He stood on the corner waiting for the light to change, watching and thinking. He walked across the street, then stopped. *I could use a live naked woman about now. Walk away. Those places are no answer.*

But I don't want to go home. But I'll get into trouble again. Ah, the hell with it, with everything. Everything's fine, great, he decided. He walked back across the street and through a set of swinging doors. A woman in black lingerie approached, her breasts almost spilling out. He laid down a twenty and she stamped his hand: "Playroom."

Everything's great, this is fun, he thought. *No, it's not.*

The place was dark and smelled of beer and cigarette smoke. At the bar a crowd of mostly men stared with something resembling silent rage as a girl wearing a G-string danced onstage, her small breasts bouncing. The music stopped. "Let's hear it for the lovely Lila," boomed over the loudspeaker. After half-hearted clapping the crowd went back to their drinks. Lila picked up her things and left the stage. After awhile she reappeared and sat on a barstool, a few down from Nick.

He took a hit of Irish whiskey; it felt warm and good going down. He looked down to Lila, and started getting aroused. Their eyes met, and she smiled. *I can't believe I'm doing this*, he thought. *I never used to go into ratty places*.... He stopped thinking and walked over to Lila.

"Drink?"

"If you're buying," she said, laughing.

He waved to the bartender and ordered a couple of drinks. Lila's breasts almost spilled out of her barely-buttoned blouse. She smiled. He smiled back, then a building with a sign saying San Francisco General Hospital flashed, and inside, Julie lying in a small, black-framed bed with white sheets covering her, and a doctor...

Time passed. "Another?" the bartender asked him.

The image evaporated; the bar reappeared.

"No. No thanks."

"Well?" Lila asked. "Do you want to...?"

He picked his fingernail. "What? Where do we go?"

"Upstairs. It's private, don't worry."

"I don't..." Nick looked at her in confusion.

"Not to be rude, but, well, I got bills to pay. It's a hundred for half an hour, a hundred and fifty for an hour." Lila waited. "What do you want? Another girl? A guy?" She got up. "Yes or no?"

"I—I think I made a mistake. Sorry."

Walking out onto the street, he felt the chilly night wash over him. He shivered, and felt sweat running down his back. After walking a couple of blocks, he took out his cell phone. He pressed some numbers and waited.

"Hello," she said.

"Hi, it's me."

"Oh. How are you?"

"Okay, sort of," Nick said. "Is—can you talk?"

"Yes."

"I just... I don't know. Want to see you."

"Are you sure?" Linda asked.

"No. But I want to see you. I'm glad you're taking care of Thad. He's a good guy. I mean it."

"Yes. He is. Thanks, that's sweet."

He started walking. "I'll call. It's getting late. I better go home."

***

A flip of the switch lit up the apartment: a big room, tiny kitchen, closet, a bathroom. In the big room, an unmade bed, a few pillows; a desk and computer; a dark-oak, seventeenth-century English armoire with gold carvings; an early-American chest of drawers. Years ago the chest had cost forty-eight hundred dollars, and the armoire over ten thousand. "Choice pieces," they were the words the dealer had used, Nick thought, *Maybe I could get fifteen thousand for the chest.* He looked at a painting of waves crashing into the rocks off the coast in Marin County, near San Francisco. It had been painted by Richard Dieberkorn, a well-known Bay Area artist. *I'm sure I could get ten thousand for that. But I love that painting.* He picked his fingernail. *Also, if I sell, that money won't last long. What when that runs out?* Nick avoided looking to a corner where an easel with streaks of coagulated paint sat against the wall. The easel hadn't been used for years.

In the park across the street, the trees, blooming with leaves, glistened in the moonlight. The cold air felt good after he opened the window. He undressed and got into bed. The market opened at 6:30 in the morning, and he set the alarm for 5:00. *Something good'll happen tomorrow*, then he made himself stop thinking. Soon he was snoring.

Before long he saw her thin, long face and thick eyebrows. Not someone who would shock you with her good looks, but closer to attractive, with a perpetual smile close to laughing.

"It was too late anyhow." Julie's eyes were small black ink-spots of despair. She avoided looking at Nick, and said, "If I had gone in when the headaches started, so what? They could have done a CAT scan. But that wouldn't have picked it up, not that early."

No, it wouldn't, he agreed. And nobody seemed to be able to help. The doctor assured them the Dilantin would stop the seizures, but it didn't. Thought Tegratal would keep petit-mal seizures from becoming grand-mals, but it didn't. Then she couldn't keep food down.

"I have to go to the hospital. They'll take some tests, but they don't know how long…"

Nick turned over. He hurt, like everything was re-occurring.

"I'll take you," he had told his wife.

"Sure."

"We'll go early."

"Sure."

Nick turned over.

"Mr. Larson, would you come with me, please?" He followed the nurse, dressed all in white, down a long corridor to a small office. After a while a doctor joined them, wearing white and smelling of cigarette smoke.

FlapFlap. The doctor riffled through a pile of charts, found one, and mounted it on a viewer. He snapped a switch, and the X-ray of the skull glowed. "This kind of cancer we can't control after it spreads throughout the brain. By the time it was large enough for us to see, it was already…"

Snap. The switch was thrown, and the skull vanished. "You should expect the worst, and I wouldn't plan for more than a few weeks. Are, are you all right? Mr. Larson?"

Nick rolled over and opened his eyes. The numbers glowing from the alarm clock read 2:33. Another long night. He got lucky and fell back asleep.

He again smelled that odor of death coming from Julie, death stinking like a rotten egg.

"Here, I'll help you to the bathroom."

It was the last time he ever helped Julie with anything.

Later, she got out of the hospital bed and put on her slippers. Her smiling cat's face slippers looked so incongruous. Nick sort of dragged Julie to the bathroom, waited with her awhile. He cried a little and turned his face away so she wouldn't see his tears, salty and hot rolling down his cheeks. He got her back to bed, and she closed her eyes. That was it. Without a trace of drama, no suffering or lightening flashes, Julie simply closed her eyes and passed away. Nick stood there wanting to save her. *How helpless I am. There's nothing I can do. She stopped breathing, but what about me? Now where do I go? What about me?*

***

Down the street from Nick's office in the heart of the financial district, near Bush and Kearny, was the trading floor of the Pacific Stock Exchange, commonly known as the "P-coast."

From the squat, gray, granite building, lights from the second and third floor glowed out into the early morning darkness. It was 6:28, and the traders were getting ready for the market opening; they had been there since about 5:30. The trading floor was a small, compact area crammed with players. The pine for the floor had been cut in Texas, had been stripped and stained, bringing out its bright yellow color, and buffed to a glossy sheen. Computer screens surrounded the floor; numbers and stock symbols in green and red flashed quickly across the blue background; the shouting started with pre-opening bids and offers and volumes and stock names; people rushed about, leather-bound order pads in their hands, cell phones glued to their ears; traders were at their spots, ready; the market-makers, those who competed in over-the-counter stock trading, against the specialist and against each other, waited for all hell to break loose.

The black, spidery hands of the clock on the wall touched 6:30. Trading started, people yelling, orders written, executed orders ripped out of order books and thrown on the floor, sweat smell, a smile here and there, pencils scribbling.

Steffie rushed to the post where they traded Nugget Petroleum. She yelled at a trader, "Hey, Weasel, what's your picture on Nugget?" The Weasel bought and sold for his own account or matched orders with other floor brokers or competed with the specialist for trades.

The Weasel studied his order book. His jaw coned almost to a point at his chin, sort of like a weasel. "Ahh, I'm at nine and a quarter to a half, and a better seller. Take your pick: I'll buy thirty thousand shares at a quarter, or can sell you up to fifty thousand shares at a half."

Steffie, a short, small woman with rings of curly red hair spilling down to just above her blazing eyes, stood there staring at Weasel. In her early thirties, she was a floor broker, executing trades for Merrill Lynch, Paine Webber, and other big firms. On every trade she was paid five dollars, and usually managed to keep 1/32 or 1/16 for herself.

She also traded options. A market player could buy an option to purchase Nugget or other stocks at a stated price. The buyer paid for that option, the amount being called the premium.

There is tremendous leverage in trading options, which are known as puts and calls. Calls are options to purchase stock at a set price; puts are options to sell stock at a set price. The call buyer only deposits a small percentage of the value of the purchase. But there's a catch: options have an expiration date. If the stock doesn't move, the options won't either, and the option will expire. But if the stock does go up, the option will follow, and exponentially. A two point move in Nugget Petroleum, symbol NUP, for instance, could make the option move maybe six to eight points, depending on the expiration date. Steffie's customers traded big, in a thousand, five thousand, or ten thousand option lots. Also, traders could profit by putting a put. If the stock declined, the put buyer could put the stock to the put seller at the pre-set higher price.

The veins in Steffie's neck protruded as she looked up at Weasel and shouted, "Okay, done, I bought fifty thousand shares NUP at a half."

Both of them scribbled into their order books.

"Not that I care, but why're you buying this garbage?" Weasel asked.

Steffie moved closer to Weasel and whispered, "The buzz, but who the hell knows if it's true, who knows what's true anytime around this place, but Nugget may be coming out with some good news. Least that's what my buyers are thinking. Least that's what the brokers of my buyers are saying."

They watched numbers and symbols running across the computer screens.

"I don't care who's buying what," Steffie said. "I wanta make my score and get the hell outta here. Place drives me crazy."

"Yeah," Weasel said, his eyes following the numbers and symbols.

"No Prince Charming in here; that much I'm absolutely, totally sure of."

Weasel studied the screens.

"One day I'll hit it big; meantime I gotta find another trade." Steffie shifted her feet, looking like she was running even though she was standing still. "I wish I could think of someone to call, someone with money, real money. I remember—what was the name of that guy, you know, the guy who went to Spain and loaded up in stocks, and everybody thought was crazy, and was right and made a bundle?"

"Who? I don't—"

"It was Rick, Rick… no, Nick, Nick Larson," she said, her voice increasing by several decibels.

"Oh, that guy. That was a long time ago." Weasel's eyes shifted from Steffie to the screen, to Steffie, to the screen. "Players keep changing."

"Just thinking." Steffie said. "I'm desperate. I'm always desperate."

"Yeah, they come and go, you know how it is. Nick Larson. A strange guy, I heard. Went nuts or somethin'. Forget him—heard he died awhile back."

***

"Hello," a woman answered.

"Yes. Brett Wells, please," Nick said.

As she went to find him, sunshine streaming in through the window was fading and the shadows were lengthening in Nick's office. He liked this time of day, especially on those days, as this one had been, where he had worked hard. Those days had become rarer and rarer. He had to psyche up now and make himself work, where before good days had just happened. But he wanted to keep going. Both computer screens glowed: "Businesses, Texas and Surrounding States. Businesses, Houston and Harris County, Texas."

"Brett Wells." His voice was crisp, that of a forty-something, busy man.

"Yes, Mr. Wells, this is Nick Larson in San Francisco, president of Investor's Research. How are you today?"

"Busy. What is it?"

"Your company keeps appearing whenever I look for cheap stocks, companies that might need help. That's what I do. Help undervalued companies find buyers for their stock and attract a following."

"How do you do that?"

"It's a whole process. It depends on the company and what it needs. Usually I write a research report and send it to people I know: brokers, portfolio managers, investment bankers, analysts. I also distribute reports over the Internet. Also, I arrange for my clients to appear at analyst's conferences and go on road shows. However I can move the stock, I figure it out and that's what I do."

"Yeah, I could certainly use some help with that... damn stock. Why don't you call me Brett."

"Okay. The thing is, is that there isn't any volume." He typed NUP on the keypad, and the screen showed, NUP, bid 9 1/8, ask 9 1/4, volume, 4000. "A lousy four thousand shares traded. Nobody cares. But the way I figure, Nugget has a cash flow of about five dollars a share, selling about two times cash flow. No oil company sells at two times cash flow; they sell at maybe six to eight times cash flow. Earn about a dollar fifty next year, only six times earnings. Most oil companies are ten to twelve times earnings. Unless there's something here I don't know."

"No, you've summed it up pretty good. But I don't know, I don't want to pay for someone to come in here and just waste my time. You know anything about the oil bid'ness?"

I have to do something with this guy, Nick thought. "I've worked in the patch, and I've done deals with oil companies. Remember Texas Resources? It used to be in Houston. It was about the same size of Nugget."

"I remember them some. Sure."

"I'll send you a report I did on them," he said, his voice racing. "I wrote it years ago, when the stock was six. I mailed it out and called analysts and traders. On huge volume over the next couple months the stock went up above nine. They kept me on after that, and paid me twelve thousand a month plus stock options. Later I lined them up with Merrill Lynch, who became their bankers and made a market in the stock. Check Bloomberg or any other source, you want to verify this."

"Trust me, I will. Didn't they finally sell out?"

"To Chevron, for twenty-two dollars a share."

"Yeah. That was a good move. And what did you say your name was?"

"Larson. Nick Larson."

"So what've you done lately?"

The shadows had grown, and Nick's office was almost dark. He hadn't even noticed, lost as he was in the conversation. He snapped on the lamp atop his desk. It threw out a weak light, most of the office staying dark. He liked it that way. "I haven't really—I took some time off and..."

His voice trailed off. *How do I tell him a lot of days I come to the office and just sit*? Nick pondered, listening to his silence. What did they call it when he went to the hospital after Julie died? Post-stress anxiety, brought on by the death of a spouse. But it could have been the death of a friend, a child. Lots of things cause a breakdown, the doctors had said. The doctors had said a lot of things. Make new friends, they said, travel, get a new hobby, play golf. Tried it, nothing worked. He wanted Julie right now to appear out of the dark, her dimples deepening as she flashed that devilish grin.

"Mr. Larson?"

Who the hell is this guy? Nick wondered, lost in his thoughts. *Come on*, he urged, *we got to close this guy.* "Yes. I've been looking at different opportunities. No, I haven't had another Texas Resources lately, but I don't need the money that much, and only want to get into a deal I'm excited about. Like Nugget."

"I'll think about it. But the timing isn't quite right, what with our quarterly reports just about due. Takes a lot of my time."

Damn, Nick thought, gripping the phone tighter.

"But maybe I could work over the weekend..." Brett mumbled, more to himself.

"Look, Brett, let's both make an investment. I'll invest a couple of days there in Houston, and you can show me your operation. As is usual, you'll pay for my airfare and expenses. If you want me to do investor relations work, that's fine. If not, I'll just write a report on Nugget and distribute it. And I'll charge just my minimum fee for the report."

"How much is that?"

He picked at his fingernail while he calculated how much he needed to survive for the next few months. "I'll write a six to eight pager for ten thousand dollars."

"Doesn't sound bad," Brett said. Nick's heart pounded. "That will include charts and graphs and earnings projections and how about I come there later this week? Say Thursday or Friday?"

"No. The rodeo's coming to town, one of the biggest damn rodeos in the world, and I'm an honorary marshal and got a lot of work. Hold on a minute, can ya?" Nick heard papers being rummaged through. "Next week'll work. Yeah, you get here early on Tuesday and let's see where it goes."

Brett hung up. Nick held the phone and didn't want to put it down. *It's been a hell of a long while*, he thought. *Too long. Can I still move this stuff*? He dialed Linda's number, and stared out into the dark office while the phone rang. He changed his mind, and returned the receiver to its cradle.

***

Nick walked in the dark night, starting at Pine to Bush, then over from Bush to Sutter. A few people were in front of a hotel, the men well-dressed in suits, the women in high-heeled shoes. Across the street homeless people pushed shopping carts under the towering buildings. Nick cut up Sutter, past coffee houses where young people dressed mostly in black were talking, laughing. Bottles of Pellegrino and wine were stacked on tables.

Farther up Sutter Street, Nick strolled, past a movie theater with lines of people, past glass-front windows of restaurants, past Polk Street, with its packed gay bars.

The city's so split, he thought. The rich were safely ensconced in their apartments on Nob Hill and Victorian homes in Pacific Heights and their cabins in bucolic Marin County. Here in the inner city, in the streets and alleyways of San Francisco, were the not-rich, people just trying to get by in this high-priced city. *Place was better in the old days, when things were cheaper.* He reached Van Ness.

Van Ness was wide with four lanes of traffic on each side. A heavy, stone building was at the corner of Van Ness and Sutter. A window on the second floor was open, and people were dancing inside. Music could be heard out on the street, the sounds of a violin, a bandonion. He looked at his watch: 10:40. After thinking it over, he entered the building.

After the dark hallway there were stairs leading to the second floor. The building had seen better days, with the paint on the walls faded. Within a glass-paneled door was a dark room large enough for about fifty people. A tarnished gold chandelier hung from the ceiling, colored lights glowing about the room. In the center, a worn, highly polished dance floor. The place was packed with people dancing, eating, and carrying plates of food and bottles of wine to tables.

On the small stage the musicians, a man and woman, started into a slow tango.

"Como estas?" a woman said, smiling at Nick. A man held out his hand, which he shook. He smiled, nodded at the faces from the old times. He knew many of them, though there were a number of younger people that he did not know. They all danced wonderfully.

Nick asked a woman to dance, a not particularly pretty woman. It did not matter. It had been awhile, a long time since he had danced. The tango quickened; he picked up the pace. Tango must be felt with the heart to be danced. Although he knew many steps, he usually only executed a few very basic ones. Feeling the woman in his arms, the crowd crushing around him, but most of all, hearing the sad, serious, lonely music drowning out all of the other sounds, all his thoughts, he surrendered to the dance.

The music played on. The crowd danced counter-clockwise around the floor. The numbers on his watch glowed red: 1:37.

Sweat covered his face and neck, and his shirt was soaked through. After awhile only the regulars were left. The women brushed against him while they performed their *ochos*, and their legs touched his during *pasadas*. Heaven, he decided once again, was a place where you danced tango and painted indefinitely, and the rest of the world and what most called *reality* vanished.

Nods to the regulars, handshakes and hugs, salutations of *mucho gusto* and *buenos noches*, and he put on his jacket and left.

Out in the cold and foggy San Francisco night, he shivered as his sweat turned cold and felt like ice. Unfolding his jacket collar and putting it about his neck, he felt a sadness rain down. He was not feeling good. When it was late and dark and he was alone was the worst time.

As he walked on, the night got chillier. The streets were almost empty. He put on a wool cap. He crossed Fell Street, then started up Polk. The glow from the lights inside the city library spilled out into the street.

He passed a closed grocery store. He stopped and leaned against the structure and looked at the empty streets. He took out his cell phone.

The phone rang awhile. *I shouldn't be calling this late*, he thought. *I shouldn't be calling at all.*

"Hello."

"Hi, it's me. Is it too late?"

"Well, rather. But it's okay."

He didn't know what to say.

"Are you okay?" Linda asked.

He did not know, but again felt like disappearing. "How about, we could meet, for coffee or something." *Not this again*, Nick thought. *It's all right, this will all pass.*

"Fine. Yes."

"I'm still bothered, you know. We never should have, and now we shouldn't."

She did not say anything.

"It bothers me," he said. "I mean, I couldn't help it before, when Julie was alive. But now I still can't. And then, when I don't think about you, I'm fine. But then everything seems empty and I start thinking again."

"Do you think I don't know? This is not fun, Nick, and you're calling me—I didn't call you, you know."

He thought it over. "No. No, you didn't. I'm sorry. I just, I just don't know what to do." *Ask her. Go ahead.* "How about Tortoni's tomorrow night. Is that okay? At nine?"

"Make it nine-thirty," Linda said. "But I can't stay long."

***

The rain would not let up. It was splattering on the roofs of the houses and apartments and restaurants and coffee houses throughout North Beach. North Beach was once home to bohemians and poets and dropouts. Most of them had moved, or had been evicted or were about to be. An apartment in North Beach cost about two thousand a month, a tiny apartment. You could not write poetry fast enough to pay that—if you could sell the words. You'd have to become a stockbroker or investment banker.

In front of St. Peter and Paul's Church, the park was flooded. A few homeless groused about, pitching a cardboard box for cover. Restaurants were filled with young, well-groomed people. Cars were racing down the rain-streaked dark streets.

Walking into Tortoni's, Nick took off his black beret and raincoat. Water puddled on the black-and-white tile floors. The place was old and funky, with just the old crowd and an occasional tourist going there anymore. There was a cappuccino machine, people sitting at tables, and opera playing from the old, nickel-slot jukebox.

He sat in a corner booth and watched raindrops running down the large windows. He kept glancing at the door, his heart pounding. *She's late, maybe she's not coming*, he thought. *Just as well. Good. Maybe that will end it*.

The door opened and Linda walked in and headed to him. He waved and tried to be casual. But he couldn't keep his heart from pounding.

"Sorry. Thad's nurse was late and then I couldn't get a cab."

"It's okay."

She sat down, leaving her raincoat on. Water dripped from her coat onto the floor.

"And how is he?"

Linda smiled tightly. "Some good days, mostly bad days. The therapist comes and tries but... he'll never walk again, we're pretty sure."

"In a way, Julie's lucky; she went fast."

"At least Thad can use his hands. Some people after strokes can't. Oh, Nick, None of this is pretty, is it?"

He didn't answer. An old, white-haired waiter took their order and left.

"It's hard, getting it together. But I think I got a lead, to make some money."

She took off her coat. "That's good. I didn't know you were still working."

The waiter brought cappuccino. Steam rose from the oversized, white, heavy cups.

"Well, yes, I got money problems."

"You?"

"I guess I kept it a secret. I've been good at keeping secrets."

They sipped cappuccinos, looked into each other's eyes. "I could help some," she whispered. "Don't take this wrong, but—"

"Don't even suggest. I just want to be honest. I'm not begging. Makes me feel better, being honest. Sometimes—don't take this wrong—but I think of when we were sneaking around when she was sick. When we went to the desert that weekend, the weekend before she died, when she was in the hospital."

Linda thought about it.

"I feel terrible sometimes, lots of times, get to where I want to throw up. No, I didn't think it would make a difference, what we did. It was exciting and sophisticated and modern and..." Nick started sweating, feeling closed in. "No big deal, other people cheat, but it is a big deal, it matters, it just does, and the more I say it doesn't matter, it does."

"What do you want from me?"

"I guess I need to talk about it. That's the only way out. Also... I miss you all the time, and that makes it worse."

"Okay. We can talk," she said. She took his hand. Together their hands warmed. He didn't want to let go. Neither did she.

They sipped cappuccino and listened to the scratchy sounding old opera records. Linda looked at her watch. "I must go." She smiled with perfect teeth.

"Yes." Nick didn't hear himself.

"He wakes up sometimes, and gets confused if I'm not there."

"Poor guy," he said, meaning it.

"He can't put his words together right. I have to do everything. He'll just be like that from now on."

Nick let go of her hand. *She should be with her husband now*, Nick told himself, as if reciting lines from a moral code printed in an ethics manual. But he didn't feel that way, not at all. She headed for the door. *This is going to be another long night*, he thought, watching her open and close the door, watching the umbrella open above her, watching the dark street now empty where before she had stood.

Two

Welcome to Houston and Enjoy Your Stay and You'all Come Back, You Hear? the sign read, with a man and a woman and a child and a modest house on a spacious lawn pictured behind the words. The sign with the perfect nuclear family smiling hung from the wall as Nick walked down the wide corridor in the Houston Intercontinental Airport.

He stepped outside. Bright sun rushed down from a cloudless, blue sky; not a breeze anywhere, just a heavy, sticky humidity that made it hard to breathe. Wiping sweat off his forehead, Nick signaled a cab.

The cab raced down an eight-lane clogged highway, oil rigs pumping in fields on both sides, cattle grazing on grass, the land flat and endless, like all of Texas. Sunshine reflected sharply off of the cars. In the distance, the tall buildings in downtown Houston looked like towering apparitions at the end of a sea of cars. When they got downtown, no people were out. A few trees were on the sidewalks, but mostly there was just concrete and the hot sun burning overhead, reflecting off of the soaring buildings.

Nick went into a rose-colored-marble building. On the top floor, he entered an office. A floor-to-ceiling window looked down on Houston. Yellow cranes were digging holes alongside the freeways, preparing foundations for new buildings. Cars were jamming the freeways. Grass and trees made the city very green.

He was led into the office of Brett Wells by a rather round man who referred to Nick as "pardner." Brett, a young man, tall and gangling with blue eyes full of sincerity, looked up from a pile of papers stacked on his desk. "Why, hello, Mr. Larson. Good to meet you."

"Thanks, you too. Call me Nick."

"Okay, Nick."

After Nick put his bags down and they bantered about the muggy, hot weather in Houston, last night's Houston Astros baseball game, and too much traffic clogging the freeways, Brett asked, "So what about Nugget?"

"What do you want done?"

"Expand like crazy," Brett said, his eyes widening. "Hell, these Wall Street types are comin around and trying to buy the company here. It's cheaper to buy us than to go out and drill for oil. I'd like to get some money, but I mean big, and drill, that's what I'd like to do. Or buy a bunch more companies. Look, ya gotta git big or nobody cares nothin about you."

"I can help, but you're exactly right. Nobody cares," Nick said. "First we have to make people care. And they won't unless we can make investors think that after they buy Nugget, others will start to care also, at higher prices. It's show biz. Stocks are dead until you can get people interested, the right people."

Brett got up and looked down at Houston.

"Let's get real," Nick said. "Do you have anything brewing, anything that I can go out with? I don't mean hype. I mean hard news that'll help me move the stock."

"Coupla things. Course it's privileged information, you know."

"Look, I know that's where we're going. You don't have to outline the rules. I'm not rushing out to buy the stock, and nothing you say's leaving this room."

Brett sat back and studied him. He opened a drawer, took out a pack of Lucky Strikes, shook out a cigarette, and lit it. The end of the cigarette glowed bright orange as Brett took a drag. He exhaled, and the stream of smoke drifted across the room. "Hate to smoke but I can't give it up. Not the worst thing you can do and, well, about Nugget. I think we're about to get lucky. They just reappraised my wells. Seems with the higher price of *ool*, I can mark up my assets—the wells, leases, equipment, all of it—about a hundred million dollars. And our foreign operation's picked up. We're really hittin it big in Argentina."

"That's all good."

"Yes. Ahhm thinkin with the markup we can issue bonds. A hundred million more in assets and we can issue about eighty million dollars of long-term bonds. We're talking to Morgans in New York right now. We might get an A rating. That's investment grade."

Wells ground out his cigarette in a heavy copper ashtray shaped like the state of Texas. Nick walked over to the window and looked down on Houston and didn't say anything.

Brett watched him and asked, "What do you think?"

Nick thought about it. "That'll help, but it won't move the stock, not a lot," Nick said. "Nugget's a nine-dollar stock with only ten million shares out,: a market cap of ninety million. Too small to show up on the radar screen of the *real* people, I mean hedge funds and big institutions. You need a market cap of at least three hundred million. That means the stock has to get up to about thirty; that'll give you serious distribution. Until then, you'll be nickel and diming with the retail buyers, five thousand shares here, ten thousand there. You need fifty and a hundred thousand share buyers to get into the game. After that you can split the stock and get into the game for real."

Sitting at his desk, Brett put his chin in the palm of his hand and stared at him, as if seeing him for the first time. "Care for some carrot juice?"

Nick wondered if any of this was getting through to him. "Sure."

After going to a small, white refrigerator atop steel files, Brett extracted a few carrots, stuffed them into a juicer. The grinding of the machine filled the air. Brett was tall and bony, and moved lightly. He poured the orange-colored liquid into glasses, and handed one to Nick. "Gotta stay healthy or life isn't worth living. Work out a couple times a day usually. You?"

"I used to. I haven't lately but I want to get back."

"Well, hell, go on and use my club. Stayin downtown here in Houston, aren't you?"

"Yes. At the Sheraton."

"Well just walk on over to Chevron Plaza; it's only a few blocks away. I'll call and tell them. Do you some good, a workout."

Nick wondered, *is he running me off or stalling or what? I need some sort of indication... something.* "Sure, fine. But are we through here? Don't you want to know more about me?"

Brett drained his glass. "Nah, no need to now. We'll get together for dinner. I'll pick you up. Say, how's about around seven?"

Nick nodded. He picked his fingernail.

***

I'm going to finish, Nick thought grimly. *Damn, I used to knock off four or five miles.* He gasped for air and looked down at the treadmill panel: Distance, 2.6 Miles. Pace, 6.0 Miles per Hour. Calories Burned, 272. He finished jogging three miles, and went and took a shower. Afterwards he sat on a chair in the exercise room wrapped in towels. Men and women were pumping iron, lifting round, black weights on the end of shiny steel bars. They shook with their efforts.

He looked at his watch: 6:42. *Be almost 5:00 in San Francisco*, he calculated, looking around at the faces of strangers in the gym. *She'll be back from playing tennis about now. I could call... no, better not.* Joking and laughing, people in shorts and tank tops continued lifting weights.

"Ahh, fuck it," he murmured. He sauntered over to a phone hanging on the wall, and called. He hung up when the phone rang. *What the hell am I calling Linda for*? he thought. Looking around the gym he pondered, *Why not call? We're friends, aren't we? Known each other a long time.* He called again, and then hung up as the phone started ringing. *What's the matter with me*? he wondered, scratching an itch behind his knee. *I want to go home.* He remembered Julie, lying in a black hospital bed and covered with a white sheet, a catheter in her arm. He reached for the phone, and again stopped himself.

"Are you finished?" A tall guy with dark eyes stood there, wiping his face with a towel. "With the phone. Are you through?"

"I, I don't know," Nick heard his voice as if through a fog.

"Hey, are you okay?" the tall guy asked.

"Am I okay?" Nick repeated to himself.

***

Steam from pumpkin soup wafted up from the plates, which were atop fine linen. One plate was before Nick, and across him Brett Wells was sipping the soup. There was an empty chair and an extra setting.

"Have you thought about my offer?" Nick asked.

Brett took another spoonful. "We need to discuss your fee."

Nick took another sip, and tried to appear unworried. His heart was pounding. "My fee for a report?"

"I'm thinking about maybe more." Brett stopped eating. "Do you really think you could move the stock? Say, over the next month?"

"That isn't enough time. It takes at least a month to get the word out. After a couple months, I've made the rounds of about a hundred people. By then, with some luck—and luck really counts—we have a twelve dollar or so stock. Then I go back to the first people I called and tell those that didn't buy, you left thirty percent on the table, Nugget's going higher, don't miss out. If you do *your* job, which is getting those bonds out with a decent rating, I think we can get the stock up to sixteen, maybe seventeen. Still a long way from a thirty dollar stock, which is where I'm aiming to go, but it's a start."

Brett placed his spoon in the dish. "So what'll you charge for that?"

Nick thought, *This could put me back, back into the show. I want them talking about me again. For that, I need stock. And if the stock goes...* He tried to keep his voice steady. "This could really work. I know I can make it. I need six months. Ordinarily, I'd ask for about a hundred thousand dollars upfront, but here I'll take my hit on the backside, with the stock. Warrants for a hundred thousand shares, half of it vesting over the first two months, the rest over the remaining four months. The warrants at today's price, nine and a half."

Nick couldn't read Brett's vacant face. He took a sip. The soup was cold.

"That's quite a bit of stock," Brett said. "A thirty dollar Nugget, you'll make a couple million."

"Sure. I earned it." *Damn, close this guy*, he thought. "And what about you? You got a couple million shares."

Brett nodded.

Still can't read him, Nick thought. "For salary, make it ten thousand a month," Nick said. "Plus expenses, reasonable expenses."

A man wearing a leather jacket appeared. His bald head was round like a small pumpkin, and he was long and thin. The man pulled out the empty chair, then nodded to Nick and Brett.

"Sorry, ah'm late," he said. "Plane jest got in."

"How was New York?" Brett asked.

"Okay, you know, *New York*. Lots of dumb-asses runnin around like ants. Hello, ah'm Butch Byrd," he said to Nick. "Do stuff for Brett." When they shook hands, Nick's was swallowed up in Butch's anvil-like grip.

Soup was brought for Butch. Brett filled him in about Nick.

Butch studied Nick as he ate. "So you think you got some time to give us? Sure can use some help. How many deals you got going now?"

Nick fidgeted in his chair. "I could fit you in. I mean I'd wind down my other engagements. They're about through anyway." *I'm lying*, Nick thought. *Yeah, but I need this job real bad, so lying doesn't count.*

"If we strike a deal," Brett said, "now I don't know if we will, but if we do, I want the warrants vested after a year. That'll make you stay a year, or you don't get any stock."

Nick thought it over, as if he didn't have the answer. "Okay. Fine."

Brett asked, "About when can you can get to work?"

"Not long. A couple weeks."

"I'll sleep on it," Brett said. "Call me when you get back to San Francisco, and I'll let you know."

***

"What d'ya got?" Brett asked Butch. Butch's plate had been picked clean. Nick was gone. Few people were left, and the busboys were cleaning up the empty tables. The air smelled of roast duck, steaks, and alcohol.

Grinning, Butch said, "That man sure can lie. Hell, he got no deals workin, hasn't had for years. Matter've fact, he's about to be evicted." Butch watched Brett take it in. "Now he did put together that Texas Resources deal, that's true enough. Then nothin. He went sorta crazy then, and they locked him up for awhile. He went to a nut house, I couldn't find out much about that, damn shrinks won't talk, but I *do* know he was under medication."

"Any other family?"

"Nah. His father was a big-shot investment banker, died when Nick was little, raised by his mother. She's dead now. He got nothin. But there's some snatch on the side, some society lady he's hosin with a sick husband.

Brett took a sip of cognac, placed the snifter on the linen, retrieved it and took a swallow. He stared at the table.

Lines gathered at Butch's mouth as he smiled and continued. "The dumb son-of-a-bitch, he went to Europe, lived a lot of time in Paris, didn't do any drugs, not that I could find out. Lived in a room near that school, the Sorbonne, studied painting. He was good, some of the dealers in Paris said he was. He showed promise, they said, and sold a few of his paintings. But he didn't show up anymore; nobody knows where he went. I couldn't find where he was for a couple of years, but he wasn't workin. Then he ended up in Buenos Aires. Ahh found some people that knew him there. Seems his wife and he used to go there and dance, when she was alive. She died, his wife, that is." Butch yawned, looked beat. "Guess he cracked up after she died. What kinda loser's he? I can get you some *real* operators."

"No. I want someone from there, from the Street. We're through with those fly-by-night promoters."

"Whatever." Butch sat back in his chair, fatigue and fury on his face.

"Hard trip?" Brett asked. He finished the cognac and ordered another.

"Turned out okay. Got Morgans all set up. Pasternak'll play ball. She needs the money."

"Don't they all." He thought a moment. "Anything from Cordoba?"

"Got it all settled, more or less. It was tough. Some damn villagers—nothin we couldn't handle—were makin trouble. We scared 'em... or killed 'em. After that I went to my place, that apartment I bought in Buenos Aires. Love it there. Sat at the safe and took out all my gold and jewels and rings, and they sure are pretty, and one day, when we make enough, ah'm just gonna stay there and count how rich I am, course how much is enough. Yeah. Well, if you don't mind, I'm gonna call it a night. Oh, one thing. Slate Gorton over at Texas Resources worked with Larson. He says Larson's good; says the deal almost broke down lots of times. Says Larson wouldn't let it collapse. Says Larson's wired into all the big money, knows how to move stocks, people trust 'em. Says the guy's driven. Least he used to be."

"Thanks. Get some sleep. Good job."

"You gonna hire him?"

"Probably. And you can watch him."

"That ah'll do, got that right. Don't trust him, don't trust anybody that acts crazy. He was makin all that money, so why'd he jest go? Well, whatever the hell you decide."

***

Taking a sip of coffee, Nick looked out the window of his new office: the Transamerica Building, a pyramid-shaped structure that jutted up into the blue sky, was in full view. Nick wore a new black Armani suit. He was surrounded by steel chairs and glass-topped tables. He sat back in a black leather chair, the leather squeaking. Plants in white pots were scattered around the office, atop his large desk, among the computers, television sets, and fax machines.

He made a call.

"Zellon."

"Lenny, this is Nick."

"Hey, Larson, where you been?"

Lenny Zellon managed a few hundred million dollars, and knew every news break on the Street, some before they were even announced. "Busy, Lenny. You got a minute? Want to fill you in on this company I'm working with, Nugget Petroleum."

Nick heard Lenny typing on a computer keyboard. "Oh, yeah,

that's a real piece'a shit you got there. What? You couldn't get honest work? Come on, Nick, nobody's recommending it, no volume. What else you wanta talk about. Baseball? Forget it. I hate baseball. How about gettin me laid?"

"Look, Lenny. Let's talk about Nugget."

"Nobody cares. Nobody cares, I don't care. Seriously. Get me laid?"

Nick laughed, thinking over how Lenny hadn't changed. "Nobody can get you laid, now *that's* impossible. And I like Nugget. And other people will after I give them the story."

He pictured Lenny: a little, thin guy, bald spot on top. Black eyes in constant motion, moving like the eyes of a cornered rat.

"Okay. You've had some calls in the past, where the fuck you been? What you got?"

"Undervalued, good fundamental company."

"Yeah, who gives a shit? What do you *got*?"

"Well, you know I can't say. I don't want the Feds havin me for breakfast."

There was large silence on the phone. Nick had just let Lenny know that there *was* inside information that was good. If it were information about bad developments he wouldn't have told Lenny to buy; he would have told him to short.

"Yeah," Lenny said.

"I've just come from Houston and seen management and gone over everything and taken the company on. This one's going to move. No question."

"Anybody buy yet?"

"You're my first call, and you know I got a long list. Take weeks."

"Yeah. You bullshitting me, Nick?"

Through the phone he felt Lenny's rat-like eyes staring through him. Nick hesitated. *Are there any problems with Nugget*? he wondered. *How well do I know Brett? Not well at all. And this Butch smells like nothin but trouble. Ah, hell with it, they're fine.* "Yes. I believe it, big."

Lenny thought it over. "Okay. I'm good for about three hundred thousand. But you better be right. And don't disappear again. Not while I'm holdin this crap." He hung up.

Nick watched the trades on the screen: NUP, 100,000 at 9 1/2; 100,000 at 9,518; 50,000 at 10; 50,000 at 10 1/8. *Lenny's trade*, he figured. *Good. The stock moved with only three hundred thousand shares bought. It won't take much to get it moving.* Looking at another screen, he saw the short interest was high, almost eight million shares. Short stock is stock sold by people that do not own it. People shorting figure it will go down and they can buy the stock lower, making a profit. Shorts panic when size buying comes in. *Good. They'll get barbecued when they have to chase stock to cover their shorts. Screw the shorts.* He hated the shorts. Everybody except the shorts hated the shorts. Often even the shorts hated the shorts.

He wiped off his sweating chin and studied the screen. Sitting over his phone like a croupier about to deal, he pushed down the speaker button and began placing calls.

***

A few blocks away from Nick's office—almost everything was close in the financial district, the area being just a few city blocks—was the office of Stanley Witter, an institutional brokerage boutique.

Ted Gunn sat at a long, wide trading desk. About thirty traders with phones to their ears were on either side of him. The traders were twenty-somethings, and Ted was in his thirties, though he looked much older. He had no neck, about three chins. Florid, fat face; gray, unruly, uncut hair. Ted was always quitting smoking, quitting drinking, quitting running around on his wife, girlfriend, whomever. Always failing at everything except being at the desk at 5:30 in the morning. He took big risks, going long or short fifty thousand, a hundred thousand shares at a time, seemingly without a care. He traded the firm's capital, then, after the market closed, he'd go get drunk.

He answered as soon as his phone rang. "Gunn." After hearing Nick he said, "What's up?"

"Nugget Petroleum. I took them on."

Ted typed out NUP: 10 3/8 on 740,000 shares. "That dog never trades. Where's all the volume from?" Clothes were just thrown on Ted. Like a bowling ball, his round belly hung between blue suspenders; the top buttons on his shirt were unbuttoned, the button-down collars as well.

"Mine. And we're still early."

"Good."

"But it's not just a trade, Ted. There's more in it than that. This is a *real* company. No hedge funds, not hot money. Real long-term players comin in."

One of the traders let out a scream. The room was buzzing.

"Nugget's got a lot going on," Nick said.

"Don't we all." Ted thought about it. "Should I buy now?"

"I'm an insider so... I like the company, that's what I'm saying."

"Okay, Nick. Thanks for the call."

They hung up, and Ted pondered: that guy's made some good trades. Not for a while though. But is he baggin me?

Shrieks came from a trader a few seats down. She had made money on a hundred thousand share trade, and had another hundred thousand shares working.

Ted ran his hand through his hair. *I need a haircut*, he decided. He remembered missing a barber's appointment last week. He had gotten looped after the market close and forgotten. It had been one of those days: his longs went down, his shorts up, so he drank. *Well, what the hell am I here for? I gotta trade.*

On the screen: NUP 10 5/8, volume 940,000 shares. "It's a hype," he mumbled, "but where *is* all the volume coming from? Larson isn't dumb. Nobody lasts on the Street if they are. Okay, hell with it." He realized he was talking to himself, made a call, and got Troster on the phone.

"Hi, Ted, how's the weather in San Francisco?"

"Haven't looked. They're showing NUP for sale at 10 5/8. How many they good for?"

"Ten thousand shares. Gets tight after that."

Ted was talking to a floor broker on the New York Stock Exchange. As a broker, Troster would negotiate trades with the NUP specialist. The specialist would buy for or sell from his own account, and in that way make a market.

"Where's the volume coming from?" Ted asked.

"Here in the States. Buying's been spotty, but it's spreading. Starting to see orders offshore, some big people. How many you want, or you just wanta chat?"

"I'm a buyer, a hundred thousand shares."

"Hold on." A moment later Troster said, "I can fill you at 10 7/8."

"Can't do better?"

"Shorts're getting squeezed. After this, it'll get even harder to buy. You want it. Don't be shy."

This smells like a score, a real score, Ted thought. He swallowed hard and said, "Buy me 200,000 shares of Nugget at 11 or better. Fill or kill." The trade had to be completed immediately or the order was cancelled.

A moment later Troster said, "Done, you're done, all at 11."

"Okay." Gunn hung up, threw the receiver down, and started pacing about the room, the other traders watching him. Was that smart? *Or was I conned by that Larson? I just don't know.* He looked at his watch. He decided to head to the bar early.

***

Every year in San Francisco they held the Black and White Ball. The affair was a society event, benefiting homeless people. The town's rich and famous, and bankrupt and fakers and wantabees, showed up sartorially splendid in black and white. White pearls, black dresses for the ladies; black tuxes and white shirts for the men. Of course, in San Francisco you never knew which sex would wear which clothing.

This year they held it at the place with one of the best views in the city: the Venetian Room in the Fairmont Hotel, located at the top of Nob Hill. The musicians played a brisk waltz. Through the window you could see the Bay Bridge, with twinkling lights on its spidery columns. Everybody was festive, with toothy smiles throughout the packed, red plush velvet wall-covered room. People were dancing, and there was conversation blaring at the long, mahogany bar. There were gales of laughter, tinkling of ice in glasses, the heavy smell of too much alcohol.

Lenny Zellon brushed back non-existent hair from the top of his head as he sat on a barstool and looked around. He was searching for the perfect woman, who he had found four times, each time leading to a marriage followed by divorce.

"Look at all these creeps," Lenny said. "Charity ball for the homeless? Half the landlords in this town are here. They've evicted half the city, threw them out on the streets and gave them cardboard boxes. They make millions and throw back a few dollars."

Nick nodded, sipped a Scotch and surveyed the scene. The mayor, his tux costing a few grand, was surrounded by beautiful, leggy women, many of them with not a hair out of place. Gray-haired men were with much younger women.

"Town has changed," Nick said. "I remember it in the sixties, when we closed down Berkeley. It was fun. We were, all of us, poor, but we didn't know it. I got tossed in jail for some damn protest, don't even remember what it was." Nick caught sight of Linda.

She smiled as she maneuvered the wheelchair carrying her husband, Thad. People stopped her and talked. Thad had put on weight and resembled a bewildered frog, smiling dully as he studied faces. It took an enormous effort for him to raise his hand in greetings.

He was well-liked, and remembered for what he had once been: a Stanford University star football player. Then, after making some money in real estate, he became a venture capitalist where the bucks got bigger, and he raked in tens of millions. Now the stroke that had come from nowhere left him a shell of a person.

Everyone praised Linda for how well she took care of him.

Nick's breathing got shallow as she wheeled Thad close. Nick and Linda shared their secret in the other's eyes.

"Hello, Linda. Thad, so good to see you," Nick said, the words feeling sour. Thad's handshake was soft and lifeless. His face had the flat, uncomprehending look of one disabled and confused about what he had done to deserve this fate.

Nick gave Linda a friendly hug. She felt so warm, her breasts firm. The moment started getting long and awkward. He let her go.

Thad mumbled something, and she bent over to him. Laughing, she said, "Nick. Thad thought you had become a tango dancer somewhere."

Nick laughed. "I don't even dance much anymore."

"Me either," she said.

"Oh."

"Nice to see you. Have fun." She wheeled Thad off.

Nick leaned back against the barstool.

"Piece of ass, that woman," Lenny said.

Nick leaned and didn't say anything.

"That woman I'd like to—she could use some. It'd be a mercy fuck, like now I'm a Peace Corps volunteer or something."

A tango started, and couples flocked onto the dance floor.

"She's untouchable, I'm sure," Lenny continued. "So I'll just sleep with these ball-busters that wanta get at my money. I get into their pants, they get alimony. Should use whores. Cheaper in the long run."

Linda and Thad were at a far corner. Nick thought she might be looking his way, but he wasn't sure.

"Course I haven't been laid in a month. Well, longer than that," Lenny said. "Way longer. How about you? You gettin any?"

She is looking for me. Good, Nick decided.

"Hey, talk to me. You getting—?"

Nick didn't hear Lenny. Trying to appear casual he walked about the room, but his stomach was in knots. Ending up at Linda he asked, "How about a dance?"

She hesitated, smiled. After whispering to Thad, she said, "Love to."

Out on the dance floor he held her close, smelling her familiar lilac perfume, her hand hot in his, the familiar feel of her hips, her legs. He got aroused—he always did. *This is poison*, he thought. *Get the hell away from this, from her.* But she felt good and soft and he pulled her closer. He missed a beat.

"This is crazy," he whispered.

"Yes." Her voice trembled.

Holding her hand, he walked quickly to the door. He could feel Lenny's rat eyes on his back. They went across a heavily carpeted corridor and past a white spiral staircase. They rushed into a dark room, one used for weddings and meetings. Shutting the door, he pulled her close. The room smelled stagnant, like many people had been there. Linda was hot. As she pressed into him, their tongues played. She felt so familiar; he was again home. Everything vanished: the packed room they had just left, Lenny leering from the bar, visions of Julie, everything except Linda.

"Nick, no." She pushed him away. "What if someone...?"

"You know what? I'm past caring."

"But these people know us. I'm a married woman."

"Yes, but—"

"And we have to get back. There *are* appearances."

"I'm tired of living for how people think!"

"Maybe you are. But that's not me. Anyhow, Thad can't stay long. You can use the side door. The key's under the mat."

"But then it's just a little while and I leave. I want more or else—"

"What? What else? What *is* coming over you?"

What do I want with her? Nick wondered. *Why am I in this room trying to cop a quick feel? She just looks so good and... I just, I just don't know any more.* "Okay," he said, "it's just that, remember? Remember when we were all gonna drop out, and you and Julie, we'd open a coffee house in North Beach and you and Julie would have serve coffee and we'd sell my paintings?"

Linda's eyes brightened. She laughed. "Sure. And you were going to paint all day and we'd live like gypsies at the coffee house, and have poetry readings on Thursday nights." She laughed. "And Thad was so stiff. He said it'd be okay, as long as he could still go to the Pacific Union Club once a week."

"We'd leave all the commercial stuff far behind," Nick said. "A different life. Remember?"

Her smile faded. "That was a long time ago. We'd better—"

He thought it over. "Okay. Right," Nick said. And then he accompanied her back to the party.

Everybody there was too drunk and merry to notice. All except Lenny, who glared as Nick rejoined him. "So you guys enjoy your little *stroll*?" Lenny asked with a phony smile.

"Nothing. The woman wanted to get some air, that was all."

"*Air*, they call it now? I got her air, hangin between my legs."

Picking up his Scotch, Nick spilled some. His hand trembled and his stomach was all knotted up.

"Come on, you can tell me."

No, I can't, Nick thought. *Not anybody*. "Just air."

"Ah, you're no good at lying. I can see it in your eyes. Now me, I can lie. Say, you and Thad, you were friends once, no?"

Nick felt like throwing up. He wanted to be alone, but also craved company. Nothing was working lately. "No, I just knew him sort of casually."

"Yeah, casually! I'm Zellon! You should get out more, Nick. You'd learn things, too. Like some very reliable sources told me you and your wife and Linda and him were all friends. Went dancing together, stuff like that. Doesn't matter. If I was screwin that woman, they'd have to stick pins up the hole in my prick to get me to admit it. Relax. Guys today, women too, come on! Affairs are no big thing. Just fucking. Especially if you're married to a person that can't even raise his arms almost. You're like that, your wife can fuck anybody. That's how I see it. Course I'm just me, Zellon. But that's how I see it."

Nick looked at his watch. Time seemed to be standing still. In a little while he watched as Linda pushed Thad toward the door.

***

The engine whining, Nick gunned his battered, old, white Porsche up a Pacific Heights hill. The top was down, as usual, and he was chilled from the damp and cold. He raced up another hill. Grassy knolls were on one side, Victorian houses on the other, and the lights of San Francisco and the black of the Bay waters were far below. He drove higher, past more houses, constructed in Queen Anne and Italianate style. Almost all of them were redwood, and featured custom woodwork. Heavy-limbed, green-leafed trees surrounded blue and peach and ivory multi-hued houses.

The town's asleep and it's not even midnight, he observed. *Stock* brokers, real estate operators, venture capitalists, all young people making millions, asleep at eight, up at five. Place used to be alive all night long, especially back in the sixties. It's changed, now all about money. The whole world's getting to be like that. I don't seem to fit anywhere anymore.

He pulled up to a white Victorian house with blue trim along the window frames.

Feeling like a thief, he opened the side door and went inside to a spare room. The hardwood floor gleamed, plants scattered about, heavy white drapes covered the large windows. In one corner, an exercise bicycle and a pair of running shoes with white socks spilling out.

Linda was waiting. "A drink?" she asked.

"No, thanks. I don't need any more."

He sat next to her, and felt himself aroused. "Where do we go with this? Gettin tired of this sneaking around."

"It *is* a problem." She smiled, showing perfect teeth, and got up. "Music?"

He nodded. She turned on Johnny Mathis, and the music filled the room: "Chances are, 'cause I wear a silly grin…"

He tried to stay calm. "I don't know what I feel about, about you, about anything."

"How about me? I can't believe this… nightmare I'm living. Caged every second of every minute of every day."

He felt helpless. Everything was so out of control…

"He may wake up any time," Linda said, guiding his hand to her breast. He felt her hard nipple, her in his arms, all lilac perfume and hair back in a bun like a proper Pacific Heights matron should wear it and her faint musky scent.

He was stroking her leg and burning up. Plump pillows were tossed off the couch. He slid into her easily, and all thoughts of tomorrow and right and wrong and friendship and loyalty were discarded. Her hair was in his face, the smell of freshly washed hair.

Three

In his office early the next morning, Nick studied the computer screen. He typed on the keyboard, and on the screen saw: Welcome to the Internet: Sports, Finance, Weather, Travel. He typed some more:

"Nugget Petroleum. State of Incorporation, Delaware. Principal Executive Offices, including Zip Code, 2233 Westheimer, Suite 405, Houston, Texas, 77057. Registrant's Telephone Number, including area code, (713) 627-5592."

He scrolled through the many pages of Nugget's filing with the Security and Exchange Commission, the SEC, the federal government watchdog overseeing the financial markets. Public companies had to file their financial statements quarterly.

About what I figured, he thought. *Lots of oil, lots of gas, much of it in Argentina, out in the Pampas*. A line caught his eye:

"… Nugget Petroleum's oil and gas reserve estimates, both international and domestic, are contracted through Byrd and Company, Houston, Texas. All references and inquiries should be forwarded to the president and CEO, Butch Byrd. The company's E-mail address is Byrdandco@aol.com"

Pretty cozy, he thought, *Brett having his friend contract out the reserve estimates. More than cozy even, not illegal, but very questionable. Reserve estimates should be done by a disinterested thirty party. I wonder how disinterested Butch Byrd is in what estimates come in about Nugget*, he thought, knowing the answer. He read on:

"The recently acquired gas wells are expected to become the largest single asset of Nugget Petroleum. As of January 15, the scheduled effective closing date, the property's proven gas reserves are over 52,000,000 Mcf, and the present value of the future cash flows are estimated at $185,000,000. These properties are expected to provide a long-lived, stable source of cash flow…"

Big numbers but, still, these reserve estimates are done by the head of Nugget's buddy. Investors think they're getting full disclosure, but who knows with these estimates just how iffy these gas wells really are.

Lot of investors glancing at the filings don't even notice the details, Nick pondered. *There are so many reports to read, how could they check out all the companies they look at? Most rely on brokers and investment bankers. But bankers and brokers get paid to do trades and deals. Are they really going to dig for negative information? I don't think so.*

But what bothers me the most are those Argentinean wells, the ones near Buenos Aires, he decided. *They're the backbone of Nugget's reserves, yet the numbers just don't add up. I could do my due diligence; I could do it the right way, the hard way. I could go and kick the tires. But, you know? None of this is my problem. I'm paid to do a job, which is to move the stock.* He turned off the computer, thinking, *But I know the oil business.* His stomach knotted. *I guess if I'm promoting the company I should know as much as I can. I don't have to guess, it's true.* He thought about it. *But I'm not paid to research Nugget.* Another voice answered, *But I should know as much as I can. People will put money into this stock.* The knot in his gut got tighter. *I just can't screw the people I'm talking to*, he decided. *Okay. All right. All right. I'll go down there and check out the wells.*

***

The best flight Nick could arrange to Buenos Aires would get into the city at the dead of night and would cost thirteen hundred dollars. He did not want to spend the money; he did not want to go. But he got tired of fighting with himself, and found himself flying for several hours, touching down in Rio, changing planes, then landing in Buenos Aires in the blackness.

He got into a yellow cab at the front of the airport, and settled back into the cloth-covered seat.

Driving down the highway, leaving the bright lights glowing from the Buenos Aires *Aeropuerto*, the cab driver looked at him in the rear-view window. "Donde?"

"The Hotel Urugray, near La Recoleta," Nick said. The district was a fashionable *barrio* containing high-priced shops, elegant restaurants, and expensive homes.

"First time you in Buenos Aires?"

"I remember this," Nick said. This smell of the countryside. Woody and grassy and dusty. "No, I've been here. A long time ago." He thought about when he came here with Julie, and now it all seemed very empty.

"You will be in Buenos Aires long?"

"Just overnight." He watched the flatlands go by. *Julie loved it here*, he thought. *Loved dancing*. He imagined her face, the black night in the background. "Then I go to the oil wells, the ones outside of Cordoba. Do you know it?"

"Si. I know muy bien."

Julie. Julie and Madrid and Paris. Most of all, Paris, Nick thought. "Buenos Aires reminds me of Paris very much," he said. "And what is your name?"

"Mi llama Oscar." After awhile, Oscar said, "Yes, especially the houses in La Recoleta, like Paris."

"Mostly when my wife and I lived in Paris we'd walk from the hotel down Rue de Rivoli to the Place de La Concorde…"

"Muy caro. St. Honore, you know that district? My favorite."

"You know St. Honore?"

"Yes. I went to school there," Oscar said, watching the road. "You ever go otro, the other way, to Les Halles, past the Musee Picasso, to the old houses?"

"All the time," Nick said. "What did you study?"

"Architecture. But I did not finish."

"Why not?"

"The times, they go bad here."

"When?"

"About nineteen seventy-eight, seventy-nine."

"Oh." *The time of the "disappeared,"* Nick thought. *The military took over the government and declared war on leftists, labor unions, hell, just about everybody. They disappeared people, who knows for what reason. Must've been a lousy time*.

"When I got home, mis padres, a sister, gone. See them no mas."

"That would be hard. A lot of things are hard."

"We must be strong, *senor*, be men, or who are we?" Oscar said.

Nick thought for a while of the job he had to do. "About the oil fields to the north of Cordoba?"

"Si," Oscar said.

"You could take me there tomorrow?"

"Si."

Slender beech trees grew tall on the side of the highway as they drove closer to Buenos Aires.

"It is not much around Cordoba anymore," Oscar said. "They drilled for water there, the peasants, long ago. They got unlucky; they hit oil. The gordo oil companies came, the gringos came, drove the peasants out." Oscar looked at Nick in the rearview mirror. "There has always been nothing but trouble at those wells. Nobody wants to go there anymore."

***

Hanging from tall beech trees along a dusty road with deep holes, a bright yellow sign: ALTO, PELIGRO, ALTO. All cars were stopped at this point. Nick looked through his binoculars and saw nothing but flatland with men milling around, the sun glaring off the long, fat barrels of their shotguns. They all looked alike: dark blue uniforms, stubby arms, fat bellies, wearing sunglasses, thick hair growing out from under their heavy, blue caps with brown leather visors. In white above the visors: POLICIA.

Through the binoculars, far off, he saw heavy, dusty oilrigs, men tending the drilling bits and scurrying about carrying tools. *But the drill pipes are not turning. Maybe they're refitting*, he reasoned. *But if they're refitting there should be more workers. When you refit you want to get back drilling as soon as possible.*

A policeman lumbered in front of him, a fat man with an ugly growth on his left cheek. His sunglasses glared from the sun. "Por favor," he said, reaching out for Nick's binoculars.

Stepping back, Nick asked, "Is there a way to get to the wells? See, I work for Nugget, and they sent me here."

The policeman stared; the lenses of his sunglasses seemed to be on fire from the sun.

"I'm with the company," he repeated. "I came down here and want to look—"

Nick didn't see the blow coming to the side of his head, just heard a thud and then ringing in his ear. The binoculars were ripped out of his hands. "Hey! What the hell're you doing?" he screamed, ducking under the ALTO sign. The policeman walked away with Nick's binoculars. Nick's heart pounded as shotguns were raised, barrels glinting in the sun. The sharp clicking of gunlocks, shuffling of feet, as fat policemen stood, guns aimed dead at him.

What the hell's this? he thought, feeling dizzy. Oscar started racing over. Guns turned to Oscar, and Nick waved him back. Blood trickled from Nick's head. Oscar turned to the car, and Nick followed. The cops lowered their guns and went back to the shade under the trees. They sat quietly in the overbearing heat deep in the Pampas.

Now he knew what he had suspected, that the well was trouble. He had flown all over the area yesterday, and there were no signs of drilling or that the wells were pumping.

Back in the car, Nick's head ached and blood oozed from the gash. "Let's go back to Buenos Aires," he told Oscar.

The cab bounced in potholes, dust flew out from under the wheels. After driving on a small road they finally turned onto a two-lane highway. There were few cars. Peasants waved happily from the open back of a dilapidated truck.

***

The Obelisk, a three-sided stone structure, rose up into the blue Buenos Aires sky. It had been built when Juan Peron governed the country. It stood at the end of Avenida Corrientas, the widest avenue in South America. Cars moved slowly in the heavy traffic, gleaming in the sun. Buses belched out black exhaust fumes. Motorcycles and bicycles dodged between cars and buses.

Nick was cleaned up, and had had a good night's sleep. *Good to be back in civilization*, he thought. *Civilization? They could still be out there; they could have followed me from—who? Who would follow? I'm getting paranoid. But the wells were not drilling. Oh, forget all that.* He picked his fingernail. *I don't care. I want to be in the old town again.*

Oscar drove past the federal buildings. The white stone buildings were square and solid, like squat fortresses. Some of the buildings had small balustraded balconies, giving the buildings an intimate effect. Evita and Juan Person had given speeches there. People had packed into the squares and listened and applauded the Perons for hours in the sweltering hot Buenos Aires summers, the freezing winters.

Traffic kept building and the cab crawled along. Walking on the crowded sidewalks, the people of Buenos Aires: the women, dark and sensual, their Italian heritage transported to sultry South America; the men, dark and brooding. There were more psychiatrists per capita in Buenos Aires than any city except for New York. The by-product of transplanting cultures. Nick watched the rootless, restless people, feeling a kinship.

Going by a stone building, so large that it covered an entire block, Nick studied the Teatro Colon. He had gone to operas there.

Blood-red crushed velvet covered the seats in that theatre. Artists from all over the world came to perform.

Oscar stopped at a crumbling building in the heart of the city, and Nick went inside. Still blinded from the sun, it took a while for him to see. Chipped, worn black-and-white tiles on the floor spelled out Cafe Europa. Atop a table in the middle of a large room, a silver samovar. Pipes ran from the top of the samovar, connected to valves that led to faucets at the bottom. Gray-haired waiters wearing tuxedoes and white shirts and black bow ties turned the faucets and steam poured out as cups were filled with steamed milk. In the room there were plants with over-sized green fronds in white pots, heavy wooden tables, chairs. Tango music came from small corner rooms.

He walked into a corner room. *That's it*, he thought. *The piano's still by the window. That is where the woman stood playing the violin*. Nick recalled the violinist in her long black gown. He touched the familiar curtains, felt the raw silk. He closed his eyes and he felt Julie as he had held her long ago, in this room, at this place. He danced the basic step, hearing tango music from another room. Nothing could ever pull them apart, nothing. He heard footsteps, but he erased them from his mind.

"*Senor*," he heard.

He opened his eyes.

"*Senor*, may I help you?" A waiter, a dark, serious-faced man, stared at Nick.

"No. I just, I just…" He wanted the waiter to disappear, wanted to forget Nugget, Linda, and that the past was gone. He wanted to dance again with Julie.

The waiter stood there, like a statue.

"Si si. Una café, por favor."

"Bueno," the waiter said. "Pase."

He followed the waiter to a table.

Without a smile, the waiter brought a silver tray containing packets of sugar, napkins, spoon, a pitcher of milk, and a steaming large white cup of cappuccino. He laid down a basket of croissants and baguettes and walked off.

Nick sat and started thinking. *Don't think of Julie, think of something else. Think of what's going down. Think of what's bothering you. Okay. It looks pretty simple about the wells; reserve evaluation is just engineering*. There are standard formulas, he knew, and that's how engineers come to their numbers when evaluating reserves. Where the hook comes is with the assumptions you plug into the formulas. The formulas are the same for oil as well as for gas. There are the well drainage area; the thickness of the "pay," the actual oil or gas residual; the porosity, or pay thickness; the gas to oil ratio, or how much of each substance is included in the pay; the temperature of the pay. There are some other things. He knew all this.

The trouble is that the reserve engineer can plug into the formula whatever numbers he wants to, depending on what he wants to prove out. Massaging numbers is no big deal. Where engineers can fudge the most is at the well drainage area, although, in certain places, like in Texas, the drainage in each field is pretty well known.

But records there in Argentina are not nearly as meticulous; the fields and their reserves estimates are not very well documented. Even in Texas an engineer could phony up the numbers about pay thickness. How much an engineer could is subject to his log evaluation. An engineer reads those logs and looks at porosity. An engineer can estimate almost any number he wants and plug it in. But estimates in Texas are pretty well known, not in a remote section of Argentina.

He pondered some more.

If Brett Wells didn't like the numbers in the reserve evaluations, he could have had Butch put in different numbers and get a higher evaluation, of course. Lots of people, like those that're looking to buy reserves, want accurate numbers. They go to major engineering firms because those firms are third party, independent appraisers; they will give accurate interpretations.

I don't like where this is going, he thought. Still... he kept kicking it around. *Well, one can take a little engineering firm, and if the firm is in on the scam, say a consulting engineer runs the place, the firm can do most anything. Butch has a degree, has a history of knowing the patch. People assume he knows what he's doing.*

None of this information was new. Nick knew it was like what real estate appraisers do. A person could take out a loan on real estate—a house, a building, whatever—and go to a real estate appraiser and say, "This is what I need and it's real important to me and, look, can you stretch as far as you can on your assumptions?" About this time you hand the appraiser ten one-thousand dollar bills in an envelope and give her a wink. Or, say that the appraiser's working for you. You tell him or her to make the appraisal values work, and that you very much appreciate it.

But pertaining to oil, recovery of oil and gas from liquids pumped is usually a pretty small number: about fifteen or twenty percent. But, sure, in a pinch the reserve engineer could jump the recovery estimate from fifteen percent to twenty-five percent or so. That wouldn't be hard. And that would make a hell of a difference in the value of the wells that Nugget has, and of Nugget Petroleum's worth.

Nick thought about this. *In fact... in Nugget's estimate there was a twenty-two percent recovery estimated in that field I looked at yesterday, the one that wasn't pumping, near Cordoba. But Nugget can get away with it, depending on who looks at the report. How many guys that know the oil business are taking the time to go out searching for holes in this Nugget story?* Nick looked around the almost empty cafe. *Just me. But that's why people listen to me, because I go and check out a story.*

Nick sipped the now-cold cappuccino.

But what am I going to do with this information? He pushed the question away.

So, suppose I'm scamming and want to build a case for Nugget, he speculated. *I could also expand my well-drainage area from, maybe, forty acres to eighty acres. The average investor, savvy ones, unless they know the oil business, don't know that the drainage area is how many acres around the bore hole that one well will drain. So if history tells me that the wells in this field drain about forty acres, and I want to show bigger reserves, what I need to do is extend a high estimate to maybe sixty acres or eighty acres. I could justify that by giving a larger number for porosity. I'd say that the sands are so loose that I'm going to drain more than forty acres. Let somebody disprove this; they really can't. It all goes back to log analysis interpretation. Really, when you get right down to it, stretching these numbers isn't even illegal, just a disagreement over interpretations.*

He stiffened. *But the point still is that those wells near Cordoba, they're outright scams, I'm sure,* he thought, staring at the white foam in the cappuccino. The image of Butch Byrd's clean-shaven head gleaming from the overhead light in the cafe appeared. Nick was no longer proud of his craftiness, his restless search for verity. He found it. Now he didn't want to see the truth he had found.

Julie appeared. She was lying in the hospital bed and her face was white, even whiter than the sheet that covered her up to her face, and a catheter was dangling from her body, emitting a yellow liquid, and already she was slipping away. Thad was there, and Linda. And Thad was vigorous and strong and had just played golf and hadn't had a stroke yet and Nick and Linda gave glances to each other. *God, what the hell did I do?* Nick thought, his heart pounding. *Okay, okay, calm down. You'll go crazy thinking about that. Think of something else.*

So, about Nugget, if Brett plays it really bad, he'll get Butch to plug in the numbers he wants for the reserve formulas. Then he'll put those numbers in Nugget's reports and prospectuses. Nobody will question them. Nobody will really read the fine points in a prospectus and take issue, not unless they know to look for something dirty.

Of course, there are accounting guidelines that public companies have to adhere to, Nick knew. But even there the information used to conform to those guidelines is open to interpretation.

He remembered working with Slate Gorton on the Texas Resources deal. Slate had bought some undeveloped reserves for two million, but in valuing the reserves to sell, Texas Resources wanted the appraisal to come in at about five million. Slate had had heated arguments with the engineering firm making the appraisals and, finally, the appraisal came in at four million. Slate grinned broadly that day.

But that appraisal wasn't bogus, like I think this one is.

He shifted in his chair.

Nick thought it would be the same if he needed to borrow half a million dollars to buy a house. He could get the mortgage company's appraiser out to the house, and say the house has to appraise out over a million to get a loan. The appraiser may nod and say that number may fit; that's honest enough. Maybe he'd say the numbers won't fit. Well, nothing could stop Nick from going to another or another appraiser until he found one that appraised the way he wanted. He'd tell the appraiser, look, just take the most optimistic approach, and there's a ten thousand dollar bonus in it if you do a good job. He wouldn't be asking him to lie, just be aggressive in his assumptions, and be willing to sign off on it. Nothing wrong with making an aggressive estimate, is there?

A good guy could make an optimistic assumption; a bad guy says sure, give me the money and I'll give you any number you want, Nick thought. *The bad guy'll sign off on it. If his appraisal's questioned later, the guy'll argue and say these're my interpretations, so what?*

Engineering, whether it's for real estate or oil or gas or whatever, is really interpretive. Engineers call it a science, but it's really not totally. Oil is under the ground; engineers are interpreting with their tools as to what and how much is under there. People are bound to disagree with estimates. Honorably disagree.

He played with the spoon. *Cut it out*, he thought, *quit bullshitting yourself. These guys aren't stretching the truth, they're manufacturing it. I know it. But I don't know what to do about it. They're paying me*!

Also, the cops at the well, they didn't look like regular police, more like an attack force, maybe paid by Nugget or partners of Nugget or... Nick's stomach tightened. *They could have taken down the license plate number. How hard would it be to trace Oscar and ask Oscar who I was and where I stayed. If Nugget's as bad as I think...* Nick pushed his thoughts away, they weren't doing him any good, and signaled to the waiter for the bill.

He went out into the bright sunshine and put on sunglasses. After walking a few blocks, he aimlessly cut across into a narrow cobblestone alley. He walked through San Telmo, the old section of Buenos Aires, where the city had started. The paint of the mostly rose- and sand-colored townhouses was fading under the relentless Argentine sun. The houses had stone steps, heavy wood doors, and flat roofs.

Coming from somewhere, the sounds of a guitar playing gypsy music. At the end of the block, a young couple on a small balcony. She wore a red blouse, had long dark hair; he was tall and lanky. They laughed and kissed, and danced to the music.

I'd like to dance and forget I ever heard of Nugget, Nick thought. *Okay, get this deal done and make a pile of money and be on top again.* Nick relaxed some. Even so, as he sauntered about the city, he looked carefully up and down the streets.

***

After flying back to San Francisco, jogging, and answering his mail, Nick got in touch with Brett Wells. He wanted to go over Nugget, but Brett was busy and wanted him to come to Houston so they could talk. They would go to the opening night of the Fat Stock Show and Rodeo. "About the biggest in Texas," Brett said.

"Brett, I really don't like rodeos."

"You ever seen one?"

"No."

"Now, pardner, this you gotta see. Will simply not believe how exciting—"

"I've seen bullfights. I've seen boxing matches. I don't like them either. I'm not one for violence. I don't even like football."

Brett chuckled some. "Well, reckon you might not like it, but still ahh want you there. The only time I got. Relax, you can look the other way if things get bloody. Some people do sometimes."

So he flew to Houston and watched as the crowd, all 80,000 people, roared.

Nick and Brett were sitting in the huge Astrodome in Houston in the best seats in the house, front row. Spectators high up in the back rows seemed little more than peanut-sized.

Once a year the rodeo came to Houston. For about a week shops and restaurants were filled with people from out of town. Everybody took on a Wild West demeanor, wearing cowboy boots, Western shirts and string ties, and ten-gallon hats. People from places like Louisiana, Arkansas, Oklahoma, joined in the fat stock shows, cattle auctions, drinking, partying. The rodeo stars did the serious work, competing in the second biggest and richest rodeo of the year. After that, the cowboys and cowgirls went on to the granddaddy of all, the National Championships in Dallas.

Up close, in the $5,000 seats in which sat Brett and Nick, you could see that the rodeo stars had affected an unconcerned look as they waited their turns. But upon closer examination Nick thought they look worried, scared even.

Kinda how I feel, he thought.

He did not like the smell in the Astrodome: horse piss and horseshit, hay and leather, beer and hot dogs, alcohol and animals and sweat and fear. Horses pranced, cheerleaders whirled and jumped, riders rode and got thrown.

Brett watched it all with wide eyes. Nick asked him why only Butch Byrd had overseen Nugget's reserve estimates, and Brett turned his way. "When I'm promotin a deal to the public, havin to use a prospectus, there's no difference than how I report privately to investors. I'll put in my estimate of the barrels of oil per well that I'm gonna hit, I think; I can only get that offa the log analysis of nearby wells. And the wells that the estimates are comin from may not be *that* close to the wells I'm drilling; may not be many wells in the field. And that's my problem in Argentina. The fields are so damned ill defined. Besides, Butch knows what he's doing."

Brett watched awhile, then started talking again.

"But I can assure you aahm gonna take the most aggressive stance I can as far as estimatin recoverable barrels. Because at the end of the day, until the wells are drilled and if oil *is* found, you're not gonna really, until you get those wells drilled, know what you have. And once those wells *are* drilled, and I'm able to do log analysis off of the drilled wells, the numbers I estimate may change. But in the meantime I'm makin assumptions about the wells, and that'll jest have to do."

He knows I know all this, Nick thought. *He's dancing around.*

Brett said, "And so, all you really want to report is how wide the area is, how porous the sands—"

"Yes. The investors I know are familiar with the recovery factor. They know it's a function of the area size and the porosity and the permeability. They're pretty savvy. But what concerns me—"

There was an announcement, a red light glowed above a holding cage, and a bronco came out bucking, trying to throw a woman. Her arms flailed as she hung on. The crowd roared. She got thrown, falling as the bronco kept kicking and bucking as if she were still on its back.

"Look, pardner, why you worrying so much? Our numbers are good. If an investor challenges our prospectus numbers—which they haven't ever, by the way—if the investor says I want to hire an engineer and do my own reserve analysis, I say, well, have at it."

Another announcement. Another light. Another duet whirl of bucking horse and flailing rider, and a rider flying through the air and landing in a heap.

Brett watched intently. "If that guy's engineer comes back and says, well, you're smoking dope if you think these numbers make sense, we'll say, fine, these are our numbers, our analysis, all contracted out by Byrd and Company, licensed engineers. Go argue with *them*. It's just their professional guess, after all. And if you really don't like the numbers, don't invest." Brett's eyes grew small, staring at Nick. "And, anyhow, none of this concerns you. Just get the damn stock up. That's your only damn job."

"I know. But I have to feel comfortable."

Brett chuckled some. "Yeah, comfortable. In this damn bid'ness dealin with who I have to deal with… Ah, come on, pardner, hell, we'll all be richer than anybody can ever imagine."

"I, okay, look, that's about all for right now. Okay with you I'll go ahead and turn in. It's been a long day."

"Hell, you say." Brett was smiling and his voice stayed low. "You'll stay right here. How'll *that* look? Honorary Marshall's friend gets up and leaves in the beginning. Yaa think I don't have friends here?"

Nick realized that he could not leave, that he was bought and paid for.

He listened to the gasps and shrieks from the crowd. A rider had gotten his boot tangled up in a stirrup, and had been bucked off the horse. The horse kept turning and kicking in a circle. The rider, like a rag doll hanging from the saddle, was being jerked around the ring. Brett's eyes were wide as he watched.

Nick thought he knew how the rider felt.

Nick flew back to San Francisco, and called Linda first thing. "Hi, it's me."

"Oh, hi. I wondered where—"

"I'm back. It's so beautiful out. Meet me."

"Okay."

"By the water. In half an hour."

"Okay."

They met. After running for a while, he was panting hard.

The waters of the bay crashed into rocks, spraying all the joggers on the narrow path by the water. The wind blew sand about. In the clear blue sky, seagulls circled furiously.

With his last strength, he sprinted and caught up to Linda and took her hand. Holding hands, they walked a little. He wiped off with a towel. In the distance, the orange, spidery beams of the Golden Gate Bridge. The water under the bridge was a sparkling blue.

"We'd better get back," she said. "He may need me."

"Why don't you just get a nurse, somebody to stay with him?"

She thought about it. "And what? We're here longer and someone sees us and word gets around that you and I... God knows what else they think."

"We're out here *jogging*. Who the hell's going to make a big deal of *that*? Besides, who cares about what everybody else thinks?"

"I just can't. Do you understand?" She started walking back. He followed. Far away, at the end of the track, Thad sat in the wheelchair, wearing sunglasses. Linda squeezed his hand. "Look, we have it pretty good, don't we?"

He didn't say anything.

"Behind closed doors, anything goes. That's what we've always said. You know that, Nick. I'm worried. What is happening to you?"

He didn't know. Nugget was up another four points. Brett Wells was happy, all the stock buyers were happy. Linda and he found time to be together, and yet... He saw the sun reflecting from Thad's sunglasses as they walked closer to him. "When Julie was alive, I don't know, she was sick a lot and I could justify, you know, you and me—"

"Is this easy for me? You have eyes—look at him."

"Yeah." Nick felt sad, wanted to cry for no reason he could see. Beyond Thad, shining brightly in the mid-day sun, was the new black Mercedes sedan that Brett had given him. He couldn't get used to the car. He missed his old broken-down Porsche.

Four

Nick sat at the computer, clicked on to "Message Boards," to "N," then to "Nugget Petroleum." He skipped through to "Argentine Equipment," from "Down and Dirty."

"What the hell's up with management? You can't get an answer out of middle management. My brother-in-law's a big investor in the company and he's been tracking equipment and says that almost nothing gets shipped to Argentina and he knows the oil business. So how come they're not hiring people if they're so busy? They haven't hired line supervisors, clerks, or engineers in years. Anybody else hearing anything?"

Guy's doing his homework, Nick thought. *I asked Brett about equipment going to Argentina, and he told me they were planning to ship big amounts. Are they*?

He scrolled through some more messages to "Killer Deal," from "Student."

"Usually this big volume and stock up-move that Nugget's getting is in anticipation of some news. Big news. Hear Nugget's about to get an A rating from Morgans. Then they're going to go out and expand like crazy. Or sell out. Anybody else hearing this stuff?"

How the hell could anybody outside of the company know what a rating agency is about to do? They can't, he thought. *This is being planted by someone inside Nugget, it has to be*. He stared at the screen. *This is inside information and it's being hyped over the Internet by someone.* His stomach tightened. *A fucking can of worms, this company.*

He scrolled back to earlier postings, looking for "Student." *Student, right. Insider market manipulator driving the stock up is more like it*. He stopped scrolling as something caught his eye. "Turkey Roasting," from "Shark."

"This bull-shit bond rating is the latest scam from that wanna-be oil tycoon Brett Wells. He and Butch Byrd go way back. They almost went to jail for selling sub-prime mortgages on homes in Oklahoma. Oil they know a little about; they used to sell limited partnerships back in the hot days when tax-shelter provisions were allowed. Bullshitting with phony filings they know plenty about. There's probably more oil in the gas tank of my car than in all of Nugget's wells. And I drive a compact."

After reading it again, Nick thought it over. *The shark's a short— I know it. The shark is shorting the stock, and it sounds like he knows what he's talking about. But maybe he's just guessing. Maybe he's another short out there getting squeezed as Nugget moves up. The shark's getting more and more desperate and is trying to drive the stock down. I don't believe the shark.*

I don't want to believe the shark. I got a job here to do: to get the stock up. Yes, somebody's passing along inside information to drive the stock and, yes, a short out there is trying to bomb the stock. But I don't make money unless the stock goes up, and that's what I'm showing up for.

He scrolled through and found another message. "From the Trenches," from "Shark."

"Is the so-called top management of Nugget, headed up by that bragging phony Brett Wells, really looking at the numbers sent by their middle-management? The answer I'm hearing from some people is Hell, No! But Wells wouldn't know what oil production numbers meant if they bit him in the ass. Okay, I know oil production is all about cash flow, but it makes no sense to show projections given on bad information from people that just want to hold on their jobs. Besides, Butch Byrd could care less about accurate cash flow reporting. You know where Byrd got his master in engineering degree? From a crummy on-line school. The school's defunct. Why is anyone working at Byrd's company? Byrd has got only one customer that I know of. Yes, you guessed it: Nugget Petroleum."

Okay, so the shark's got a good information pipeline, Nick thought. *Big deal. So do I.* He started typing on the keyboard: "From the Top," from "Spear."

"All you interested in Nugget Petroleum: don't be fooled by Shark. I don't know what he's got against Byrd and Wells and Nugget, but the company is sound, well managed" (The fat policeman in Mexico ripping the binoculars out of Nick's hands appeared. Nick hesitated, took a deep breath, and went on.) "and management is capable and committed to building value. The Shark doesn't understand the oil business. Brett Wells runs Nugget in a decentralized way to maximize his field talent. Look at the price of oil: West Texas Crude at $32.00 a barrel, the highest since the Gulf War. That makes Nugget worth more than its market price in terms of net asset value. I don't know what it is with Shark. Maybe he missed buying NUP cheap and now wants it lower to get in? Or he or she is a short and getting scorched. I say jump on Nugget and enjoy the ride.

He clicked "Send" and watched his words appear on "Messages." Reading his words he felt hollow. *God damn it, I don't believe what I've said*, he thought. He turned off the computer. *The shark's right; everything he said sounds right.* He looked at the dark computer screen, around at the empty office, out of the window to the three-sided Transamerica Building in the distance. *And I don't care. I want it all again, and I'm getting close.* He snapped off the lone light on his desk and he left.

***

"Hey, you hearin anything?"

"Ah, like what?" Nick cradled the phone receiver on his shoulder. The Transamerica Building started to glow in the early morning sun. Crumbs from a croissant, the leavings of coffee in a Starbucks cup were on top of a stack of papers.

"What, you're askin? Not how many times that rich bitch piece of ass you're fucking in Pacific Heights gets off every night. Hell, I've screwed every whore in the city. My shrink says I should find someone to speak to. *That* can ruin a good fuck. Nugget Petroleum I'm talking about. Hello? Helllooo??"

Nick went cold. *You just don't lie to the Lenny Zellons*, he thought. *Not lightly anyway. The Street will hunt you down, and it doesn't forgive bad information.* "Uh, nothing new, Lenny."

"Nothing new, your ass," he screamed. "There's a story around that a bunch of peasants, farmers—hell, I don't know, they're all the same down there in South America, don't have shirts, fuck all the time, wish I was one of them, hosin them hot brown-skinned women. Well, they were shot at by police, Pampas, some damn hell-hole, you know, where Nugget's reserves are. C'mon, you got anything? Why do I suddenly feel like I'm sitting here holding my putz?"

Nick pondered about telling Lenny that he was standing there in a field, and some fat policeman tore off the side of his face with a gun and grabbed his binoculars. Would've blown him away if the driver wasn't around. But, then, Lenny would sell Nugget and people would ask why.

"Hey, hold on," Lenny said. A few moments later, "Sorry, Nick, but this guy on the Market Channel, the ugly guy, red hair, well, the moron's talkin about the price of wheat's up for the fourth day. Well, I'm long wheat and makin money, but I'd rather be losing money than have to look at him. So he says Nugget's going higher. And I'm thinking where's that pretty piece of ass with the blonde hair? The one who's on at the market open. Now her I'd watch all day. And so where are we? Do you—hey, sorry, but hold just a minute."

Nick shivered, was freezing though the office wasn't cold. *All Lenny, all any of them respect in this business is the money*, he realized again for the millionth time. *Ahh, so what? Just do your job.*

Lenny came back. "So about the blond, the one at the market open who looks and talks like a perfect WASP, and I'd love to suck her toes, she said this morning that nobody can account for Nugget making a new high. Interesting, but I'd give up all my stock just to get a sniff of her panties, maybe after she plays, what do they play, WASP girls? Racquetball? Learned it at Smith or Radcliffe or some damn place. Her friends Buffy and Muffy and their dog Radcliffe and all that. Gives me a hard-on watching her talk. I'd take a hundred Viagras before screwin her. Die, but it'd be worth it. Look, I can't talk about her anymore. I got a half million shares of that shit, up five. Do I sell?"

He felt Lenny's rat-eyes staring at him through the phone. *If I tell the truth I'm dead. But it's him or me*. Nick thought about it. "Hold the stock, Lenny. Would I steer you wrong?"

Lenny thought, then said, "No. I don't think you would. But I worry about you. Why *wouldn't* you screw me? Ahh, maybe you're wearin blinders, and that works. But watch out. Maybe that piece of ass you been hosin turns on you. Or maybe those guys at this Nugget you're pumping up get pissed off. You screw up and they come after you, with machetes. No, you don't see it. You know what? Maybe you're right. Whatever you're smokin, send some to me."

Nick laughed. "I'll keep you up to speed about Nugget. And, Lenny, about Thad's wife—"

"Okay, okay. I'm through talkin about her. What do I care? I get mine. I just may call a whore. My therapist tells me sex's better when it's part of a relationship." Lenny cackled. "What the hell does he know?"

***

Linda and Nick hiked up a mountain in the Marin Headlands, just across the Golden Gate Bridge from San Francisco. Trees towered above them. Heavy clouds muted the sun. Far below, waves crashed into boulders, sending white foam into the air. Reflecting sharply off the water, slivers of light came out from behind the clouds. In all directions you could see the green ocean, towering mountains topped by heavy trees and gray skies. The muddy path was filled with faded, dead, brown leaves. Dirt spotted Linda's sweater. Her blue boots were caked with mud.

When they reached the top, off in the distance the buildings in the San Francisco financial district were tiny. The Transamerica Building looked like a large toy. Linda sat under a tree in heavy grass. Pine needles stuck to her jeans. Nick sat alongside her and watched the water swirling in the distance and felt defeated and sad and didn't know why. He didn't want to talk but had to talk about it. "Uh, you know, I think I figured out—"

"This isn't going to be one of those conversations, is it?" She closed her eyes and leaned against the tree.

"Yes, afraid it is." He did not like where the conversation would go. "I think I figured out that when I'm with you it feels like Julie's still alive. I mean, we, I, cheated on Julie, and now we're still together and I'm still cheating on Julie, so she's still alive."

Linda looked at him with barely opened eyes.

"Don't you see?"

She did not speak.

"But Julie's dead. And all we're really doing now is cheating on Thad." He tried, but couldn't stop. "And Thad's not a bad guy, and doesn't deserve it just because he's had a stroke. And you're not a bad person either, and neither'm I. But it was exciting before, you know, to sneak around. Now... I just feel bad, and rather... helpless."

"I don't see what this means."

"Except maybe not seeing you anymore, like this I mean, I'd feel better."

Linda's mouth turned down.

"I want to feel good again."

Tears started down her cheeks. "What do we do?"

They sat there, not wanting to leave. The flat gray light got darker, the air colder. After awhile he got up and said, "We'd better get back." When he tried to hold her, she brushed by him and started down the trail.

They walked down the mountain, got into his black Mercedes and sped off. Heavy trees over the muddy sides of mountains flashed by. The moon glowed heavily over the highway.

She took his hand as he drove toward the city. He warmed, just feeling her touch. *Damn, I don't want to feel this much. How can I ever get away?* He relaxed, thinking, *Loosen up, you've always been too rigid.* He drove faster. *It'll all come together. Don't worry.*

***

Ellen Pasternak was frantic. As the senior analyst on the grading team for energy and chemical companies at Morgans, the old-line bond rating firm, she had three projects she was wrapping up. There was that bonus the partners promised her for getting these done, and she could use the money. They promised an additional fifty percent of salary if she could get the Nugget Petroleum package sent to the partners by next week. That, they especially wanted completed. Well, Nugget was finished, she had sent the package off, and she was dog-tired.

Nugget had been tough to do. She had spent weeks in Houston, and it had been painful to get hard numbers out of Brett Wells and his people. "I'm not even sure of those numbers," she mumbled, sitting at her desk. She had no background in the oil bid'ness (they all called it bid'ness, and now she was also, she thought, smiling), but she supposed numbers are numbers. She did the best she could. She needed the bonus.

She looked around her office: on her desk, a framed picture of her husband, their two kids, aged eight and ten. Out the window, traffic clogged Fifth Avenue. People packed the sidewalks, they walked in and out of the expensive shops and restaurants. She rested her head in her palms; the headache was worse and she wanted to go home.

She jumped when the phone rang.

"Ellen Pasternak."

"Hello, Ellen. This's Nick Larson. I do some investor relations work for Nugget Petroleum. I'll be in New York for a few days, and need to get together with you. Not a big deal, just a few minutes."

"Oh, yes. Brett did tell me."

"Good. When's a good time?"

Kneading her temple with her hand, she said, "I don't think I could be of much help. Sorry."

"Just want to see about Nugget's bond rating."

"But, Mr. Larson, I can't comment on a rating consideration. That's confidential, as I'm sure you know."

"Look. Five minutes. Check the chat-rooms. It's no secret that Morgans might rate the bonds highly."

What does this Larson really want? she wondered. *I don't want to get into Nugget again. The bonus money's already spent.* On Pasternak's desk, her keys to a sixty thousand dollar Lexus SUV. In her pocket, keys to her West Side apartment, half a million for something not all that fancy. She looked at the picture on her desk: private school for two. "I'm snowed here. Maybe next week."

"No. I'm here now. What time do you get off work?"

"I've gotta dart out of here at five to make my yoga class so I can get home at seven."

"I'll come to your place. We can go get coffee, or talk there, or—"

"No, that won't work." She took out a tissue and wiped her damp forehead. "That's when I do homework with the kids."

"Where's the yoga class?"

"Midtown, Seventy-Second just off Fifth."

"Name of the studio?"

"Power Yoga by Ramanad, at five-thirty, but I don't honestly see—"

"I'll be there. Just five minutes? Ten at the most."

She thought it over, realized he wasn't going away. "Okay, but how will I know you?"

"I'm slightly balding. And I'm not that tall, and I'm thin, and I'll wear black shorts. You?"

"Dark hair, sort of tall, full formed—well, I don't mean it that way, you wouldn't turn on the street and watch me, but I'm on a diet. I'll wear a gray sweatshirt that says Banana Republic."

"I'll find you."

***

Nick got to the studio before class started. He pushed open a door with a sign: Power Yoga by Ramanad. Walking up the dark stairs he smelled incense burning alongside yellow candles, aglow just at the top of the landing.

A sign said: PLEASE LEAVE SHOES. TAKE YOUR VALUABLES. PEACE.

He took off his shoes and walked across the wide expanse of the studio. Through the wide windows, he looked down into busy New York City. People passed hurriedly; cars and cabs clogged the streets. The traffic light at the corner turned yellow, then red.

Stripping down to black shorts and a T-shirt, he surveyed the dimly lit open space. The smell of sweat and bodies permeated the air.

Photos of an old bald-headed man of Indian descent, in pretzel-like postures, were hanging on the walls. The faint sound of a sitar came from somewhere.

He picked up a thin, spongy mat from a pile and unraveled it in the front of the room. Sitting down, he watched as people started pouring in.

People kept arriving. After awhile, it was filled: men and women in their twenties and thirties with sculpted bodies; a gray-haired woman, her hair back in a bun; a few older guys but mostly women, shapely and some in skin-tight leotards. One woman stood on her head. A pencil-thin-bodied man sat and casually put his leg behind his head.

A rather large but attractive woman, her hair cascading down in ringlets over her shoulders, rushed in. Banana Republic was printed on the front of her sweatshirt. She spread her mat in the back of the room. Nick walked around the sea of mats and people separating them.

Ellen Pasternak's eyebrows knotted and her eyes darkened as he approached.

He waved. She nodded back. He mouthed, I'll see you after class.

She nodded and smiled faintly. Nick went back.

Appearing in the front of the class, the old but ageless bald-headed man whose photos were hanging on the wall. Standing straight, his light eyes surveying the room, dressed in a crisp white linen loose-fitting shirt and shorts, he waited as the room quieted. He put his hands in prayer position and closed his eyes. So did the class. Nick, glancing around, did the same.

Then, "Oooooom" the old man chanted deeply. The class did the same, the sound filling the room. Softly the man said, "Chataranga Dandasana," then dropped to the floor and executed a push-up, moving quickly and lightly, like a cat.

The students were crowded together. Nick followed their movements: hands to the floor, kicking his feet into the air, ending stretched long into a pushup, then with his head between his arms and his butt stretched toward the ceiling, as a dog would stretch, on all fours, he stayed in the "downward dog" position. Then jumping forward, his feet landing on the mat, then reaching up toward the ceiling, Nick felt sweat soaking through his shirt. Back down, hands to the floor once again, another kick backwards, the students repeated the posture. Nick's feet hurt when they hit the floor. He sweated and panted and tried like hell to keep up with the movements.

The old man continued, muttering the desired postures in Hindi: "Vrksasana, Dirkasana, Dandasana." The class followed, the smell of bodies filling the room.

Nick wiped off with a towel. His arms and legs and stomach ached. He would not quit. Whatever it took, he would keep up. His mat was sweat-soaked. He sweated and stretched with the other students on all sides of him.

He started thinking, *She's afraid, and hiding something. Only reason she'd be scared's if she's covering up stuff about Nugget. Maybe in on it*. Gasping for air, he thought, *Later. Figure it out later*. Yet his mind raced. Thoughts came pouring back, right to that time. *Julie's funeral, here it comes again*. Ratratrat as dirt was shoveled onto her casket; as the casket got buried under a mountain of brown and black earth; as he walked away from her grave, and the light San Francisco mist hung in the air; as the smell of freshly cut grass, just dug earth, mingled; as the Golden Gate Bridge stood heavily in the distance, its orange towers barely visible through the mist.

I'm going away, he had thought at that time. *I'm not coming back. Where can I go?*

Memories kept rushing in, and he recalled when Julie was sick, and she'd be home for days at a time, then go back to the hospital. Nick would often travel, between hospital visits. He remembered sitting in the stands of a bullring. Cerveza Carta Blanca, the sign under the lower tier of seats read, its words in green. Bienvendo a Ciudad De Mexico, those words in black on a sign in a higher middle tier of seats.

The fight was on a Sunday: *Domingo*. Crowds in the stands yelled and stomped their feet as below men and horses dragged the carcass of a freshly killed bull out of the arena. The bullring was much smaller than the grand *Plaza Del Toros* in Spain. The sun reflected off the sand, creating a white glare in the center of the ring. Pools of brownish red blood were about the ring.

This is sadistic and cruel, Nick had thought. *Take his sword away and see how brave the matador is then*.

He took off his sunglasses and looked around.

Dark eyes in back were looking at him.

"Ola," he said to her.

"Halo?" The dark-eyed woman said.

"Theresa? We met at the Ambassador's house?"

"Si. Yo soy. And you are Senor Larson, the rich American who is buying up our country."

He laughed. "Hardly. But I am buying Mexican stocks."

She smiled. Maybe she was thirty or thirty-five years old. Thick black hair matched her black eyes.

He turned back to the bullfight only to see the picador pierce the bull with a lance. He turned to her again and gestured at the empty chair next to her. "May I?"

"Por favor," she said.

Later, much later, Nick now remembered, after they had made love in a tony, small hotel in the *Zona Rosa*, they lay quietly. Moonlight poured into the room, illuminating their discarded clothes, lying on the floor.

"You long separated?" Theresa asked.

"Actually I, I'm still living with her," Nick said. He felt nauseated. "My wife, she is ill, and, and..."

Theresa stared at him. "You love her? You love her, yes, very much."

He had started crying. Far away from where Julie lay in a hospital bed, he hadn't run far enough. "Very much," he whispered.

"Why are you here?" she asked, gesturing around the room that included herself.

"Why am I here," he said.

In front of the class, the old man said quietly, "Bakasana." The class responded: hands on the floor, knees up under elbows, the students rocked forward and balanced on their hands. Nick kept trying.

Memories rushed in. Run-run-run back to Mexico City, after that night with Theresa, after a day of trading Mexican stocks, after betting right on a peso devaluation. *Damn right Mexico did not devalue, just as I thought*, he had gleefully thought, throwing open the heavy golden door of the *Bolsa*, prancing down the street. About a million dollars, he made, he figured. *No, more than a million; maybe a couple*.

On the wide Zona Rosa he watched the swaying stroll of a woman, long black hair shifting with the rhythm of her hips, skirt above her knees. A blonde joined her. Talking excitedly, they strolled down the boulevard.

Nick followed them. The city smelled like a giant tortilla, the streets flooded with cars, white and green cabs, horns honking. A man dressed in dirty, soiled rags in a storefront begging, his hand outstretched, grinning with a toothless mouth.

They stood on a corner while the light changed. "Pardon. Habla Ingles?" Nick asked. "I am rather lost."

"Si," the black-haired woman said. "Pero... but no perfecto." The woman whispered something to the other, and they laughed. Nick laughed. The blonde shook her head, and mumbled something in Spanish.

Planting himself between them, he said, "Look, it's getting late, and I've made some money—mucho dinero—and why don't you have a drink with me?"

They hesitated.

"Here's the cell phone number of the Minister of Finance for Ciudad de Mexico. Call him. We just made a bundle together. He'll vouch for me. Esta bien."

Looking at each other, chattering in Spanish, the women giggled and appraised him. "Okay," the dark-haired one said. "Pero uno drink."

After entering a dark restaurant, enormous plants scattered about a large room, they sat down. His hands brushed the fine tablecloth. He surveyed the wine list, told the waiter to bring two bottles, "Uno rosa, uno blanco." The women laughed, he laughed. Everything everybody said was very funny.

The blonde said something about a boyfriend. The black-haired woman answered and laughed. Nick laughed. Then the image of Julie in the hospital bed, pencil-thin, appeared to him. Julie with great effort reached over, she took his hand. He couldn't help it—he started crying. The women's eyes grew large. He took a sip of wine, but he couldn't stop. The women signaled to each other, pushed back their chairs.

"No, no, don't," he said. "We'll have dinner. It's nothing," He didn't want to be alone, not now. "Hey, look, esta fiesta," he said, trying to laugh.

"Navasana," the old man said.

Memories flew away. Nick did as the other students: he sat and raised his legs up, toward the ceiling, his arms stretching forward, his body shaped like a V. His stomach muscles hurt like hell.

He held the posture, legs trembling. *Stop thinking*, he told himself bitterly. *Just forget all that. The doctors said to put it behind me. It happens. So why can't I?*

He remembered the black, iron sides of a hospital bed. The hospital where Julie was: white walls, smell of cleaning fluids and medicine, women and men in white uniforms walking in and out of the room. Julie'd manage a smile every now and then.

He watched. Then the heavy smell of the antiseptic room had made him want to leave. *Where? Where*, he asked himself, walking toward the brown door. In the cold San Francisco night he dropped down the top of the Porsche and roared off.

He followed the others as they put their hands in prayer position and exhaled a deep "Ummmmmm."

Wiping sweat off, he caught Ellen Pasternak at the door.

"Coffee?"

"I only have a few minutes," she said. "Really."

"That's all I need."

She shrugged. "I can't help you any."

"That's fine too."

***

The Oak Bar, on the Central Park South side of the Plaza Hotel, used to always be full, with people spilling out of the bar and into the hotel corridor. But since the World Trade Center was destroyed the crowds were heavy only on the weekends. So tonight most tables sat empty. Dimly lit and crammed with tables, the room had a mahogany bar running its length. The trees of Central Park were visible across the street. People hustled by the window.

Nick sat at a small table in the corner sipping a martini, his third. Surveying the almost empty room, he realized he missed the people, people crammed in at the bar and lots of boisterous talk. Again he realized he didn't like change, especially the kind where people are missed.

He decided to think of the work at hand.

She's the key, he thought. *Pasternak's the ticket to Nugget making it. That rating agency she works for is like all of them, sort of an oligopoly. Everything in the credit markets has to flow through those big agencies, gotta get their blessing. They're arrogant, all those companies are, but can they can afford to be.*

He had worked with the agencies at one time or another. Just five agencies controlling all of the money flowing through the U.S. credit markets. They were all pretty much the same: big corporate bureaucracies.

When you got a rating, you end up working with just one officer. That person gets committee approval for the assigned rating. So that one person is crucial. Take Ellen. Members of the committee didn't have the time to scurry around checking out the numbers she showed them. The way she presented Nugget, favorable or unfavorable, if she was lukewarm or showed she hated it, made the difference in how the committee voted Nugget's rating.

He squirmed in his chair.

She's very young, he thought. Most gatekeepers at these agencies were, and inexperienced. They could be easily fooled—or bought.

She seemed scared, he decided. *Let's say she was bribed. It'd be simple: she goes to the committee and shows Nugget's reserve numbers. They wouldn't even question her about who did the analysis, just want her findings. They probably don't know the oil patch. Ellen's the specialist in that industry and they rely on her. They wouldn't even know which questions to ask. Now if oil analysts came in and grilled her, they'd know exactly what to ask. But the committees deal with their analysts, then go to lunch.*

It was her pauses, her body language, he decided, that tipped him off to thinking that she'd give Nugget an A rating. She didn't flinch when he mentioned that possibility.

The ache in his gut told Nick that Ellen had sold out. He told himself to get off it.

You're too suspicious. He stopped thinking, not liking where he was going. He took out his cell phone, put it back, took it out again, and called Linda.

***

A movie flickered black-and-white from the TV screen in the bedroom. The sound was low, almost too low to hear. Linda watched the movie, her mind elsewhere. Thad slept, with his mouth open. From outside, the chirping of crickets, a few cars passing. Pacific Heights was quiet, most of the hard-working residents asleep; they would rush off to work in the morning before the sun showed first light.

She wondered about Nick, what he'd said on the trail. Did he mean it about not seeing her anymore, or how did he mean it? And he had said that before, both of them had, about leaving each other, but couldn't or didn't want to stay away, and what did it mean? What does any of it mean? They had discussed that too, many times.

The phone rang. Instinctively, she went into the den to answer the phone.

"Hi," Nick said. "Can you talk?"

"Yes, he's sleeping. Glad you called. We had a bad time of it today. He tried to walk, he always does." She just wanted to forget the day. "How's it going?"

"It's, about the same. I don't know about this company I'm working with. It might be more than I can handle. Anyhow, I just wanted to say hello."

"Hello."

He laughed. "Hello."

"When are you coming home?"

"Oh, not for awhile."

"Sorry. I miss you."

There was silence on the line. Glancing back to the sliver of light coming from the bedroom, she thought, *Oh just leave and join him*. Almost as quickly she thought, *How silly. What would people think*?

"Did you mean what you said? On the hike?"

"I always mean it, don't I, Linda? And then I miss you and see you and the wheels of my resolve just come off."

She laughed. "Yes."

"Besides, we're too old for anything to be a final final, aren't we? At a certain age you don't know about tomorrow or how many more you have, so you, I guess, enjoy what you have."

She laughed. "Something like that. So, when are you coming home?"

He laughed. "Soon as I can. You know I don't like to be far from the jogging track."

"Call. I got a new jogging outfit. Black."

"Yeah, okay."

"Well, get a good night's sleep."

"Oh, my mind's taking off. You know how that is."

"Yes. I know."

"And the future's worrying me. Never did before."

"Maybe you're getting smarter," she said.

He laughed. "Goodnight."

She walked toward the sliver of light, then into the bedroom, lit only by flickering images from the TV screen. A dressing table and mirrors were near the bed where Thad lay, now snoring. She snapped on lights, and the large mirror in front and the smaller mirrors on the sides reflected each other, so that many Linda Thackerys reflected back to her. Glowing along the mirrors, the light bulbs illuminated her face. Many Lindas started brushing their hair. Brushing her hair always relaxed Linda.

Surveying herself, she smiled: perfect white teeth, short bobbed hair, warm brown eyes. *A handsome woman*, she decided. *No, not pretty, and not young anymore, but fifty, well, almost fifty-one was not old.* Her firm breasts, shapely legs, thin waist—men still came alive around her, she could tell. And she loved knowing that.

If he wants, we can be friends. That's okay. We're no good at this sneaking around. Is that what we're doing? We are friends, and we do have sex, and he has a life, doing stock deals or out there with whatever he does. And I wish I were with him, wherever he is. Anywhere. Just something exciting. When he holds me, and he's all worried and confused and horny and all tongue and fingers and... Linda was brushing her hair furiously.

Slowing down her brushing, she felt herself getting wet. *So we have a good time and the rest, it's all chemistry*, she decided. *That's all. Nobody knows and nobody gets hurt.*

She turned out the lights. Her face disappeared from the mirrors, and she looked at Thad, then at the TV screen. She watched the figures in black-and-white, speaking about something.

***

After Nick hung up, he knew he couldn't sleep, so he stayed at the table in the almost empty bar.

He started thinking about Ellen again. That if you were just bribing one person, it's all so simple. He knew that Ellen was the conduit for information that gets through to the rating agency committee. That even though they made the decision about improving Nugget's credit rating, her recommendation is what they use. *And these big rating agencies, they're not as calm, as collected, as people think.*

He stared at the empty martini glass and pondered that he was drinking too much. He ordered another, rationalizing, *I can't sleep. Back to rating agencies, yes, they're always scrambling, like any bureaucracy: this analyst left, that analyst is getting up to speed, always a feverish sense of filling the holes, getting the ratings done, making decisions. There's always room in that kind of frenzy for cutting corners or cheating. And it would be so simple: Ellen Pasternak, lots of bills, kids, nothing wrong with taking a little cash here or there to hurry things along.*

Except that it's illegal.

He continued pondering. That they were all young people, the analysts at the agencies. Lots of turnover. The good ones got hired away, mostly to Wall Street and at big salaries. The bad ones got fired, or stayed and got passed over. *Ellen, she's good, probably just waiting for a fat job offer to come her way.*

A fresh martini appeared, frost covering the chilled glass. He took a sip but didn't even taste it. He again wondered why he couldn't sleep. He thought about the fact that everything goes through the rating agencies. The industry was so huge because nearly all instruments had to be rated. Corporations, their senior debt, their preferred stock, their junior debt, their collateralized debt—pretty much everything.

But rating agencies extend to other areas, he thought. Even homes. In fact, home finance rating was bigger than most industries. Sub-prime lending was huge also. *But Pasternak's in over her head and she doesn't know who she's playing with.* He wondered if he was in over his head, and dismissed the thought. *They wouldn't dare touch me.*

He ruminated that if a guy had fraud in his heart, he could make it work through a paper trail. Maybe set up a phony real estate company, create a bunch of paperwork to make it look like people out there had loans against the houses that his phony company was financing. Or people could have loans, but not know about false loans that were recorded for additional houses.

Nick knew how easy it was. A scammer could create records of everything. Anybody could lease office space and hire temps to fill the desks; give them make-believe jobs to do. For a few thousand dollars, an Internet scammer could build a website, state-of-the-art to impress the loan underwriters and securitizers. At the rating agencies, someone like Paternak could be in on the take, and get a company a BAA, maybe an A rating, and sell bonds through an investment banker or broker.

He took a sip. *Cut it out, you'll drive yourself crazy.* But he couldn't stop the thoughts. *And Pasternak'll put her kids through school with the scam, and nobody'll even notice. And the investors'll be swindled, but so what? They'll never know until later, if the deal unravels. Like Nugget's a fraud or something.*

He scratched behind his knee, and tried to make his mind go blank. He finished the martini and looked around. Again he wondered how he had gotten tied up with Nugget. Telling himself to forget it, he thought, *You could set up an office scam for under $50,000. Hire some temps, hell, go out and hire real sales people and set up an office, and raise money. Isn't that what Nugget's doing but on a mega-scale?*

He stumbled upon the answer to the question that he'd avoided asking himself: using Pasternak, Nugget was probably getting the paperwork and reserve estimates and drilling records past the rating agency. Maybe investment bankers would want to securitize the bonds to lower the risk. The bank would then send the paperwork to a trustee, Citibank or someone who would attest to the existence of the collateral. The trustee would never check out the numbers, just note that they received the paperwork, then file the documents in a warehouse somewhere. Probably never look at them again.

And nobody cares about any of this, except me. Why do I care? I've just never been tied up in something like this. So, where else can I go? I'm over fifty and nobody's gonna hire me, not when they ask, so how long did you have your last job? And there's that warrants. I have to be around for a year or I get nada.

What about going to see Brett? Maybe he'll let me quit early. I got the stock up pretty good, so maybe we can work something out. Nick decided that Brett would understand, and he felt better, knowing that he could now sleep.

***

Brett Wells stood on a concrete platform, surrounded by a crowd of roughnecks, oil patch workers who did the tough grunt work that was needed to drill a well: set the drill pipe, keep the drill lubricated, and keep aiming the drill toward its target.

About twenty yards from the platform, Butch Byrd leaned out of a battered truck, sweat pouring down his face, and hollered, "Hey, Brett, let's go have lunch."

Straining to hear, Brett turned toward him, but the noise from the drill was deafening. A tall, gangly man came over, his bony face wet with grease, and shouted into Brett's ear, "Guy's comin to see you. Let him in? Name's Larson."

Wells nodded, then waved to Butch. Butch crawled out of the truck, and walked across the mud to the concrete platform. They watched as Nick walked up.

The incessant buzz from thick clouds of mosquitoes was everywhere, there in the heart of the muddy, dead-water swamps in southeastern Louisiana. Trees towered over the swamps, and above the concrete platform containing Byrd and Wells and Larson and the oil-field roustabouts and field hands. Above all of this hung the omnipresent sun blazing from the sky, the air still, no breeze anywhere.

Nick stepped onto the platform, nodded, and asked Brett, "Can we talk?"

Brett wiped off sweat. "Sure. What's on your mind?"

Nick shifted. Brett and Butch stared at him as people raced about the drill.

"Well, I got the stock up and I'm wondering—no, I've *decided* there's no sense in me continuing. I have some other business I'd like to do."

ClankClankClank, from the drill pipe. Nick slapped at a mosquito buzzing about his nose. Another was biting his ear. Butch took out a handkerchief and wiped his neck.

Brett said, "You'll see. We're just getting started."

"No, you're doing fine. You don't need me. I'm always there for consultations—"

"We do."

"Well, couldn't we..."

"See where this stuff's goin," Brett snapped. "Bottom line, you'll be out of a job, and lose yer stock options, which I might add're worth quite a bit now. And as for a reference from me about you, I wouldn't hold mah breath."

Nick felt like a knife was cutting through his gut: stock options gone, no income, no recommendation, all gone. The gold buckle on Butch's belt reflected the sunlight in blinding flashes. Nick sweated.

"Yeah, also forget Ellen Pasternak helpin you. Fact is, you can forget her, period."

"Yes, well..."

"Ain't nothin but gettin that stock higher," Butch said.

"Now, let's not be hard on him," Brett said. "He's gonna continue, aren't you?"

Wrong, he thought. *I made that stock and I can take it down.*

"A simple yes or no'll do." Brett said.

Nick swallowed. *Where the hell have I got to go*?

Brett spoke louder, over the racket from the drill. "Crunch time's about here. We'll go on a road show, grab a couple of our top people, the CFO, couple of board members. Go out and tell the world to buy these new bonds we're comin out with. You're good at that. And just think, we sell those bonds, we got plenty of cash to work with. We buy a company or two, you get out the word, and every point Nugget goes up, another hundred thousand to you. Not bad."

Nick found himself nodding.

"Sound good? Rich again? You like that?"

Nick nodded. So did the others.

"So let's get to work."

Butch and Bird turned back to the well.

"Okay," Nick said, hating himself.

Five

Sunshine streamed into the huge ballroom and washed over the seated people. Through large windows that looked down over the city, the crowd could see the lush tops of trees all over Houston, making the city appear a vivid green. Outside, very few people walked under the blazing sun. Dogs lay under the shade of green-leafed trees in a park across the street.

The air conditioning blew freezing air into the large room. Women were scattered among the white-faced, gray-haired men that were wearing dark suits and white shirts.

The crowd listened intently as the speaker continued "…and ah'm so proud to introduce him right now. The man who put this company together and is makin us richer ever day. Now, let's all just welcome our friend and Chairman of Nugget Petroleum, Brett Wells."

Hoots and hollers and clapping erupted. After mounting the podium and standing for a while, Brett put up his hands for quiet. "Thanks to all of you," he boomed into the microphone. "I've been traveling around the world, and let me tell you, it's good to be back. I have just one thing to say: every day, just stop for a moment and think, and then thank God you are privileged enough to be in the great State of Texas."

The crowd roared approval.

"You've all been given handouts 'bout our financials. These figures were presented to Morgans, the big rating agency in New York. Those people looked us up and down and crunched the numbers and gave us a new ranking."

The crowd buzzed.

"And I'm proud to say as of this morning we have been informed that the rating on Nugget Petroleum debt has been raised to a good solid A."

Sitting in the front row, Nick looked around at the smiles. *Never told me*, he thought. *Nobody did.*

"We'll soon get to your questions," Brett said. "But I want you to know that we appreciate all of our stockholders and what you've been through with us. Damn low-priced stock's no fun for anybody. But we're takin care of bid'ness, don't you worry none."

Smiles and laughter filled the air.

"And anyway, ool's not stayin at this price long. Hell, no, we're seeing a worldwide oil shortage coming, maybe even rationing, like we had in the '80s. You just wait, Nugget's gonna have a bond offering, then buy other companies and leases and reserves. Be a major player, that I promise you."

Applauding along with the others, Nick thought, *He just might pull it off.*

A hand went up in the back of the room.

"Yes, what is it?" Brett said.

Standing in the back, a woman wearing a black suit, white bow-tied scarf. "About your reserve estimates. I could only find one consultant listed. Maybe I overlooked others, but I *did* read the financials carefully. Also, in the balance sheet section—"

"Yes," Brett snapped.

"Much of the long-term debt has maturity dates of a year or less. This should be carried as short-term debt, which affects the liquidity rations in a negative way."

"Well..."

"And the footnotes don't really help. They reference the maturities but don't catalogue them as is usual. These are important issues, as I'm sure you're aware."

Brett's face reddened, but he spoke in a friendly way. "I'll look into that. When you're rushin to get a rating, like we were, then also runnin a growing bid'ness, it gets all frantic. I'll get with my accountants. As far as the reserve estimates, there is no set rule. Look, our lead underwriters have covered all this and they've been around for about a hundred years. Maybe we *did* switch some debt around. Happen. Hell, maybe the printer just put in the wrong numbers."

She's dead on right. So obvious, the maturity dates, I skimmed right over them. Faces in the crowd were blank. *Nobody'll care*, Nick decided, *not if the stock keeps going up.*

"Well, that's why we're here," Brett Wells said. "To answer all your questions. Hell, these things always get screwed up, but we'll get 'em straightened out." He looked to the back of the room, and said, "They're setting up."

Heads turned. A woman in a white apron rushed to a long, linen covered table carrying loaves of bread. A man carrying a silver pot with steam escaping from its nozzles placed it in the middle of the table.

"Talk this over lunch," Brett said. "Plenty of experts here. There's Margaret Anderson, with Fidelity in Boston." He waved and a woman waved back.

"And there's Nick Larson. You all remember him? He got Texas Resources sold. Well, he's working with us now. Right, Nick?"

Nick felt chilled by the cold air. He shivered. *Do I really have to admit I'm tied up with these people*? he thought. *Do I have to lie to them about this scam company*?

Brett smiled. It seemed to Nick that all the faces in the ballroom turned his way.

"Hell, Nick knows us better'n anyone. Been busy showin us how to handle our investor relations person. Right?"

Nick asked himself if he had to. A tiny voice within him said yes. *Yes you do. Otherwise you have nothing, maybe sleeping on a park bench. Do I have to*? *I'm not going back to being evicted, not ever again.*

"You know what I did with Texas Resources," Nick said, rising and facing the crowd. "That was nothing compared to where Nugget's going." He observed himself speaking as if the words were coming from someone else, rather surprised at his capacity to equivocate. "I was just waiting for the right deal to bring me out of retirement. Nugget's the one."

Brett beamed. He said, "Look, enough of this. Let's have lunch, lunch and drinks and we'll answer all your questions. What do you think we're here for?"

***

The sun was setting as Nick walked down a narrow cobblestone street in Buenos Aires. For the past two weeks he had been at Nugget Petroleum's road shows, speaking before groups and having one-on-one meetings with important investors. He arrived at the wide Avenida Corrientas, finding a parade spilled out into the street. Black and brown and white people in scanty costumes; a man inside a gold swan float; masks with rhinestones; black breasts nearly bursting out of bikini tops; a woman wearing a tiara; faces painted in gold, silver, with sequins; a woman with a yellow parasol above her head, dancing down the avenue.

Carnival time, and next stop: Rio.

He walked hurriedly, thinking that there was another damn road show in a few hours. Again he'd have to avoid telling about the hidden side of Nugget. He kept walking.

At the intersection of Avenida Carlos Calvo and Avenida Defensa in the 800 block, in the heart of the old San Telmo District, near the port of Buenos Aires, he passed the Freria café. Piano music drifted out to the street. A few doors further on was a heavy black door with gold letters: Estacion de Policia. Nick opened the door and went up to the second floor and down the hall. Stenciled in chipped gold lettering on a glass door: Capitan Hector Pugliese.

Inside the office, a lit lamp stood next to a desk. There was an adjoining room with barred cages: a holding area for prisoners. A middle-aged man sat behind a desk, holding a cigarette. He had sleepy-looking eyes.

"Senor Larson?" he asked. "I am Capitan Pugliese. You wished to see me?"

"Yes." The chair scraped on the floor as Nick brought it closer to the desk. He sat. "It's about... I was here a while back, and got attacked then by some policia guarding the Nugget Petroleum wells, out by Cordoba."

"Si. That is much out of my jurisdiction."

"But you see, don't you see, the police, they were, I don't know, except they weren't legitimate."

Capitan Pugliese watched him, as one might watch a caught fish squirm on a fish-line. After dragging on his cigarette, he sighed. "No, *you* do not understand, senor. A group here hired those policia in Argentina that, though they are not registered with your government, are connected tightly to big oil companies. Nugget Petroleum is, I am sure, one."

The heavy cigarette smoke drifted across the room. Pugliese shifted heavily in his chair. "All related to this group, maybe they do drugs, maybe other things, like blowing up buildings. Even the international agencies can not penetrate them. Borders mean nothing to them. They go where the money is. Trouble follows."

Nick said, "That squares. I come up with, through other investors they control the shareholders' votes of Nugget. I don't know how. Not yet."

Pugliese looked at his fingers, holding the almost burned-out cigarette. "Do you have a gun?"

Feeling a chill run down his back, Nick said, "Why, why would I need—?"

"They will come. Sometime, for something, they will come." The captain thought it over and said, "Because they will see you may betray them, from what you told me. Not like that Wells. He is a thief, they know. They own him. But you they do not own. You are helpful to them just now. When you are not..." Pugliese made a sign of his throat being slit from ear to ear.

Nick thought about it. Surely, nobody would cut his throat. He was just a money manager doing his job.

"Do you have a gun?" Pugliese said.

"No, I..."

"Buy one," he said. The meeting was ending.

"This's silly. Certainly you don't think—"

Pugliese looked tired. "Might I show you the victims that these people, we call them the Invisible Hand, because they are everywhere and nowhere, the ones they have slaughtered? Do you want to see women beaten and stuffed into garbage pails, or bodies with their eyes torn out—we think while they were still alive."

What the hell'd I get into? Nick thought. *Maybe I will buy a gun. Is this guy just trying to scare me? It's working.*

The police captain got up. His chair rattled as it was freed from his weight. "Now I must leave. We are known for tango in this city, senor. I say, go tango. Enjoy yourself. You can not fight them, senor. I wish I could help you but... " Pugliese shrugged his shoulders.

Nick made his way downstairs and went out into the black Buenos Aires night. Walking down the wide avenue, he crammed his hands into his pockets. Lights from tall buildings twinkled in the distance. Remnants of the parade were strewn about: sock; broken pieces of a float; discarded masks and paper tiaras, torn and with their strings missing.

I don't need him anyway, he thought, walking faster in the cool air. Nick figured he'd stay in there and do his job. He started calculating: Nugget was up over five points, that was half a million to him. A little longer and he'd have that up over a million. He'd never have to work again. He decided he wasn't a moral policeman for Wall Street. He couldn't know everything that was going on.

Music came out of the dance halls, over the sidewalk teeming with people. Getting jostled by the crowd as he walked along, he headed back to the green and blue twinkling lights of Cafe Europa. After sitting down on a hard chair and ordering a *mate*, he surveyed the people: couples holding hands, intellectuals with short beards and wire-rimmed glasses, deep in conversation.

He imagined that in the empty chair across from him Linda was smiling brightly, her perfect teeth, short bangs over her forehead. He thought then of Julie's dimpled cheeks, her blue eyes.

How could I? he wondered as both images morphed and vanished. *Julie in the hospital and Linda and me skiing in Lucerne. Some guy I am. Linda in a pink skiing outfit, me in black, riding a lift over the Alps, skiing off.* He remembered the swwshsh from the skis as they raced down the mountain, the bite of warm cognac going down at the end of the day, a fire burning in the corner, Linda smiling, far away, far away from the woman in the hospital—

A couple burst into laughter at the next table. The snows of Switzerland disappeared.

He started to think that maybe he could take Nugget down and make some money, big money. At the same time it would be illegal, but he figured that nobody would ever know, how could they, not the way he'd set it up. His brow tightened. *But it's illegal*, he thought. *Yeah, but so's what Nugget's doing*. He squirmed in his chair, then got up, dropped some *dolares* on the table, and started for the door. *Everybody's crooked*, he decided bitterly, throwing the door open into the black night.

***

"Trudy Schlanger, please."

"Certainly, sir. One moment, please."

Looking out the window of his hotel room, off the main thoroughfare in downtown Buenos Aires, Nick looked into a restaurant in an alley. Although early in the morning, men sat in blue work clothes; the heavy smell of steaks and fried eggs, fried potatoes, coffee. The city's *portenos* ate heartily, especially the men who did heavy work, such as machinists, carpenters, and dockworkers.

He wasn't hungry. Moments ticked by.

"Trudy Schlanger. May I help you?" the woman asked in a German accent.

"Nick Larson. Remember me?"

"Why, Mr. Larson, of course. It's been awhile. Are you still in San Francisco?"

"Well, I still live there, but I'm on assignment and… Trudy, is my numbered account still open?

"But of course."

"Good. And Nugget Petroleum, NUP on the New York, can you get me protection? Say on a hundred thousand shares?"

He heard the clicking of the computer keys as she typed.

"That would be no problem, Mr. Larson. We could get protection for that and much more."

He needed to get protection to make a short sale so that when the stock went down, which he hoped, and he wanted to buy it back, the stock would have been "protected," been reserved for his buy order.

"No, that's enough. Also, you better go ahead and make the account margin." That way, when he sold short he only had to put up about fifty percent of the sale.

"All right. And do you wish to place an order today, Mr. Larson?"

"No. Not yet."

"And your address? Still on Washington Street?"

"No, it's not." He remembered that house in Pacific Heights. Julie and he had lived there, just down the street from Linda and Thad, in a miniature Victorian with a riot of bougainvillea creeping up the weathered wood of the house. *I thought I'd live there forever*. He kept picturing the house, on the corner of the street with the view of the green bay below.

"Mr. Larson? Mr. Larson?"

"Yes. For now let's just use my e-mail address. Keep any correspondence there at the bank."

"Yes, certainly."

"The trade confirms—you can hold the hard copies and e-mail me the details."

After hanging up, Nick looked across the alley. The men in blue outfits were drinking coffee, sitting and smoking. Empty dishes sat on the tables. The coffee and steak and eggs smelled good.

Putting on his pants and cinching his belt, he went through the scenario again. *It's illegal. If I sell or short stock, I have to register as an insider*. He knew it was an SEC regulation. And if he didn't, he would be in violation; people go to jail for things like that. *But nobody'll ever know. There're no records, not in the States anyway. There's no way anyone can know.*

He pulled a wool sweater over his head and brushed his hair. He knew it was wrong, whether they caught him or not. He never cheated like that—never. *Yeah, but times've changed. Look, you can scrape together some money, maybe go in with Lenny. You short that stock here at about twenty, you can cover at about two. That's eighteen points, and on a hundred thousand shares, close to a two million dollar profit.*

He brushed his hair furiously. *Oh, great, in with Lenny*, he thought, studying his face in the mirror, not recognizing the face staring back at him. *But for two million—I don't know. I just don't know anymore.* A cold feeling went through him, as if he knew no one, everybody was a stranger. *I just don't know*, he thought again.

On instinct, he picked up the telephone. He told himself not to call. That he'd be right back into it, not good. He replaced the receiver. *Where do I go?* He lifted the receiver again. His fingers felt frozen in ice.

"Hello," Linda said.

"Hi. Am I bothering you?"

"Of course not. Where are you?"

"Away, on business. About through. How about... can we get together tomorrow?"

"Afraid not. Thad's cousin is coming up from Hillsborough. The day after?"

He wanted to put the phone down, wanted to hang up and never feel guilty again. *Where is there to go?* "Sure. I'll call you."

"Will you? You're sure?"

"I'll call."

"Lovely. It'll be fun."

"Yes. It's always fun."

"Anything new? That you can tell me about?"

"No. Just miss you and want to get home. You're the only thing that's familiar anymore. Does that bother you? Me saying that?"

"Come home, Nick. We can talk then."

***

Nick stood on the corner of California and Montgomery Streets, in the heart of the financial district. The office buildings had long ago emptied. The day started at three or four in the morning and by late afternoon most traders, analysts, brokers, and investment bankers had put in about twelve fourteen hours. Many stayed, however, and worked fourteen to sixteen hour days. Then the back-office people, and the overseas traders, and the computer night crew showed up. Wall Street never slept.

With its bells clanging, a cable car loaded with tourists rumbled down California Street. Its iron wheels went *ClacketyClacketyClackety* on the steel tracks. A boy on the car snapped pictures, while a little girl beside him studied the people on the sidewalk. Nick thought that they were cute kids, probably belonged to a nice family. He'd settle for that, to go home to a wife and kids. That scenario used to look boring to him, and now he figured that's about all the excitement he needed. Another cable car climbed the opposite way, up California Street, past the large plaza fronting the carnelian granite Bank of America and the other glass and steel buildings.

Down the hill he studied the Port of San Francisco building on the waterfront. Beyond its long front façade loomed the Bay Bridge, connecting the East Bay and Oakland; the lights of Oakland twinkled in the gathering darkness. *Now that would make a great painting*, he thought. *So who's going to paint it?* He shrugged his shoulders, knowing that this was not the time to think about painting, that he had work to do.

He walked through an alley and came out on Kearney, the street teeming with tourists. Bells chimed as he pushed open the door of a small shop. Rows of pistols enclosed in glass cases on both sides of the aisles; rifles stacked up, their chestnut stocks gleaming. A small man wearing a bowtie and white shirt with the sleeves rolled up stood behind the counter.

"Hello. What can I do for you?"

"Oh, just looking," Nick said. "I'm not crazy about guns, in fact, I'm opposed to them, but, something's come up, or may come up, maybe I may have to protect myself. But what do you have, something small, so no one would know."

"Hey, look, it's not about liking. But if you need one, fast, nothing like having something." The man smiled, an avuncular, understanding gesture. He placed a compact short-barreled pistol on the glass-topped counter: Clunk. About the size of a cell phone, the pistol gleamed black in the overhead lights. The sound of *Ratttratt* as bullets were dropped onto the counter, each about the size of a long finger. "Only three inches overall, the derringer packs a wallop, the man said. "Comes in a 38-caliber model. You could tear a hole through a man's chest with that." He smiled. "Stainless steel, it's rugged, and got a special price, only for this week. Just three hundred forty-nine and ninety-five cents. Plus tax."

Nick looked at it like one would eye a poisonous snake ready to strike. "How do you carry it?"

From a rack, the man snatched a leather belt; he looped a small holster onto it. He placed the pistol into the holster and snapped a button. "Nobody can tell you're wearing it. Just keep the pistol around your back."

Picking it up, Nick was surprised how light it felt. "I'll think about it."

"You ever fire a pistol?"

"Once in the Army, well, a rifle, in basic training." He laughed. "I was a clerk typist. That was my MO."

"Nothin to it; you'll catch on. But it only has two chambers. Gotta make 'em count."

Nick thought it over.

Later, the bells chimed as he walked out of the store carrying the small package. Music was coming from Dexter's stand about a block away.

"Hop right up, Mr. Larson. Get you ready for the street."

"Thought you'd be gone."

"After you, will be," Dexter said, snapping his rag. Nick sat upon the rickety chair and rested his feet on the steel shoe stand. After slapping on some polish, Dexter started working it in, his black hands moving in a whir. "Hear you doin all the good, Mr. Larson. You the man, back on top."

"...hey, good lookin momma, c'mon and back that thing here; you good lookin and you back that thing here..." Rap music played from Dexter's radio, on the pavement next to the stand. The music's rhythm kept time with Dexter's hands, slapping and buffing all in a whirl.

"I guess so."

"Why you say that? You not?" Dexter asked, glancing at Nick from behind his gold wire-framed glasses.

"Guess I am."

"... ine lookin woman, I got what cha'need and you know you want and back that thing here..."

Nick said, "Thing is, used to be all the market people, we'd make a lot of money and go out and, hell, it was one big party. Don't know where everybody went. Anybody partying anymore?"

Dexter shrugged. "Yeah, hell, that's all of us, never happy. Least that's what my old lady says." His face creased into a grimace that showed his brown-tinged teeth. A few gray hairs grew around his temples. "Is what it is, that's all. That's not what *she* says; *I* do."

Taking out a heavy brush, Dexter started polishing furiously. "Say, didn't you write or somethin?"

"Paint. It's been a while," Nick said. He thought it over. "Found something in painting, something bigger than hustling and buying bigger houses, was an art major. Not much you can do with an MFA in art. Not these days. Loved it, but never could make enough to live on, then got into making money. Never thought I'd paint again, started again after Julie died."

Nick studied the blinking red lights on the sign across the street: Enrico's. Live Jazz. *Live Jazz. Tinkling glasses*, he thought, *jazz until three, four in the morning; tables packed, knew everybody.* "Used to go there."

"Enrico's?"

"Yes."

"Yeah, but now listen, listen to that rap. Hell, that's what Coltraine and them other cats was tryin to say. They was sayin 'we're angry, but we're gonna make it pretty.' These rappers, hell, they're sayin fuck pretty. We're angry. Times change, gotta change with em, that's what my old lady says."

Nick thought about it.

"Caan't last. No, sir, caan't last."

"What?" Nick asked.

"Shoe leather I see today, every day. People, hell, in their twenties, younger even, the assistant's assistants have these shoes from Italy, fine as silk. Shoot, costs a fortune, everybody's got money, everybody's buyin oil stocks, like they used to buy tech stocks and Internet. They keeps goin up. No, sir, caan't last."

Nick watched Dexter work. "Say, you'd know. Who's *really* wired into the Street with the oils?"

"A broker?"

"No, they just sell what they're told. I mean somebody connected with the institutions, the right ones."

Dexter finished off a shoe, shining brightly in the streetlight. "Don't know no one," he said, thinking, then, "Oh, yeah, maybe I do. There's the Weasel, sometimes they call him the Dart, hell, Weasel, Dart, makes no difference, and sometimes this girl, Steffie, comes here. Ain't no tellin how much money they make, all wearin *Gucci* leather and stuff like that, 'course complainin, like they can't make enough money to eat or somethin. Think they're homeless the way they talk about…"

"Who're they?" Nick asked, sitting up on the seat.

"The Weasel trades all them oil stocks. The big ones, I mean. Her, I don't know what the hell she does, trades for whoever pays her or somethin. They both over there on the P-Coast."

Scratching an itch behind his knee, Nick said, "That'll work. I got this stock, and those people'll bid it up or blow it up. Whatever puts money in their pockets.

"Got that right. Lately Weasel's sayin oil stocks're goin to the moon. I made plenty money here shinin shoes last thirty years. Plenty, don't you worry about me none. Bought me some broken-down buildings right here in the city. Hell, with what I made in the dot-com days, worth millions now. I could quit this shoe shinin. But I like it, like the people. Keeps you young. What my wife says. Yeah, everybody knows the Weas. Market's all he cares about. Oh yeah, and cars. Caan't get'im to stop once he starts talkin 'bout cars." Dexter snapped his rag. "You ready for the street, my man."

Nick slipped Dexter a twenty. "Where can I find him?"

"'Bout every mornin at four he's at the Alley Café. In Lombard Alley, right next to the exchange. Weasel always wears a Giants baseball cap. Oh yeah, he loves baseball, too. Loves money and women. Hell, the Weas loves lots of things." Dexter laughed, and tossed the rag into a beat-up wood box. "Weasel jest like the rest of you guys. He nuts. You all nuts."

***

It was warm early in the morning as Nick set out for his office. He thought about how it was going to be clear and bright and in the low seventies, a perfect San Francisco day. In the real world, which was anyplace outside of San Francisco, days could be hot as hell or bitter cold. Here the weather was usually moderately wonderful. Dressed in a black Armani suit, black knit jersey, a beret cocked jauntily on his head, he walked briskly. The air was clean and fresh.

He walked down Nob Hill, then cut over down Market Street. The street was a hodge-podge of glitzy condo high-rises, a Radio Shack, Macy's, and old movie houses long ago turned into porno parlors with signs saying *Live Girls, Real Live Girls.*

What other kinds are there, he thought.

Sleeping in the storefronts and on the streets were entire families. The homeless never made it into the slick brochures sent out to attract tourists. They were pushed into dark pockets of the city, rousted by police when the sun came up.

The street people were waking up. Families in tattered clothes and smelling badly picked up battered, homemade signs: Please Help, Need Work, Have Children. At the entrance of a towering, glass-fronted building, a man lay on old, torn cardboard, barefoot, his dirty, red beard matted, red sores on his neck. Next to him, a sign propped up: Lost Job Will work for Money.

Since the dot-gone bust, there were more and more homeless. Nick hesitated, dropped a five-dollar bill near the passed-out man. *That could be me*, he thought. *Could be anyone*.

He passed a just finished building with a printed announcement: BARGAIN RATES—PRE-SALE SPECIAL. ONE BEDROOMS, ONLY $1.0 MILLION. A few people walked out of the building, thirty-somethings dressed in jeans and sport coats. *Some dot-gones with money*, he thought. *Very few of them left*. Few people could afford to live in the city anymore. *But at least those people living in the street, they don't have to—damn, do what I have to do*.

After stopping for a coffee-to-go, he arrived at his office. The phone was ringing as he walked in. He answered right away, and sat down in the dark. The leather chair felt cold.

"Hi," Brett said. "How's it going?"

Sunshine started creeping into the office. Nick loved these clear mornings. Usually they were followed by brilliant blue skies later.

"Good, keep pushing. The stock's acting well. Figure I need to get into the bigger institutions now. Want to hear my game plan?"

"A couple of things first. To the members here on the board, you're famous. Ahh'm hearin there were a coupla Nugget hundred-thousand share buy orders this morning, already. Look, the story's getting out big, and we want to offer you—it's gotta be approved, you know, not done yet—but we want you to join our board. Hell, you'll have an expense account, go anywhere you like, stay in the best hotels. We'll increase your salary also, but the best thing is that we'll double your stock options, to two hundred thousand shares. You know damn well you can move the stock another ten points. A slam-dunk for you. Hey, look, you can use two million dollars, can't you?"

Two million, Nick thought. *And I can get in with other companies once I make this work. On the board I'll meet the directors; they'll have contacts*. He watched the sun through the window, and heard cars honking on the street below, and pictured himself entering through the glass doors of the Lodestock Apartments, the chicest building in the city, located on the top of Nob Hill.

"Can't you?" Wells asked.

Nick could use the money, but had to think about it. "Thanks for the offer. I need some time to think about it."

There was silence on the line. Then Brett said, "Well, yeah, think it over, take your time. Say, we're all meetin in Houston next week, the whole board. That'll be a good time for all of us to get ta know each other."

The receiver felt heavy in Nick's hand. "I'll be there."

"Thursday, about nine, in my office."

"Sure."

After hanging up, Nick looked at the packet of papers on his desk: "Earnest Money Contract. THE LODESTOCK APARTMENTS, 333 Jones Street #423, San Francisco, Calif., 94113."

Okay, so I spent a cool million, but I gotta live somewhere, he thought. *In this town makes no sense to rent, not when you can buy. Going on the board I can probably get five thousand more a month, that'll cover the mortgage.* He scratched an itch behind his knee, watching yellow sunrise flooding into the room.

Nick thought it over. The phone rang. It rang again a few times. Nick absently picked up the receiver.

A man said, "Ted Smiley here at *The Wall Street Journal*. I write features mostly for the front page, exploring the more high level companies, and the top people that run them. You know, the personalities, what's really going on in the inside. Can you give me a few minutes?"

Nick figured that this was exactly what he did not need right now. His stomach knotted up. "Why me?"

Ted said cheerily, "We're hearing that at Nugget you're the man. We'd do a feature on Brett Wells or Byrd but we're having a hard time getting people to talk to us about them, you know, as people. We tracked down Ellen Pasternak, but she cut us off, and next thing we know, quit Morgans. So you're the only player we can reach there."

"Well, you can just review our prospectus. I'm really pretty dull, just do my job, don't socialize with Brett or anybody." He started sweating. "Nugget's a great buy and the management team's savvy; they know what they're doing." *I can't lie to these guys, can I*? he wondered. Standing up, he said, "Look, I can't help you. And I am busy, very, very busy."

"You're supposed to be good at moving stocks. Doing a hell of a job there."

Nick felt his blood starting to flow, like the old days when his lines of patter made things happen, big. "I am. Yes, I moved Texas Resources—check out what I did there—and I'll make Nugget even bigger. Nugget'll probably make three dollars in a couple of years. Put a twenty multiple on that and the stock goes to sixty, maybe seventy dollars a share. That's just for starters." Nick knew the press was a great way to move a stock. His mind raced as he saw this opportunity to get the story out. "I'm going to New York next week to see Merrill and Webber. Both have natural resources funds and neither has bought

Nugget yet, not real size. And there are also the hedge funds. I haven't even talked to them, but you know their huge appetite." *What the hell was I worried about? I'll get this stock up thirty, forty, points and pocket three or four million dollars and make even more on the next deal.* "They'll buy in New York, then I'll take this story to Europe. Nobody can put away shares like I can."

"That's all well and good, Mr. Larson, we know your reputation. But in the prospectus there are footnotes regarding a group from Mexico and Argentina. They control a majority through interlocking shares."

Who is this guy? Why these questions? Nick thought, looking at the receiver. "Sure, maybe some foreigners are involved but these are good, honest investors…" Sweat dripped down his cheeks. He wondered if he had said too much.

"I have to go," Nick said. He hung up.

***

The sun was setting as Nick drove up Pacific Heights to Linda's. The ocean below was brilliant blue. Workmen were packing up rakes, lawnmowers, shovels, onto their trucks. *You need a full-time army to keep these places going*, Nick thought, and remembered his house, long ago, just down the street from Linda's. He had planned to live there the rest of his life. Suddenly a long, black Jaguar sedan beeped its horn, the driver almost forcing him into the cars parked along the sidewalk. Lenny Zellon was laughing, waving frantically from behind the wheel of the Jag, and motioning for him to stop.

He pulled over.

Lenny jumped out and ran over.

"Where've you been?" Nick asked.

"South America, all over," Lenny said, bouncing as he talked. "Hey, Larson, you ever fuck a pregnant girl? I mean, here I am in Mexico City, ya shoulda seen this whorehouse. Chandeliers, thick rugs, long bar, and walking around this young snatch is hitting on me. I'm tellin ya, just fifty dollars for that stuff. So, there's this sweet, young pussy, I mean, she couldn't've been more than seventeen, so she approaches me—her belly's stickin out, I mean she's ready to deliver any time. I'd never fucked a pregnant woman. Have you?"

Nick shook his head.

"So, I pay her. We go to a room, she takes off her clothes; like a watermelon's in her belly. So, I crawl on her, she spreads 'em, and I'm hard, man, I haven't been hard since—" Lenny shrugged, as if to say, maybe never—"So, I put it in, and damn, I'm pumpin, pumpin, and ya know what she does? This beaner? She makes the sign of the cross. Get it? She's prayin, tryin to, I don't know, get close to God. I'm watchin her cross herself, this crazy Mexican, and I'm fuckin her..."

Nick watched him, totally fascinated.

Lenny asked, "You ever fuck a pregnant woman?"

"No. I'd remember it, I'm sure."

"They're starvin down there, all of 'em. The bartender told me no money, no jobs. These girls, their parents bring 'em to the place, wait for them while they get hosed. You imagine takin *your* daughter to get hosed?" Lenny laughed and laughed. Suddenly he stopped. "Hey Larson, how come I keep hearin stuff I don't wanta? Like Brett Wells is fronting the company for drug guys. Bad guys."

Nick's stomach knotted. "That's news to me."

Doubt flickered in Lenny's dark, grasping eyes.

"Yeah, well I'm bettin you won't lie to me. Wouldn't be that stupid. What d'they say in Hollywood, 'You'll never work in this town again?' We're bigger than Hollywood." Lenny smiled. "Hey, Nick, come along with me to Cuba. You know you can buy a woman for the price of a meal? I mean, you take 'em out to dinner, beautiful young girls—you know that hot Latin pussy—then after dinner you fuck 'em. Maybe fuck her mother, sister, too. Then, I'm hearin this from a buddy of mine, he trained a girl. Best blowjob ever, and for only fifteen dollars. Costa Rica. He says the women down there—"

"Look, Lenny, I gotta go."

Lenny looked toward Linda's house. "Yeah, okay. Like I don't know who's waiting."

"You're hallucinating," Nick said, starting the car.

"What do I care, Larson? Think you're the only guy who's gettin his?"

Nick drove off. *Damn*, he wondered. *Where did Lenny find about Brett and...?* He looked at himself in the rear-view mirror. His face was twisted with conflicting thoughts. *Lenny does things. But at least he's not lying to his friends.* He looked away.

***

Linda was waiting. They drove in darkness down Pacific Heights to the entrance of the Golden Gate Bridge. After parking, started walking across the bridge. The bridge was suspended over darkness, and they reached the middle. The water was far below, all they could see was a black void. The damp sea smell was heavier at night. Lights twinkled on the bridge towers and on the boats far out on sea. The buildings of the city stood behind them as they walked at a quick pace. Linda wore Shalimar, Nick's favorite perfume. Julie had worn it, also.

They walked in silence until the end of the bridge. No one was around. He took her hand. She held on.

"Does he know you're out?"

She studied the black void that was the ocean. Lights from Alcatraz Island glowed in the clear night. "I don't know what he knows. We really don't talk much."

Walking along, feeling her hand warm in his, smelling her perfume, inhaling the damp sea air, he felt at home: that feeling that everything was familiar and just like it had always been.

"Maybe we ought, I know it would be hard, but if you put Thad in a hospital he could have full-time help, and you wouldn't have to worry." The air, the smell of her, being home. "We could get married, not right away, of course. We'd wait. But later."

She looked at him, her face broke into a smile, and she laughed. She tried to stop but laughed some more. He let her hand go. She said, "I'm sorry, that was rude, but what*ever* are you thinking?"

Nick said, "It's not totally silly." To him, the night looked very black, the smells were gone.

"But. I know people in this town. And I like them and where I'm invited and, I hate to say this, but people are talking about you. That at the Black and White Ball, who were you hanging out with, Lenny Zellon. He's so gross. He would be *déclassé,* but he's never had class. You don't *deign* to go to the Pacific Union Club anymore. What's going *on* with you?"

"I don't know." His voice was a whisper.

"You and I, we have a good time. We *see* each other."

"I know." Nick started sweating. *What is the matter with me?* "I don't know."

"Oh, well," she said, "forget it." Her hand was warm as she took his. "Will you stay the night?"

"I'm going to New York early in the morning."

"Will you... the maids are off." She slid his hand under her sweater and under her bra. Her nipple was hard.

Nick did not say anything. Of course he would go home with her.

***

The minute hand circling the face of the giant, round clock, Colgate Palmolive printed on the face, moved slowly. The clock was on the New Jersey waterfront, across the brilliant blue water from New York City. The sun was hanging in a clear, cloudless blue sky. The giant, steel buildings towered over the plaza of the World Financial Center. The World Trade Center buildings, which used to be a few blocks away, were gone. People walked about the plaza; pigeons flew over and walked on its stone surface. Offshore, boats bobbed in the water. Helicopters flew overhead. Nick sat amid the crowd, shirtless, and soaking up the sun. The Statue of Liberty looked toy-sized in the distance.

He typed numbers on his cell phone, turned on his laptop.

A woman answered crisply, "Pattie." He gave his name and she said, "Oh, hi. I heard you were around again."

"I got a company I really, really like."

"I'm sure you do. What? The meter's on."

Typical portfolio manager, he thought. He'd made Pattie Levin tons of money in the past, but had to sell her again. She was beautiful and smart and managed about five billion. Pretty serious, even by Wall Street standards. More than that, people know she was good. Funds have to post their holdings quarterly, and Nick figured that if she bought, the other PMs would see she owned Nugget, maybe they'd buy too.

"Nugget Petroleum. The stock could double at least from here over the next six months. Forward year's earnings could be about three dollars a share; cash flow at four times, versus eight times for the group. There're big new hits in Argentina expected and major new money raised by bond financing."

"Nugget, Nugget," Pattie Levin repeated, clicking her keyboard. "I've been wondering about that company. The numbers work but there's such bad buzz about it out there."

Nick swallowed heavily. "And I'm telling you the buzz is wrong. And the stock moves big, starting in about two weeks. Have I missed, even once?"

"No. No, you haven't."

"Pattie, just do this. Buy a hundred thousand shares. That's nothing for you. And I'm telling you it works."

"Are you sure? Come on. This company's been around for years and finally it's adding some assets and their bond ratings went up. But there're questions about their financing, and let's face it, Nick, the guys running Nugget are not exactly angels. Okay, maybe they've gotten lucky lately—"

"More than that." *Give me a break*, he thought. *I need you.* "I can't tell you much, but Nugget's Argentine properties, there's a whole story..."

She'll get it, he hoped. *Assume I'm talking code for a big hit. It's only a little lie.*

Her voice wavered. No one, not one portfolio manager will ever buy anything without grilling the pitch. "If I want oil and gas, why not just buy Chevron or one of the other big companies?"

"At thirty times earnings? Nugget, what if Nugget sells at thirty times? That's ninety. A home run."

She hesitated. He pressed. "A hundred thousand. Just stick your toe in."

"Is that like putting it in just a little?"

He laughed. "Sort of. How was it?"

Pattie laughed. "The worst was wonderful."

She's hooked. Don't talk. Don't talk.

"Okay. I'll talk to my trader. It'll be more than a hundred thousand, though. Actually, I've been looking at Nugget. But Nick?"

"Yes?"

"You change your mind, you'll call? Early?"

His stomach knotting, he said, "Sure. I'll be on it."

"You can make a mistake, but I read on the Internet something material before you let me know, Nick, you know what you can do with my number."

"Gotcha."

He sat awhile looking at the phone and listening to the Buzzz of the dead line. Looking at his laptop, he saw NUP: Bid, 21 3/8; Ask 21 1/2; Last 21 5/8; UP 2 1/8; Volume 9,285,000. Nick knew that that was a lot more volume than Nugget usually traded. Looking over the trades, he found that a half a million share piece had been executed about five minutes ago. *She did that one*, he thought. His stomach tightened. *And you screw her, and there's no place in the world far enough to run.* Lenny Zellon's face appeared in his mind. *I gotta move this stock*, he thought. *I'm just doing my job, what I'm paid to do.*

Then he stopped thinking.

***

"Enjoy your stay in Houston, sir."

Nick smiled at the flight attendant, and walked from the plane and through the airport's wide corridor. After catching a cab, he looked out the window at the sun burning in the blue, cloudless sky; green flatlands, heads of cattle grazing; shopping centers and two-story apartment houses; a sea of cars reflecting the sun as far as he could see. Gleaming off in the distance, the glass and steel buildings of downtown Houston. No people out walking on the baked-hot, wide sidewalks.

On the top floor of the towering building, Brett came out to get him, his jacket off, his tie loosened. "How'd it go in New York?" Brett asked as they entered his office.

He smelled liquor on Brett's breath, and thought how very unlike Brett it was to be drinking early. He sat. "I probably put away three million shares, the stock up over four points. Once I started rolling, it was easy. A lot of people remembered me."

"Way to go, pardner. You're the best. Hell, that's why we hired you."

Nick smiled, enjoying the compliment. "But questions keep coming up out there about the Argentinean reserves."

"Yes, well, just what the hell about them? They're fine, don't worry, ah'll send you down there if you want."

"I think we're okay. I allayed their fears." Nick's pride started to dissipate. *What have I put my people into? Might as well know it all*, he decided, feeling the way he did just before the dentist started drilling. "Then I never did ask you about an organization called the Invisible Hand."

Like a cornered animal, Brett's eyes went wide and alert.

"They're some sort of group. I've gone through the stockholder records," Nick continued. "Large blocks of stock're registered in nominee names, the addresses are of banks in Uruguay. America has no reciprocal agreement with that country so I can't find out who the real holders are. I figure about thirty percent of the stock is held that way, well over control."

"Now, look here, leave it alone. You don't know where you're going—"

"I need to know before I put any more people into it."

Butch Byrd walked in, wearing his usual khakis, black Western boots, khaki shirt, his black belt cinched by a large gold buckle.

Standing up, Brett said, "Larson here's askin about something named Invisible Hand. You know them?"

"Yeah. Bunch'a drug dealers in South America. Heard of 'em when I worked in Government Intelligence in '73, during Nam. Rumors about 'em durin the Gulf War, then they got tied up in that mess in

Afghanistan. Wherever oil was, they were. Ain't no thing. They're long gone." To Nick he said, "Stock's sure doin good."

Nick beamed, thinking that he could still move stock.

"Don't worry none about them, they're sort of a legend."

Nick wondered why he was asking dumb questions that didn't go anywhere or make anybody any money. *What the hell does Pugliese know? Who cares*? "Okay. But, Brett, I have a few other questions."

Smiling, Brett said, "Okay, okay. We'll discuss 'em at dinner. I got people comin in from all over. You'll see everything." He put a hand on Nick's shoulder. "Look pardner, hang with us. Everybody's gonna get well, you know?" Opening a cabinet, he took out a bottle of Jack Daniels. "Enough of this damn business. How about a pop?"

Brett filled glasses for the three of them. The phone rang, and he answered it.

Nick studied the photos on the desk: Brett with a beautiful woman; on a horse, in boots and a ten-gallon hat; with the Mayor of Houston; with a sheik, in front of a mosque in a desert. Nick wondered why he'd worried: the guy was solid.

After hanging up, Brett said, "Nick, come on with me. Jest a quick stop, won't take long. Then we'll go eat."

***

In his long, black Cadillac sedan, Brett drove through the night at a hundred-ten miles an hour. In the dark Texas sky, distant lightening flashed. After turning off the highway he headed toward a house that was hidden by the darkness.

Brett parked and Nick and he got out. Fireflies blinked on and off, like tiny light bulbs. Gravel crunched underfoot as they walked. There was high-pitched neighing coming from an old, weathered barn near the house. Through the open barn door, the horses were seen pacing restlessly in their stalls, their breath visible in the night air. The odor of horse dung mixed with the smell of hay.

"Drew Lane sure does love his prize Arabian horses," Brett said. "Keeps 'em all over Texas, Arizona, Mexico. Costs him a ton of money. Now, look. Ol' Drew's gonna sell us his company. They're in the oil service bid'ness, been in it for years, hell, they're up to a few billion in sales. He's balkin about getting Nugget stock, and heard about you from the Texas Resources days. Need you to reassure him. Take a few minutes."

"Reassure?"

"Hell, sell him on our stock. That's what you do, isn't it?"

Drew Lane, a bald-headed man with a round face, stood waiting inside of the house. He opened the screen door and led them into a large dining room. The room was dimly lit. They all sat down.

Leaning forward, Brett asked, "What d'ya think?"

"Don't know if ah want'a sell." Lane leaned back.

"Hell, your little piss-ant company can't keep up with the global players unless you pump in a billion or so. You'll be able to compete, with us."

Lane took a deep breath. "Well, maybe I'll sell, but only for cash."

"No deal. Our stock's better'n cash, and I don't want you mad at me when Nugget goes up over a hundred dollars a share, and you're pissed and tell everybody at the Houston Club golf course what a bastard Brett Wells is 'cause I didn't make you take the stock."

Lane thought. "Maybe I'll hold off for awhile."

Brett gestured to Nick. Nick thought, then said, "I've just been on Wall Street and got big people to put away a few million shares. This is just the beginning. We need you along, guys like you, real oil guys." Lane listened intently. Nick went on. "Nugget's gonna work out. Big."

Drew sat looking at Nick. "You really think so?"

"I know so."

Brett winked at Nick. Nick's stomach tightened.

Drew looked down at his hands.

"C'mon, Drew, what're you waitin for? I trust yer word, you heard Larson. I'll get the papers to you tomorrow."

Drew thought about it. "You sure?" he asked Nick.

"No question," Nick said quickly.

"Okay, okay. Let's git this done, I wanta git outta town," Drew said.

Getting up and motioning to Nick, Brett said, "My guys'll be at your office first thing tomorrow."

After they got outside, Brett said, "Good job," and slapped Nick on the back. Nick cringed. "That's what I mean. Show you got a commitment. We're all gonna get well, so what're you worried about? Enjoy yourself."

**

As people filed in, the restaurant got louder. Black-suited waiters rushed around red, crushed velvet chairs. At the bar, men and women drinking, talking, white teeth gleaming in the dim light. At the table next to Nick, large plates with pink-in-the-middle chateaubriand, parsley sprigs, boiled potatoes, sat on a white linen cloth.

Taking another swallow of wine, Brett started slurring his words.

"Don't know what happened to 'em, can't rely on anybody nowadays to be on time."

Nick fingered the stem of the cut-crystal glass. "The financial people coming tonight?"

"Nah, the CFO and the others couldn't make it. But I got plenty more people for you to answer all yer questions." Brett ogled a short-haired woman poured into a dress spangled with sequins. He said something to her. Laughing, she sat down. After bantering loudly with her, he looked at the restaurant front door and said, "Here they come now. Damn about time."

Waving, they gathered around Brett. Their boisterous laughter filled the room.

He said, "Sit down. *Caan't* do business on an empty stomach." Chairs were pulled out. "Y'all meet Nick Larson. He's the guy I told you about pumpin the stock."

Brett gestured at a man with dark hair and movie-star good looks. "That's Manuel Santos, from Argentina." About another, he said, "That's Assad Yousef, from Iraq. He's first cousin to Sadaam. That's his brother Abdul. And that's Ronaldo Roses, from Argentina. He's on our board. The others, we'll get to 'em later." He told the waiter, "We'll start with caviar, and Dom Perignon. Then steaks all around, the thick cuts. There'll be more people joinin us. Bring 'em the hell over."

A big bear of a man wearing a wide brimmed hat came into the restaurant, nodded at Brett. "And that's Hammer," Brett said. The man sat at a table alone, his eyes guarding the door.

Reaching for the glass, Nick thought, *What the hell. When in Rome...*

The night wore on. Nick kept drinking.

About fifteen men and many more women showed up at their long table in the middle of the restaurant. Most other diners left. On the tables, empty plates, wine bottles, empty, full, half-full. Men and women made their ways to the rest rooms and returned from the rest room, with white powder traces under their noses.

Nick watched, got drunk.

Brett put a hand on Nick's shoulder, his breath replete with alcohol. "What d'ya think, pardner? These guys control, well maybe not directly, but through friends, relatives, shoot, maybe quarter of the world's oil supply, maybe more. Some of them're on our board. We're just getting' started, ya know that?"

Then Brett moved on, putting his hand on another shoulder, breathing into another face.

More bottles arrived, empty bottles taken away.

About twenty men were there now, most speaking with accents from around the world. The women spoke with Southern accents, and wore skimpy dresses showing lots of leg and cleavage. Couples kissed, joking and laughing.

Nick stumbled to the rest room. After fumbling with his fly, he stood swaying at the urinal, relieving himself.

Manuel Santos staggered in. Standing a few urinals down, he unzipped, swayed drunkenly while trying to urinate. Flashing a broad smile, he said, "Brett, he in good manner tonight. You make him happy with our stock."

Through a drunken haze, Nick saw his opportunity. "I'd raise it a hell of a lot higher if buyers didn't worry about certain things."

"Such as, senor?"

"The stockholders that control the company. What the Invisible Hand has to do with all of it."

"Do not worry about the Hand. As long as you do your job."

"Who… how can I contact them? Just in case."

"In my office, at the foreign ministry. His job is not important, nobody pays him any regards."

"It's… who is it? Probably I met him."

"Of course you did. Rosas, Ronaldo Rosas."

"Rosas? The board member?"

Manuel nodded, finished, stood there shaking the last from his penis. He looked like he was going to collapse.

Heart pounding, Nick asked, "Is he the only contact?"

Manuel shrugged. "Nugget is very confusing. Nobody knows for sure anything."

"What else?"

"Rosas works with the banks in Uruguay, finds names, holders of Nugget. My friend, there are people that have been dead for a century, some never born, listed as owning our stock."

The door was thrown open. Brett staggered in, smiling, but his eyes were hard. "Hey, you all're missin out. There're some awful pretty, lonely women out there."

Nick zipped up, and started to leave.

"Life's too damn short, anyways." Brett unzipped, stared down.

Leaving the men's room, Nick glanced back into the mirror. Brett and Manuel were close to each other, whispering furiously.

***

Nick was waiting in Brett's office. A mountain of papers was piled on the desk: "MERGER, TRITON OIL; MERGER, BUCKINGHAM PETROLEUM; ACQUISITION, WEST AFRICAN GOLD, INCORPORATED." Nick figured it out: Nugget was getting ready to merge with good companies and hide how weak it was. Then Wells and the others would skim the assets off into shell companies that they would create, and if and when Nugget blew up, the stockholders would be left with an empty bag.

"Sorry I'm late, pardner," Brett said, walking in. "Hell of a night. Took off with some of the ladies and just never did make it home."

Brett wore the same clothes as yesterday, shirt wrinkled, tie unknotted, shoes scuffed. His hair stuck out at all angles like a porcupine.

Nick's head throbbed. "Great party. I'm thinking, for this morning you mentioned I could get with the CFO."

"Ahh, hell, just wait 'til you come to our board meeting."

"You know, Brett, I'd rather speak with him now." *Maybe there's some good stuff about this company*, he thought, picking his fingernail.

Brett pressed a button on the phone. "Hi, Shirley, listen sweetheart, could you please get me Pete, Pete Ralston, right away?" Brett listened, and then put the receiver down. "Too bad. He went to some damned-fool seminar up in Dallas."

"So who can I go over the financials with?"

Gesturing at the pile of papers on his desk, Brett said, "Ahh'd like to do it with ya, but I'm just snowed. Let's see, who *is* here?" He pressed some numbers on the phone. "Wells here. Say, is Roger there? Well, all day? Yeah. How about Willie?" Brett listened, then hung up. "Well, pardner, ahh sure am sorry, but there's nobody around here that can do ya any good. Look, you'll be comin back soon, nothin has ta get done today."

Nick took the news grimly. The last thing he wanted to do was go back there and waste time. *While I move the stock up, the lies keep growing.*

The phone rang. Brett picked up the receiver and said to Nick, "Hey, pardner, I won't be but a minute or so." After listening on the line he said, "Now don't you worry none, leave it all to us. Hell, people're sheep. And we'll buy all the politicians we need, here and South America. Doesn't make no difference what country. Only thing that changes is the language or the currency." He chortled.

Nick looked through the window at Houston below: yellow cranes over deeply dug pits; freeways choked with cars; more cars sitting still on the feeder roads under the hot Texas sun.

After hanging up, Brett asked, "What else, pardner?"

"Just one thing, but it can wait."

"Like what?"

"Well, in reviewing our drilling prospects from the county's plat maps, they're shown as belonging to drillers other than us."

Brett smiled. "No need ta get into all that. Just a mix-up on recordin properties, I'd guess." He stood. "C'mon, Nick. What we really gotta talk about is you goin out and keep gettin people ta buy Nugget big. The newspapers, the newsletters, the brokerage analysts. We wanna get Nugget into every institutional account there is, both here and overseas. We need you, and hell, you're gonna be on our board!"

Brett picked up a pen, tossed it down. "Look, this is bigger than us. But we'll own everything and you'll be a part of it. C'mon, let's go to work. We got a call to make."

***

Standing in the rear of a large den with a crowd in front of him, Nick could see very little up front. Brett stood next to him, smelling of a too sweet, lilac-scented cologne, liquor still coming through his pores.

"That's Buck James." Brett pointed out a round, short man. "One'a the richest damn man in Texas. That's his daughter who's gettin married."

The bride stood in the front of everyone, in a white veil and gown that appeared to shine like an apparition in the crowded room.

A big, burly man dressed in black said, "I now pronounce you man and wife," and closed his Bible. "You may kiss the bride."

The groom, skinny and with a long sober face, lifted the bride's veil.

"Well, let's go see'm," Brett said, starting to push through the crowd.

Buck James stood in a group of people circling the bride.

"Hey, Buck, right fine wedding," Brett said.

Tears welled up in Buck's eyes. "Should be. Cost me a ton."

"Yeah, well, you got tons. Say, this's the fella I told you 'bout that's helpin us with Nugget. Guy's really wired into Wall Street."

After studying Nick, Buck James said, "Let's talk later. Now, let's go eat." He led them all outside into the blazing, stifling day. The bride's heavy white-lace wedding dress rustled as she followed her father.

Crowds of people milled around a huge pit where hunks of beef turned on spits. The cooks—white, black, Mexicans—scurried around in white uniforms with tall white hats. Multitudes of beer bottles, Dos Xs, Carta Blanca, Coors, Tres Xs, and Texas Pride (Made-in-Texas-by-Texans), bobbed in steel barrels filled with ice, the glass glistening in the sun. On oak tables scattered over the huge green lawn, bowls of potato salad, ranch-style beans, white bread, red and spicy barbecue sauce. Plastic chairs and chaise lounges had been placed over the spacious green field.

There was the sound of Zapzapzap as flies, mosquitoes, and an occasional flying roach flew into bug traps which were hung high in trees. "That there's our state bird," Brett said, laughing and gesturing to a flying roach.

He nodded to a man named Joe Brown, who stood in the bright sun, his Adam's apple bobbing as he chewed. His face had the deep lines of late middle age, and was tanned, showing the results of being in the sun-washed oil fields for far too many years. The rim of his ten-gallon hat was just over his skinny face and gray, serious eyes. After taking another bite of rib, he washed it down with big swallows of ice-cold beer.

Brett and Nick and Buck James walked over to the huge swimming pool, its blue water shimmering in the sun. Joe Brown followed them. They all sat down.

Turning to Nick, Brett said, "Ah was jest tellin Buck here, 'course it's hard to tell Buck anything 'cause he knows everything, Haahaahaa, but, he'd better have his little ol foundation load up with Nugget stock. Buy it before we merge. 'Course we *caan't* talk about mergin, not while we're in registration for a bond deal."

"Well, yeah, but what about the price of *ool*?" Joe asked, his sunglasses reflecting the sun, the pool. "Our damn-fool government don't have the sense of a stupid-ass mule. How the hell're we gonna know how much ta drill when we don't know what those sons-a-bitches are gonna do 'bout freezin the price like some'a them damn liberals are threatenin? Damn ool's goin to a hundred dollars. Ya' reckon?"

"Ahm tellin you just buy Nugget Petroleum, let us worry about the price'a oil." Brett turned to Nick. "Fill 'em in."

Wiping sweat off his face, Nick thought, *On exhibit again*. His stomach tightened. An angry inner voice said, *Come clean. Let's just leave and make a clean slate, and enough of these nasty, dirty, damn illegal lies*. But he also thought, *Where do I go? Back to find another company and push their stock? Work for an investment banker or broker and push their IPOs, tell people what great buys they are when I think they're shit? Ordered by some damn twenty-five year old sales manager to sell the stock or else. Shove it down customers' throats! I'm not giving up my new condo, the view of the Golden Gate, birds flying over the water. I'm not giving up my car. What do I do? Take the bus? To where?* Linda appeared in his mind, smiling with perfect teeth under bobbed hair, her nipples hard, lying under him on the couch. I want to go home, he thought, worn out with his struggle, the heat.

"If Nugget's exploration plays hit about thirty percent of what they predict," he said, staring into Joe Brown's clear and steady gaze, "the stock could double and still be undervalued." Nick figured it wasn't much of a lie. It could happen. *But nobody hits anywhere near thirty percent on exploratory wells, more like ten.* He hesitated, and started scratching an itch behind his knee.

Brett cut in, saying, "You got no idea what we're gonna do in block twenty-seven in the North Sea. Hell, bigger than British Petroleum hit. Bigger maybe even than the monster we brought in in Argentina."

You've got a very little interest in the North Sea block, Nick thought, slapping a mosquito that was feasting on his arm. *And Argentina's probably a big dry hole. We're spreading bullshit. I want to go home.* Sweat dripped down from his armpits.

Buck squinted at Nick through the sun. "Well, maybe I'll buy some. I'll look at it anyway. What'ja say your name was?"

"I'm Nick Lar—"

"He's Nick Larson," Brett said, "the guy that put Texas Resources on the map. Took the stock from ten to forty in six months. Gonna do the same for us."

Buck said, "Well, give me yer card. Can't get too much help in the market doesn't make sense to me. Better yet, give me a call, maybe next week."

Brett winked at Nick; Nick did not respond. It was the heat, that, and the sun and the lies. Nick was guessing that he felt like a fighter does in the fifteenth round on a stifling, breezeless night in an outdoor ring. Or a bullfighter who has failed in his kill ten or so times. Linda's face appeared and faded in his mind. He was left with the chirping of the birds, the sight of the distant white cows and brown cows, standing and stupidly staring in the hot sun. His wool trousers itched, the fabric appropriate for the cold dampness of San Francisco but not today in Texas.

Shrugging his shoulders, Joe Brown said, "Yeah, market only does what those damn Washington pea-brains want it to do. You own any Nugget stock yourself?"

"Hell, he's got plenty optioned," Brett said.

"Yes, I have options," Nick said, "but they're no good unless the stock goes up. And the truth is that the stock won't move unless I move it. And I'm having trouble talking about Nugget anymore. I need to know who the players are holding the stock in nominee name. There's a bank in Uruguay with a lot of Nugget stock in the vaults, and I'm not sure who the holders are."

"What the hell're you talking about?" Brett said.

Screw these people, Nick thought. *I'm going home.* "You know. Also, how come I go down to Argentina and I'm hit in the face by a cop making sure nobody can get close to the wells? I'm not convinced those wells are pumping even."

"That's enough," Brett said. He smiled to the others. "You know you gotta be careful down there. Hell, in South America—"

"Bunch'a communists," Joe Brown said. "Sure gotta be careful."

"Sure do," Buck James said soberly.

"Nuff this frettin." Brett clasped Nick's shoulder. "This's a weddin day."

The three Texans sat back in their chairs, while Nick stayed straight. They did not speak. Finally Buck James struggled out his chair, the chair shaking noisely. "Gotta git goin. But, ya know what scares me?"

"What?" Joe Brown asked.

"That somethin happens to make oil stocks blow up. That this stuff we're drillin for goes back down to maybe thirty, maybe even, hell, twenty dollars a barrel. I seen it down there not that very long ago. Hell to be paid, that happens."

Brett said, "No way. We'll never, hell no, allow that."

"Okay. Y'all be good now," Buck said, walking off with Joe Brown. "They'll be lookin for me ta pay the bills. Everything costs money today."

Brett and Nick left the pool and headed back to the car.

"You crazy?" Brett snapped.

"Yes. I was. Now I'm not. I'm giving up this charade. *You* move the stock, or hire someone else, or do whatever you want."

"But we got a long way to—"

"It'll be without me. I quit."

***

Nick walked out of the hotel into the steamy Houston night. He crossed the black asphalt of the parking lot, and got into a long, black Mercedes. The smell of its rich leather filled the interior.

He raced down the freeway toward the airport. In his rear-view mirror, the bright lights of downtown Houston grew smaller and distant. Cutting through the blackness, headlights from other cars flashed into his eyes.

He squinted and thought that he'd done it now. Brett would never trust him again. *Ah, to hell with him; to hell with everybody.* He drove on awhile, then suddenly wondered where he would live, and what would he drive.

He turned on the radio, and turned it off.

He thought about that new leather smell. He looked over to the passenger seat and imagined Julie sitting there. She smiled at him. He felt better.

It started raining, and he remembered water dripping from her hair onto the new leather seats. That was when they'd driven out of the Berlin airport years ago, rain splattering on the windshield of a new BMW. He drove fast, about a hundred and forty.

"Will you always love me?" she had asked.

"Always? That long?" he'd replied, laughing. "Yes, always."

He drove awhile, then glanced over. She was gone. The rain pounded harder, and he could barely see through the windshield. But it wasn't only rain on the windshield; tears ran down his cheeks. He didn't understand. All that was supposed to be over. He had mourned, he cried, how much was he supposed to cry?

Damn therapists saying this pain passes, time heals all. Bullshit! I miss her as much now as the day she died. Self-help books say "resolve your grief," whatever the hell that means. "Let new people into your life, and start anew." New people didn't change anything.

Nick thought about it, decided he'd better keep his job. Otherwise, where would he live? *Maybe I'll call Brett, apologize. I'm still good at moving stocks.*

In the black night, a few oil derricks near the highway pumped, the wheels of their valves turning slowly. Nick snapped on the radio. Hank Williams Senior's voice filled the car, "I'm so lonesome I could cry…"

Six

Walking hurriedly down California Street, Nick yawned, looked at his watch—4:03 A.M.—and yawned again. No light yet, no one but him out on the street. Off to his right, the Bank of America building, the black marble floor of its plaza glowing, reflecting the streetlights.

Cutting off of California Street, he entered a narrow alley.

At the end of the alley a bulb had burned out on a glowing sign that now read, ALL Y CAFE. Halfway down the alley he saw a figure flit across a doorway. Turning to see, he heard a noise behind him. A piece of metal crashed down on the side of his head. Nick put his hands up, but he got hit again. It didn't really hurt, he just went numb. He got hit again, and that hurt a lot. A fist crashed down the front of his face, and he heard his nose crack, sounding like a broken twig. Blood spurted from his nose, feeling sticky on his shirt. A kick in his stomach and he couldn't breathe. He fell down, gasping for air.

Lying on the pavement, he saw the stars twinkling in the black sky. Another kick in his ribs, more kicks, he moaned, wondering, *What the hell...?*

A skinny man sat on his chest and grabbed his shirt, bringing him close, and said, "Hey big man, feel big now?" The man stank of alcohol, sweat, and filth. Nick thought, *This can't be happening.*

Nick looked up to see another man, with a beard and mean eyes. *Holy shit.* A long-bladed knife reflected in the moonlight, the knife near his left eye. The skinny man said, "I can blind you, mother fucker, like carvin out an oyster. And don't think for a moment that I haven't done that plenty. Haahaahaa." The other man laughed also, sounding like a horse neighing.

"Hey, look, you got the wrong guy," Nick said, coughing. "I'm a stock market consultant. I'm not tied up in—I'm not a cop or whatever—"

"Better yet." The man with the knife unzipped Nick's fly. "Maybe you'd like to see, but not fuck anymore. Haahaahaa." The blade felt cold on Nick's penis. Sweat pouring down Nick's face, he shivered. "One snip, and you'll know what a lesbo feels like. Course you like to talk, that's what I'm hearin, don't you, mother fucker? Yeah. Like to ask questions. Maybe we'll cut off your mother fuckin tongue and stuff it up your ass." The knife gashed Nick's leg. He started to scream but a huge hand covered his mouth.

With all his strength, Nick squirmed and grabbed the man's hand and bit it as hard as he could. The man yelled and pulled his hand back. Nick had an instant to reach to his back. He slid his hand under his jacket and pulled the derringer out. "Son of a bitch," the skinny man said, looking at the gun. He reached for it and Nick fired point blank into his stomach. Nick was blinded as blood spurted from the man onto his face, feeling like warm, sticky oil.

The bearded man made for Nick. Nick pointed the gun at his face. "Come on, you bastard, I got one more. Come on."

The bearded man stood there; the skinny man lay on the street.

"Ahhhhh," Nick screamed, his voice echoing in the alley.

"Fuck outa here," the skinny man said.

Nick rolled over, watching the bearded man drag the skinny man to a car at the far end of the alley. He closed his eyes once the car pulled away. The pavement felt cool as he lay there, feeling blood spurt from his nose. He could have fallen asleep very easily. *Get up*, he told himself. *You have to get up*.

He arose. His sides hurt with every breath. *A rib's broken*, he thought, *maybe a couple*. His nose throbbed, and he hoped it wasn't broken. The derringer felt heavy and friendly as he stuck it back in its holster.

After hobbling up to the cafe, Nick opened the door.

There was an orange fire in the corner fireplace. People were at tables scattered about the small room; worn planks covered the floor; eyes looking up at him, men and women, small ink dots staring. Nick staggered by a counter crammed with pastries, croissants, bagels. Behind the counter a girl, her back to him, poured coffee into a huge urn. She turned, and looked him up and down, startled. He figured he was a mess, hurting. He hurried toward lights glowing bright red in the far corner: MEN.

Inside of the tiny room, hanging under a light bulb on the ceiling, a metal cord. He pulled it. In a large mirror he saw blood under his nose, around his mouth, and down his neck. Dirt and grime were plastered over his face. A purple bruise was just over his left eye, the eye starting to swell. After feeling his nose, he decided it wasn't broken, but it hurt bad. He took off his shirt and pants and looked at the cut on his leg, raw and wet, blood still oozing out.

"Hey, anybody in there?" a man asked, pounding on the door.

Nick jumped, his heart racing. He pulled out the derringer.

Easy, easy, he thought, his hand shaking. "I'll be a little while."

Using lots of paper towels, running out of them and then using toilet paper, he washed off his face, dabbing around the bruises. He cleaned the gashed leg. *Those bastards*, he thought, pulling on his pants, brushing dirt off his clothes. Smelling the blood on his shirt, he put it back on, buttoned his jacket up high, trying to hide the stains.

Looking in the mirror, Nick asked himself, *What the hell did that guy say? Talk too much? It had to be about Nugget, maybe me talking the other day in Texas. But he wouldn't have tipped me off, not unless he planned to... kill me.*

He shivered. He thought maybe the guy had been just high. Maybe it had nothing to do with Nugget at all. He dropped the bloody paper into the toilet, and flushed until it disappeared. A final glance in the mirror. *Bad, yeah, pretty bad.*

He pulled the cord, and the room turned black.

Over in the corner of the cafe a guy sat, eating a croissant. He wore a black baseball cap with the words SF GIANTS printed in orange. His thick black hair was over his ears. His dark eyes glowed in his skinny face. The young woman sitting next to him had a riot of curly red hair spilling over her face. Cups of coffee sat in front of them.

Hurting with every step, Nick walked over to them.

"Hi. I'm looking for—are you Weasel?"

"Yeah. I'm the Weas. Who're you? Better yet, what the hell happened?"

"Had a bad-hair morning. Can I sit down?"

"Better. Before you fall down."

Nick pulled up a chair. "Somebody, I think two, jumped me. I'm Nick, Nick Larson."

"Prob'ly some druggies," Weasel said. "Alone around here? You gotta be careful."

"I'm Steffie," the woman said. "Crime's terrible all over the city."

"Yeah, but they didn't take any money. I don't know what the hell they wanted." Nick coughed, and his ribs ached. He shifted on the chair but it didn't help.

"Hey, Nick Larson," Steffie said. "Sure, we were talking about you the other day."

A waitress came over, took a pencil from her hair and asked Nick what he wanted.

"Cappuccino—a double," Nick said. "And a chocolate croissant. And a glass of water." She left. He studied Weasel for a bit, then said, "Look, you trade Nugget Petroleum…"

"Yeah. Also, I'm tradin them, the others. All the oil stocks, some golds. You know, you 'oughta load up on Nugget."

"Why?"

Weasel took off his cap, smoothed his hair, put the cap back on. "They got lots of oil, price of oil's flyin. I trade 'em, know what I'm doin, and I say they all look higher. All's I know is I'm buyin a Porsche for cash. You do the math."

Nick was sweating. He was nauseated from smelling his blood.

"Want to call an ambulance?" Steffie asked.

"No, I'll go to the emergency room in a minute. So, where're the orders coming from mainly?"

"A lot now offshore," Weasel said. "The hedge funds, the big ones, are starting to buy. But this is all new, for the big players to come in. Before, the stock hardly traded."

"International now?"

"Yeah. The banks in Switzerland, 'specially the big ones."

"I know. I've been the one pushing them."

"You work with them?" Steffie asked.

"As their IR person. For awhile now."

Nick's mind wandered as he again realized what he had to do. That those bastards had planned to leave him dead in the alley.

"Where's Nugget going?" Steffie asked.

I have to lie down soon. "Straight up I think. How can anybody stop them? I see it as a monster grab by Nugget and the other companies to jack up the oil price. By merging the big companies and buying up the little companies, they collude on the price of oil by joint venturing their drilling and have their limited partnerships the stock. By holding oil off of the market until the price goes up." Wiping off his forehead Nick said, "They did this before, in the nineteen seventies. Oil went from twelve to fifty dollars a barrel, and was on its way to a hundred when the market broke. Everything collapsed when oil went down to nine dollars. This time they're raiding the patch through the stock market. You watch: a whiff of inflation, and gold, silver, real estate'll take off like a rocket, with oil stocks in the lead."

He coughed, his ribs hurt. "I don't know how big this thing is, but Nugget's in some kind of conspiracy with world-class players, and they're not going away. Think of it. You control oil, you control the world." He coughed again. With a check in hand, the waitress asked if they wanted anything else.

Nick couldn't talk anymore.

The cafe started filling up with people.

His hand shaking, Nick nibbled on the croissant, sipped the cappuccino. *They only ran when I shot*, he thought. *Would've killed me. It was Brett. I know it.*

He pushed his chair back, got up and dropped some bills on the table. Barely audible, he said, "I can see it. Long lines at the gas pumps again. Raging inflation, and all those guys jumping me, they'll win."

"Well, whatever," Weasel said, getting up. "Meantime, I gotta go make some money."

They started toward the door as daylight started through the window. Nick shivered and thought, *Next time they come after me, they'll finish the job.*

***

In a tree-shaded park in Houston, children got on and hopped off swings in the playground area. Pigeons pecked here and there, and flew up on benches. It was sunny and hot, typical for Houston.

The park was downtown, surrounded by glass and steel buildings. In the corner stood a freshly painted, white, ancient cabin, looking incongruous amid the modern buildings. It had been home to one of the Allen brothers, the founders of the city.

Brett sat and waited. Butch came walking up in thick-soled, mud-splattered boots. Butch was a gangling man who looked as if he'd just come out of the oil patch: brown shirt, brown pants, brown boots. His bald head reflected the sun. His dark eyes were too large for his narrow face.

Shielding his eyes from the glare, Brett said, "Hello, Butch. Fine day."

"Yeah. Hot as hell, though."

"When isn't it?"

"I called Larson," Brett said. "Left word for him to call me."

"Yeah. Good. Saw the guys. They really messed it up."

"Well, you better get them out of town. Lota good they did us."

"Ah'll take care of it. That's what you pay me for." Butch smiled tightly, showing no teeth.

"Larson'll call later." Brett gave him a long look. He could never tell what Butch was thinking. But this job with Larson had been botched up, big time. "He might come at us."

"With what? Larson's got nothing. What's he gonna fire at us? That little stupid-ass-pistol that those dumb bastards didn't even have the sense to know he might have? Maybe his dick?"

Brett slapped his palm on the park bench. "Damn, I told you we didn't have to kill him! Just like when you had your guys wipe out that village, in Argentina."

"Ah, hell." Butch continued smiling. "They wasn't nothin but peasants think they got a right to higher pay after we put up all the money, done all the work. Did the same we did to lots, in 'Nam. Weren't no traces left, who cares? Was smarter in the Gulf even, just shoveled dirt on top of 'em—saved on bullets."

Brett squinted through the sun and thought about how Butch had been at the top. He'd been the top colonel in the Gulf War. Fumed because the Army didn't take over the Iraq oil fields; kill Sadaam; take the fields and negotiate with the Saudis, and control most of the world's oil supply. Why the hell fight if not to take over? Butch had questioned to anyone who would listen. But the Army got tired of his raging and early-retired him. *Then he and I went out and made a fortune trading in sub-prime mortgages and oil leases, then hooked up with the guys at Nugget. Sorry we got with them, hell, we were makin good money, but Butch wanted the big time. Now he's losing it. Maybe I am too… but murder? That's too much, even for me.* Brett watched Butch study the top of his boots.

"Too damn hot," Butch said. "Let's go to my office."

Brett nodded, and followed him across the street and up into a towering, modern building. Butch's office was filled with animals: Dead animals. From high up, hanging on a wall, the head of a brown deer, its glassy eyes staring. A giant, white, lifeless, stuffed bear stood in a corner, its mouth opened in a snarl. On the floor were stuffed rabbits; quail hung motionless from the ceiling.

Brett studied them, thought, *Should'a known he couldn't stop.* Butch put a shot of Jack Daniels in a glass, offered it. Brett shook his head.

"Son-of-a-bitch had a gun," Butch said. "Wasn't expectin no gun."

"Damn it. You should've told me you planned to kill him. That's crazy."

"Now, now, just slow the hell down, I can explain everything." Butch slugged down the whisky, poured another glass. "He started it.

He's gotta start askin about the Hand. And how about his blabbin at the wedding? We need that, to hear stuff we don't want to talk about? Had to protect us."

"But killing Larson?"

"Come off it, Brett. If I didn't order the hit, the Argentines would've—eventually." Butch took another slug, poured another. "And maybe us too."

The ringing of his cell phone made Brett jump. He answered, and recognized Nick's voice, sounding frenzied. "Jumped me... crazier... No, didn't recognize them. Just need to get back to work... scared me to death... see some institutions in Dallas next week."

"Hell, go on and see everybody," Brett said. "These things happen, I mean with you and me. Don't worry none, all part of gettin a deal done, you and me arguing and stuff."

Nick spoke rapidly, "No, no sense at all. And I wish I had never opened my mouth at the wedding. This damn... made me see how lucky I am to be alive. I'll drive this stock through the roof. You have no idea."

"Hell, just get a good night's sleep. Take a few days off, then let's talk again."

Brett hung up and said, "Guy's scared shitless. Maybe it helped, sending those guys, who the hell knows? But now he's not gonna cross us."

"Maybe he's bluffin," Butch said. "Can't trust a man I don't understand. Why'd he bad-mouth us when he makes money with the stock up? Can't trust a man that can't be bought."

Brett laughed. "But you're the one that said all's he got's his dick to shoot with. What can he do to us? A puny has-been who's so scared now he can't breathe? We'll crush him he crosses us in any way. Can always sick the Hammer on him. What're you so worried about?"

Butch thought it over, poured another, drank it down, thought it over some more. "Reckon so."

***

After finishing the conversation with Brett, Nick stood staring into the receiver, then hung up. He was satisfied, thinking he had done a good job of convincing Brett he was panicked to the point of blind obedience.

Nick stood in the phone booth by the jogging track. The wooden booth was worn, its paint faded from ocean breezes and constant sunshine. The booth leaned slightly, and vandals had torn off both doors. Usually the phone didn't work. Homeless people had pried open the change box, and its cover had been removed. Nearby, the ocean splashed onto the rocks, spray pelting joggers. The wind got stronger, and blew sand about.

He pulled a sweatshirt on. He was chilled although the sun was beating down. He peered at the blue ocean, then past it to the distant green hills of Marin County, shimmering in the sun.

Nick hated to leave San Francisco, but… he muttered to himself about Brett Wells and all the Nugget players being bastards. He went down and sat on the beach. The sand was hot and felt good as he sat. *I'll destroy Nugget*, he thought, looking out at ships coming into port. *I'll blow them to bits*. He figured he'd have to be careful, no way they should find out what he was thinking. He wondered where he'd live if he destroyed the company. *There's gotta be a way to come out of this okay. Just has to be*.

***

The audience walked up from the side and center aisles. They always rushed to leave when the performance was over. Through the dimly lit theater lobby, its walls covered in red-velvet, its overhead chandelier glowing with orange lights, Linda and Nick strolled with the crowd out onto Geary Street in the San Francisco theater district.

Waiting vehicles stretched for about a block on the wide street: black limos, white limos, yellow taxies, black and white checkered cabs. Nick waved at one after another, and finally snared one.

They drove off and he said to Linda, "I'll drop you at your place."

She took his hand. "Why so early?"

He took his hand away. Neither said anything as the cab climbed up steep Taylor Street.

"Okay," she said, "going to be another of those nights? Honestly. This is getting more than difficult." She looked out the window.

"I've been thinking," Nick said, "about those times I brought zucchini, fried zucchini, to the hospital. Me and Julie, we ate it and laughed and wondered why we didn't have fried zucchini more often, we liked it so much. And I wondered how many more fried zucchinis we could have before she… couldn't. And I didn't want to think about it or know how sick she was…" He stopped talking.

"Oh, Nick, what is the difference now?"

"It's just that same feeling's here. About us, and how much time we have."

She laughed. "We're young, sort of. Years maybe."

He didn't say anything.

The cab climbed Nob Hill, then started up the hills of Pacific Heights. She told the driver where to go.

Everything moved in slow motion for Nick: lamp posts with lights atop, rays of light shining through the mist; neat, miniature Victorian homes; doormen at The Comstock Apartments, walking through the large glass doors after parking cars. He thought that he should go home, and end it with her right now. *Ah, the hell with it. How many more nights will there be?*

After going up steep Taylor Street and across Sacramento Street, they stopped at a deserted, dead-end street at the very top of Presidio Heights. From this height everything appeared lit up: the Bay Bridge, black beams and girders making the long structure look like a giant spider. Along the side of the bridge, white and red lights blinked in the misty night; glowing beyond the bridge, lights from homes in the East Bay.

They got out. As the cab drove off, the red glow of its taillights got dimmer, then vanished. A streetlight illuminated the area. There was a murmuring from the blackness where the sea was far below. They stood in front of a low, stone wall. The night was cool and damp.

"Should we talk about what you said?"

"Well, things are coming up," Nick said.

"And?"

"I don't think I can keep it up much more." She studied him. "With my work."

"And?"

"It'll affect... I may have to go away."

"You've gone away before."

"This time I don't know when or if I'll be back."

"Oh, Nick." She looked about to cry. "I don't want to lose you too."

He didn't answer. He held her, smelling her lilac scent and the sea air, he heard the sound of a far-off foghorn. "I don't want to leave either. But afraid it's coming. I wanted you, I need you. Except, the world's bigger than that. Bigger than us."

Sighing, she said, "I guess, I just wish things could've changed, or would change, or—"

"But they can't. And I'm sorry, and that doesn't change things."

"No." She looked off. "Will you change your mind?"

"Then I'm back in it again. And I'll regret it. Eventually I will."

"I know," she said in resignation. "I know." She took his chin and put his face to hers. A simple kiss, but familiar. "I don't know if I can live without, I mean, it's all so… sad." She started sobbing.

Like snow in spring, his resolution melted. "Let's go." He took her hand, started walking to her house. He thought about going home. *Just drop her off and go home and then you're free of her.* He also wanted just one more night, but also knowing that he'd always be wanting just one more night. *Cut it out*, he thought, *all of you quiet. Maybe this is the end, maybe not. I'm making no more promises, and tonight I'm having one more night.*

***

Nick prepared to leave San Francisco the next morning. He jogged, did some yoga, a practice that was growing on him—just fifteen or twenty minutes a day he found was sufficient. Then he looked at the easel in the corner of his apartment. *Paint, fuck it all, just start painting*, he thought. *Not yet. It's not finished yet. Maybe only just starting.* He caught a cab that was driving about Nob Hill, and an hour later was at San Francisco International. About half a day later he checked into the hotel.

An enormous chandelier hung from a white, gold-trimmed ceiling. Nick stood by a pair of small French chairs covered in heavy blue brocade; he stood on a long, rust-colored Persian rug with stars and moons on its corners. French doors opened onto a small patio outside of the room. In the distance, the orange sun was fading in the blue sky.

The hotel was three storied, built in colonial style. Ferns and palm trees covered the hotel entrance, which was near the water. At a nearby dock, tires bobbed, a cushion for boats to keep them from banging onto the pilings. Deck chairs and plants in large pots were scattered on the lawn just above the dock.

Nick stroked his two-day-old beard, with tinges of gray hairs interspersed with black. He wore a blue blazer, and gold cuff links on his white shirt.

Mr. Jeffers sat on a couch. A thin mustache accentuated his white face. He looked as if he had never been out in the sun. Jeffers said, "We at Barclays Private Trust assure you that as long as you're here the securities that you trade will be governed solely by Bermuda law, and provide you all the protections of Bermuda law."

"And, so, if I trade with a Swiss bank, I can take delivery of the securities here in nominee name, and there are no public records. That is what you're telling me?" Nick asked.

"Precisely so."

"Okay, good." His mind raced. He could short Nugget in Switzerland and open an account at the Bermuda bank in nominee name. Barclays was one of the best. Nobody would know where he was or where the trades were domiciled. The SEC, if they got nosy, wouldn't be able to trace the trades here. Not easily, anyhow.

"Branches of the world's largest banks are here in Bermuda, and our experience over the last two hundred years—"

"Yes, yes, I'm very familiar." Nick led him to the door. "Thanks for coming in, I'll let you know."

"But of course, sir. Just call."

Watching the door close, Nick thought, *So far, so good. Brett's thinking I'm here selling the institutions. I wouldn't tell anybody again to buy this crap. Just lunching with people from the old days, meeting new people, damn, money game's changed. They're all thirty-somethings, scary smart. If Brett asks if I've had any luck, I'll tell him sure, the institutions are all placing trades through Europe. I don't have to push the stock; Nugget's got legs now.*

A small voice asked, *Then how do I stop Nugget from running up when I'm ready*? Picking at his fingernail, Nick pushed the question away. He wondered if he should align with the shorts? Then he could force the stock down. On his laptop he checked on the short interest. There was very little stock sold short. To make waves now would just alert the stock watchers, and wouldn't move the stock down.

Ah, hell, do I just call in the cops? The enormity of what he was going to attempt washed over him. But he wondered what he would tell the police? That he got beaten up and he suspects the management of the company he works for? They wouldn't believe him. Brett would cover himself and... he might as well draw a bulls-eye on his forehead, because next time they would finish the job.

Then how'll I blow Nugget up? I don't know.

He went to bed, and barely slept all night.

***

The morning sun hadn't come up yet. Outside of his room, Nick heard the ocean pounding onto the shore but couldn't yet see it, the water appearing only as a black void. A boat with its fishing nets rolled up bobbed on the heavy waves outside of his window. A chattering flock of seagulls flew about it.

Light shined from the dining room across the grass. Through the windows of the dining room, he saw waiters in tuxedos standing by tables and using tongs to place rolls onto plates. There were Mercedes cars, Jaguars, and BMWs parked on the side of the hotel.

Wearing jeans, a white button-down shirt, and running shoes, Nick took a cup of coffee from the room-service cart. He picked up the phone and made a call. White paint speckled his fingertips. In the corner was an easel with the beginning of a painting: a cobblestone street reflecting sunlight.

"Gunn," a man answered.

"Hi, Ted. Nick."

"Oh, hi. Been leaving messages—"

"What's your picture on Nugget?"

"The bond deal's oversubscribed. The oils're all going crazy on the upside. Just pandemonium. You in the City?"

"No, sort of vacationing."

"Good for you. You know, most guys your age are retired."

Nick laughed. "Last time I tried that I ran out of money. Look, Ted, why am I seeing so little short interest in Nugget?"

"Hold on."

Ted went to check it out. Nick knew that many big traders would leave orders with institutional traders like Ted. There were lots of things going on not known to most traders. Lots of secrets on the Street.

"No interest out there in shorting," Ted said. "Some big short size lower. Nugget goes down about ten points, the shorts'll start kicking in. No damn chance of that happening, though."

"No. Guess not."

"So wha'd'ya have? Anything?"

"No. Just checking. See you later."

They hung up. Nick typed out NUP on the keyboard, and it came up on the screen: 43 1/4. *I'd have to drop that below 33 to get it to really crumble*, he thought. *How the hell can I do that*? He went outside. The sun was rising. The blue and green ocean raged. The waves roiled and crashed onto the shore. A storm blew in the distance. The sky darkened, then lightning flashed. Gray clouds gathered overhead.

Sitting on a chair near the dock, his straw hat on the grass, Nick watched men in dark suits and women in basic black and pearls walking to the front door of the hotel. He figured they had been out all night gambling. He had done his share of that.

The ocean clapped onto the shore. Some spray came his way. He wondered if he was hungry, and decided he wasn't. He'd eaten nothing for days, a little soup, a few crackers, a roll. He wondered why wasn't he hungry.

A boat started up and sent black smoke into the air. Smelling the smoke, he remembered something from a long time ago. Sitting in the back seat of a cab, the sun reflecting from a yellow bus in front, just about blinding him. They were stopped along with all the other cars and buses, all lined up on the Avenida Corrientas in Buenos Aires. The bus finally moved, belching up heavy black smoke. Diesel fumes mixed with the hot South American day.

Nick sat and remembered the cab moving, cars honking, people scurrying through the traffic; signs were posted on buildings lining the wide avenue. The cab cut off and sped down a narrow street barely wide enough to get through.

Waiting by the doorway of a small townhouse at the end of the alley, a short, red-faced man. His round belly hung over his belt.

Getting out of the cab, Nick said, "Osvaldo, I... well, she's not here. I mean she won't be. She—Julie died. I just left everything and I... I just don't know where to go. I want to dance again. I need to practice. Will that help?"

"Si, si," Osvaldo said. "Por favor."

Nick followed the tango teacher into a bare room, the sun reflecting from shiny parquet. An old, battered cassette player was in the corner. Tapes were piled atop, and more tapes spilled over and onto the floor.

Osvaldo opened large the French doors facing the avenue. Street noise rushed in, along with a breeze. He flipped a switch on the cassette player, and the beat of a tango filled the room.

Nick felt raindrops, then more, and the dream vanished. The sea churned wildly, while people ran out to the boats, and sails flapped savagely.

Grabbing his hat, he ran back to the porch outside of his room and sat. The rain came down in white sheets, and he could no longer see the ocean nor the boats. The hotel entrance had disappeared.

Closing his eyes, he again remembered the tango music. "Let's dance," Osvaldo said, extending his arms. Nick held his shoulders, Osvaldo taking the woman's part. Nick went through the basic step, guiding him through *ochos, boleros*. Linda's face appeared, and he took her hand, warm in his. She smelled of lilacs. *I want to go home*, he thought. *I want to wake up tomorrow in my bed, and know she's just cross town.*

Osvaldo's face reappeared, red and sweating. He said, "Many

people, too many, they come from all over, different countries. They try to dance the world away. Thinking that the morning will not come."

Craack: thunder boomed through the white blinding rain. Osvaldo, the music and the studio, disappeared. Linda's lilac smell was gone. All that was left was the constant hissing of heavy rain falling on emerald-green grass.

Chilled from the damp and cold, Nick thought, *I can't go home... there isn't any. I started this trip a while ago. I just didn't know it.*

He went inside to his elegantly sterile hotel room. Atop the bar was his computer, its screen glowing. He studied the screen, last night's information still showing: "Big Action: Your Research Source." He typed in his password, scrolled to: "Stock Holders, Institutions, Nugget Petroleum (NUP)."

"DEVON VALUE MANAGEMENT, Westport, Conn., 400,000 shares. Portfolio Manager, Joseph Grogin.

TOPPER VALUE MANAGEMENT, Boston, Mass., 170,000 shares. Analyst, Mark Barney.

FIDELITY INVESTMENT MANAGEMENT, New York, N.Y., 250,000 shares, Portfolio Manager, Lisa Allen.

KOGA NATURAL RESOURCES FUND, Boston, Mass., 600,000 shares, Portfolio Manager, Shirley Schuss."

Scrolling through, he identified the biggest holders of Nugget. He copied the names onto the hard drive, saving them as *Nugget Masters*. After he had copied most of the shareholders, he clicked *Save*, slid open the glass door and walked outside.

The storm had let up, and the rain was coming down in small, quiet drops. The wet grass smelled sweet; above, white clouds floated by. He still wanted to go home. Remembering his old office, he thought, *Yeah, the door would stick, but, so what? Hell, that wasn't so bad. Where am I now?* He started sweating under his arms. *Keep going, don't quit. Not in mid-stream.*

Back in his room, Nick pressed the redial button on his cell phone. After a few rings, he heard, "Gunn."

"This's Nick."

"Hold on." Nick held, the minutes ticking by like hours. Then, "Sorry. I'm jammed here. Lots of orders at the close."

"Want me to call back?"

"No. It's okay now."

"Look, let me ask you—"

"Uh, gotta be right back."

Nick picked his fingernail as the minutes ticked by. "Okay, Nick, what'cha got?"

"Trying to get a handle on Nugget. You got some time? Fill me in on what you know of some holders."

"Shoot."

"Lisa Allen at Fidelity, in New York."

"Tough and smart and a ball-buster and got in Nugget early. I showed her some bids. She doesn't want to sell. She loves the stock."

"Okay. How about Shirley Schuss at Koga Resources, the fund in Boston?"

"Don't know her. Them. They don't take calls. Think they're too damn smart to need..."

"Okay. Mark Barney? At Topper Value Management in Boston."

"Topper? They're value investors? Maybe that's what they *call* themselves. Bunch of flippers is what they are. Whore around for hot deals and promise all the commissions they'll pay us and we never see a trade. Nugget? They're in it as long as it's climbing."

"Devon Value? Joseph Grogin?"

"Don't know them. Must be nobody."

He continued identifying weak holders of Nugget, prone to sell if they heard bad news. They went on, and Nick thanked Gunn and hung up. Going back to the screen, he calculated that the Nugget Masters controlled about nine hundred and eighty-six thousand shares. *Well, it's something*, he thought. After that, he knew he had the big institutions like Grogin to go after. He needed more, a lot more, but it was a little size. When he was ready, he figured he'd go to these guys. But he'd have to convince them Nugget was a fraud, and that maybe would not be easy to do. They'd probably think he was just another short-seller out there trying to drive the stock lower. No, he didn't have much stock, less than a million shares to sell into the market. That wouldn't be good for much, probably drop the stock down a half point at the most.

Walking around the room he figured, *I need ten points, at least. Maybe... maybe I can't take this stock down.*

For a while he thought about it, scratched the back of his leg. He made a call. A woman answered and said, "Ellen Pasternak."

"Hi. Nick Larson. I don't know if you remember me."

A long silence ensued. Coldly she asked, "Yes, I do. I... how can I help you?"

"Oh, just wanted to catch up with you and see how you're doing."

"Fine. Thanks."

"Saw you made a change, and I'm doing some due diligence and wondered if you can help. Who would be our contact over at Morgans now?" Bringing up her new employer on the screen, he studied the information. Bank of Frankfurt. Good firm, he knew. It was based on Wall Street, an international investment bank, one of the majors.

"I don't think anybody. We did the bond deal, there's nothing else in the pipeline. To tell you the truth, I stopped following Nugget once I left."

I'll bet you did, he thought. *Washed your hands of it.* "I also wanted to ask if you knew—" Careful, he thought. *Don't go there. She's one of them, took their money. Don't go near questions about the Hand.* "—about what you see in the way of earnings for Nugget next quarter. I'm putting together a consensus estimate, and maybe there are some not good things you see about Nugget or management. Whatever you got."

"No. No, I can't," Ellen said. "I told you, I've left Nugget behind."

"Well, I just—"

"And I have a motto: Live and let live. I only speak well of people or I say nothing. It's a good way to operate, I've found."

Wish to hell I could, Nick thought as they signed off.

He made another call.

A voice boomed into the receiver, "Nick, heard you were away." Lenny Zellon had the phone on the speaker mode. Nick felt as if he was at the bottom of a well and Lenny was shouting down at him. "How are you?"

Lenny scoffed. "Lousy. I ain't been laid in who the hell knows how long! My shorts've gone up, my longs, down. Enough about me. So what do you think of this Nugget bond deal? Should I buy?"

"Lenny, I don't know. I—"

"You don't know? How the fuck could you not *know*, you're the friggin IR guy, the maven. Hey, I got lots of that stock because of you."

"No, I mean, I've gotta make some calls. I've been away."

"How many you buyin?"

How the hell do I get out of this? Nick wondered. Sweat trickled from under his armpits. He thought fast, and found the answer: "I can't buy. I'm an insider, and public orders have to be filled first."

"Yeah, true, the deal's oversubscribed." In the background, a phone in Lenny's office rang. "Hold on, I gotta grab this."

Nick listened, the receiver to his ear. He heard the rustling of papers, the slamming of drawers, the scuffling of Lenny's shoes on the floor. *The Street's tiny*, he thought. *It stretches around the world, and with instantaneous communications, most secrets last a nanosecond—if that long.* He knew he had to be careful, even with Lenny. Especially with Lenny. He pictured Lenny's bald spot, his darting black eyes. Moving in quick jerks and stops.

Lenny exploded on his other phone, "What do you mean you can't get me Nugget bonds? You'll take an order? You don't have an account set up for me? What are you, brain-dead? I told you a million bonds, even if I have to pay up a half a point in the after-market. So put the order in. Are you still here? Don't you know me? I'm Zellon. So go buy already!"

He came back. "Sorry, Nick. I gotta open up a new account, they make it a major project. All these damn brokers are hirin MBAs. What the hell can an MBA know? Only what the other MBAs know. They all took the same courses, so they all follow the same damn, stupid theories, which lead them to buy the same stock at the same damn time. Me? I got my MBA at Stanford. Trees, green campus, pieces of asses wearin little glasses and with brains. Got laid about once. Took me years to forget what I learned there. I fried hamburgers at McDonalds to detox from that friggin tree-lined boring prison. Learned more about the market short-changing those cheap professors. I hire MBAs now as clerks. Pay 'em eight bucks an hour, no benefits."

"Well, at least they get the benefit of your warm personality."

"Yeah, that's true, and I... hey, hold on."

Lenny went to the other phone. "Okay, sure, open the account. My investment objectives? Forget that. Only objective I got is gettin laid, haven't been in a month, and I'm bragging 'cause it's been longer than that. 'Course, I don't count whores, I know every hooker in every corner of this city and there're plenty. Okay, you want an objective? Make money, that's what. My financial profile? Profile this: I got a huge shlong, at least I think I do. You ever fuck a pregnant woman? I'm sure not, you MBA queen." Thonk, as the phone was slammed into its cradle.

"Sorry," Lenny said, coming back to him. "Can't even open up an account anymore without these guys hassling me. Uh, about the Nugget bonds, I need some good information. You know, trustin these brokers's like trusting my first four wives. Ya gotta deal with these liars or, hell, you won't get any good deals. And look, about women? Just out to rob you. But you and me, we go back, don't we? I ain't worried about what you tell me. Should I?"

"No, and Lenny. I have to talk to you about something else."

"Yeah, yeah, sure. What d'ya got?"

"It's about, well, I need some money. I don't mean I need it, but if I want to go short, I mean—"

"Short what?" Lenny snapped.

"Don't know yet. Could I borrow from you?"

"How much?"

His hand shaking, Nick stared into the phone. *I got nowhere else to go. Using margin I can short double the amount of cash I put up. With a half a million cash, I can short about twenty-five thousand shares. Nugget goes down to about five, I can make a million. No, I want more. I don't ever want to be broke and have to run around like this again.* "I need a million." Breathing came from the other end of the line. Nick felt Lenny thinking.

"What's my incentive?" Lenny asked. "I mean, the deal whatever the hell it is doesn't work, I'm left here holding my putz. I'm often left holding my putz; but I like to know that I'm left holding my putz."

"I'll give you twenty-five percent of the profits. And sign a note for the loan."

"Yeah. But then you have my money and I just have a note. Toilet paper is worth about the same."

"And we'll do the trade in a joint account."

"So—"

"That the million you lend me will be in *your* brokerage account. That for me to make money the deal has to work. You trust me that way?"

"You bet your rich girl WASP panties I do—after she's played soccer all day."

Nick held the phone with a shaking hand. "Deal?"

"Yeah. When do we pull the trigger?"

"Soon. But it has to be done my way. We'll short in Switzerland so the specialist won't know where the short's coming from. Then we'll clear through a bank in Bermuda…"

"As if I give a shit. Just let me know."

The room felt empty after Lenny hung up. Nick stared at the phone, thinking he could make about a couple million bucks. He wondered about whoever said that money didn't buy happiness. He thought it must have been a very poor man. *Easy*, he reminded himself. *Not home yet. Barely even started.*

Back at his laptop, sitting atop the bar, Nick clicked on to Message Board and found Nugget Petroleum. He wondered who was out there, and what they knew. For the hundredth time he wondered if he could take Nugget down. His stomach knotted.

He scrolled through to a message sent earlier: "From: Down and Dirty. Anybody else hearing about the phony baloney act Nugget's putting on with its road show, starring this over-the-hill, used-to-be-real Nick Larson, their IR guy? Anybody out there hearing what I am about Larson going off his rocker and disappearing few years ago? He sounds like the flaky type that would fit in with Nugget. Oh, yeah, I'm hearing that all the equipment that was shipped to Argentina is just sitting in an open field, gathering rust. Stock's going down, you can bet it."

Nick stared at the screen, thinking that the guy was a short, a serious short. But that information about the phony wells in Argentina, he had to work to find *that* out. *Probably he, or could be a she, maybe went down there herself and found out about the well.* Nick figured that the message was sent to drive Nugget down, that was for sure. It dawned on him that if she or he couldn't drive Nugget down with this information, how could he? Again he reminded himself to keep going, just keep going.

He scrolled to the next message.

"From: Student. Deal Maker Strikes Again. Looks like Nick Larson, the genius who saved Texas Resources and made stockholders rich by selling off the company, is about to do the same with Nugget Petroleum. I'm hearing Nugget's going merger crazy after its bond deal raises billions. Hang on for the ride—BUY, BUY."

Studying the screen, Nick thought, *he, or she's, a long. Who's so sure Nugget's going to buy other companies? Must've had information from the company. Student's obviously out to drive it higher. Brett's not letting that stock go down. Not without a fight.*

Another message: "From: Shark. To the Bottom. Okay, so now Nugget's trying to get its bonds out and raise a lot of money. The deal won't get done—not if the Street reads the prospectus. If you figure Nugget's income from operations, not from damn phony sales of leases to the thieving companies that it's colluding with, Nugget has a net loss—because, damn it, I crunched the numbers. Even if the bond deal gets done, and Nugget buys a lot of companies, Nugget's going nowhere. Wells and his buddies will just drain the acquired companies dry, and the stockholders will be the losers. As usual."

"He sees right through the scam," Nick mumbled.

Another one from Shark, a pretty recent one: "From: Shark. Got any Dirty Dish Towels? Because you can put them with the rest of your laundry and ship them off to Nugget Petroleum and say you'll pick it up over the weekend. Just leave it there with the other cleaned laundry, tell Brett Wells and the other sleaze bags to launder your stuff along with all the money they're laundering. I'm hearing that's all Nugget's good for, to launder money. From Mexico, Argentina, hell, I'm hearing people from all over the world show up with bags of money. Drill for oil? Why? And one day Wells and Byrd and the others, who the hell knows who else is in this, will disappear. With bags of money. Cleaned. There's an invisible hand out there. Ciao."

Picking his fingernail, Nick stared at the screen. *Of course*, he thought, *that all makes sense. Nugget's the biggest home for dirty money in the world. That's the only reason for its existence.*

He scrolled through more chat room messages. *Nothing. Shark's sent in one a day, sometimes two, and after that last one, zilch. The sharks got to the Shark. I wonder… anytime the Hand is mentioned, things happen. Maybe I'll get bit, but am I just dreaming about this guy*?

He typed in "From: Spear. Hear About the Invisible Hand? Just an observer, of late; I've dumped my Nugget stock, but thinking of jumping back in. Anybody hear about this group the Invisible Hand? That it's out of Argentina and are big holders of Nugget. Anybody hearing anything?"

Nick looked at it, hesitated, pressed Send. He ordered up coffee from room service, and studied the screen. *Maybe I've bought it now. No going back anyway.* The coffee came and he took it to the couch. Sitting far from the screen, on a couch across the room, he sipped the coffee. It was strong, with a touch of chicory. He made himself wait ten minutes, looking out of the window, half expecting men with knives to appear outside.

Back at the screen, he scrolled through and read: "From: Student. About the Invisible Hand. Sure, I've heard about that outfit. Smart bunch of guys. Loaded up on oil stocks, I'm hearing, before the advance. E-mail me, Spear. I'll fill you in: rigor2@aol.com"

Nick re-read the message. *I'll e-mail you and somehow, I don't know how the hell, you'll find out my name. Back in San Francisco you'll be waiting, you and Brett and all the others. Okay, Invisible Hand. I get it.*

He shut down the computer. He was drained. It had been a hell of a long day. He took a final sip of coffee and started packing his bag.

Seven

Nick slept twelve hours after he got back to San Francisco. He stared at the phone, finally summoned the strength to get up. After picking up the receiver, he looked out the window of his Nob Hill apartment. A large park across the street showed a sea of green, and beyond were the blue waters of the Bay. The Golden Gate Bridge was off in the distance, followed by the hills of Marin County, everything looking tiny.

Nick noticed a man almost hidden behind a tree, across the street in the park. He walked a few steps forward, then backward. Nick wondered what the man was waiting for, or who. *Not from this neighborhood, obviously.* A giant, hulking man, his dark brown camelhair coat was too warm for San Francisco. A wide-brimmed hat hid his face.

Go ahead, light up, Nick thought.

The man lit a cigarette, cupping his palms to protect the flame. Resumed his pacing. Nick looked from different angles and finally saw his face. His heart pounded. *That's Hammer, the guy at the restaurant in Houston. What the hell's he following me for*?

He called Linda. The phone rang, but the line went dead. He called again.

"Hi," Linda said.

Nick heard a faint sound: click. "You hear that?"

"What?" she asked.

"A click, something, on the line."

"I... I'm not sure."

"You didn't hear anything?"

"I don't think so. What's the difference?"

"I saw a guy. Maybe they're tapping my phone."

"You're—you're making me nervous."

"I... oh, maybe it's nothing. Are you ready?"

"Not quite. Give me half an hour."

After hanging up, he looked out of the window. Hammer was gone. He thought maybe he *was* going nuts, that the click on the phone (which he wasn't even sure he had really heard) could have been anything. *Was that Hammer? Maybe just another strange guy in the city. Like they're not all over. But why would anyone follow me*? He then answered himself, *Why did they try to kill you*?

He got dressed and drove to Linda's.

"Hi, Thad."

Thad Thackery looked into Nick's face. Showing no signs of recognizing Nick, he resumed staring across the room. His gaze was aimed out of the large window, its white curtains half-drawn, into the quiet streets of Pacific Heights. Thick trees, their limbs heavy with green leaves, obscured the view of the street. Thad seemed to be deep in thought about something, the thoughts lost somewhere in his mind.

Linda said, "He doesn't recognize you, he doesn't recognize anyone." Pouring half a glass of wine and bringing it to Nick, she said, "He won't get better than this, not ever."

Sprinkled in her dark hair, Nick noticed a few gray strands.

"All right. To bed," she said, turning Thad's wheelchair toward the thin slice of light shining from their bedroom. Its wheels squealed as they moved over the thick-carpeted living room.

She came back, took a sip of wine, and looked at Nick for a moment. The stem of her wine glass tinkled as she placed it down on the glass coffee table. "I drink too much. Almost every night, a half bottle."

"That's not too much," Nick said.

"Yes, but it's almost every night. No, it *is* every night."

"I'm glad I came while he was still awake. If I just come later, and don't say hello, I feel like I'm sneaking around."

"Really, he doesn't know the difference. Probably will forget he's seen you."

"But *I* know. I look at him and think, Do you know I'm sleeping with your wife, and how could you not know, then I know I'm cheating him, but I'm not sure from what, and... I guess I'm asking you to make me feel better."

She took a sip. "I don't need this conversation, not just now. I'll think about it tomorrow." She took a sip. "Oh, Nick."

Admit it, he thought, *you need her; maybe love her. I miss Julie. If I could just keep living in the past, I'd put up with Julie in the hospital again. But the reality is that I don't know what the reality is.* "I, I just feel better when you're near."

Smiling, Linda said, "I feel the same."

"Let's go away, for a few days."

"Oh, I don't know. Thad needs..."

"He has full-time help. Come on, it'll do us both good." Feeling his fears melting away, like taking off a heavy coat on a summer's day, Nick put his arm around her. She moved closer to him. "It'll be like old times." He tried hard to believe that.

***

From the antique filled, thick-carpeted lobby of the Ritz Carlton Hotel, you could look down to see waves lapping up onto the white sand at Laguna-Nigel. About an hour's drive south from Los Angeles, Laguna was known for its wide beaches and lush green golf courses, and yogis and millionaires and high-tech firms and mansions. Near the end of town were the homeless and hippies. Very rich and very poor and very fringe people: a typical California community, with the sun shining constantly.

Nick and Linda walked across the lobby and into the dark dining room of the Ritz-Carlton. People walked about in bathing suits, golf shorts, Hawaiian shirts. All were attending the Spence Trask Oil and Gas Stock Conference, the biggest conference of the year.

Nick glanced around, having been a past regular at these major events. Stock analysts, investment bankers, stock promoters, and brokers met the officers of the companies that presented there. The players schmoozed and sniffed out a company's problems or promise. Do they buy or sell a company's stock? Does a banking deal need to get done? Lots of hustle and deals and whispering, and false and honest camaraderie.

Linda wore black shorts and a sheer linen shirt. Nick had on jeans, a white Armani shirt, black linen sport coat, white tennis shoes.

He tried to avoid Lenny, but it was too late. Lenny's dark eyes found them. They went to Lenny's table for a minute. It was near a large open window. Enormous white curtains, blown by the ocean breeze, fluttered into the room. The sun glowed in the late afternoon. Lenny offered them drinks, and Nick and Linda ordered cognacs. A white-jacketed waitress wrote it down. Lenny ordered another martini.

"Oil stocks're on fire," Lenny said. He wore white shorts; his skinny legs were like a spider's. "I'm hearin the Nugget bonds're all allocated already. Deal'll come in about a week. I got a few hundred thousand. Should I get more?"

The salty smell of the ocean blowing into the room, the memory of Linda lying next to him in the sand, the hypnotic blue of the morning sea and sky, the mindless drift of doing nothing all day, all faded away as Nick stared into Lenny's unblinking eyes. He felt dizzy, wanted to go lie down, be with Linda and stroke her hair, forget all about Lenny and Brett Wells and... everything.

"Nugget's still okay. You'll do fine," he said in a voice he didn't recognize. He forced himself to look into Lenny's eyes. "Buy as many as you can. Don't worry." Nick scratched behind his knee. He wiped away some sweat from under his chin.

The waitress brought the drinks and left.

Lenny waved across the room. "Hi, Wild," Lenny said as Willie Bornstein approached: tall, handsome, a thick head of black hair starting at just above his eyes; swarthy, standing straight, as if movie cameras were focused on him.

As the managing partner of Spence Trask, Willie Bornstein had to get the Nugget bond deal done. Spence Trask was the lead underwriter in the deal. Willie was known for spontaneous combustion outbursts: yelling at assistants, cursing, telephone throwing, computer screen crashing. Anything could set off his wild outbursts: a stock going down after he bought it, a trader getting him a bad execution, a trader getting him not a good enough execution. Almost anything.

After handshakes all around and an introduction to Linda, Lenny turned to Willie.

"Just tryin to squeeze the inside out of Larson here. Guy won't open up." Lenny was smiling but his eyes were very serious. "Heard you were down there, in Argentina," he said to Nick. Each word felt like a pointed dagger. "You never told me."

Nick tried to not appear shaken, but his voice betrayed him by coming out thin. "Yes. Yes, I was."

"Well? How was it?"

Ah, fuck it, Nick thought. Maybe it was the sand, sun, or just the debilitating weight of being a liar. *Blow Nugget up now. Run later*. "Yes, I was down there. A damn cop hit me with a rifle, stole my camera, wouldn't let me through to the wells. You know what else? I didn't see any drilling going on anyway." He sat back and waited for the explosion.

"Yeah," Lenny said. "I sent a guy down there. Same thing happened to him."

Pulling his chair closer to the table, Willie said, "Nugget did have some problems earlier, with bandits. Maybe they dressed up as cops, who knows? Anyhow, it's all been cleared up."

"Has it?" Lenny asked. "You still can't get to the wells. Not as of, uh, yesterday." He kept looking at Nick.

"Ah, these things happen. They like to steal cameras down there. It'll be cleared up, certainly in the next week or so," Willie said. He tried to get the waitress's eye.

Taking a sip of the cognac, Nick felt it burning his insides. He figured that Willie had never been down there, near the wells. Willie didn't want to know or see trouble. Willie wanted his banking fee, well into the millions. The whole Street was like that. *The Street's got a stake in Nugget, a big one. And they won't let Nugget fail. And I can't read Lenny*. The knot in Nick's stomach told him that he didn't control much of any of this.

They chatted about golf. Lenny kept looking Linda up and down. After a moment Nick said, "Wild. I should come see you guys, as part of my due diligence. To keep up with the offering."

"Come next week," Bornstein said. "We're getting ready to full-court-press the deal. I got to get this out. The partners, they've been on my back a lot lately. The rankings, those fucking rankings, that's all they care about, don't you know."

***

Willie Bornstein stood up from behind his desk as Nick walked into his office.

Behind Willie, an oil painting of a large-fanged tiger hung on the wall. Against another wall a claw-footed table was filled with small, toy motorcycles; framed pictures of Willie and others on Harleys and BMW bikes; Willie standing next to a row of black motorcycles, his shock of hair mussed from the wind. More framed pictures of his girlfriends, ex-wives; his four children; photos of leading financiers, one taken on a yacht; thank you notes for doing this deal, that deal, from the governor of California, the mayor of New York.

Far outside through the window the waters of the San Francisco Bay shimmered blue in the afternoon sun. The houses in North Beach in the distance looked toy sized. Among them, Coit Tower stood tall and gleaming white; the site was famous as the location for the ending of the movie *Vertigo*. Nick recalled its Diego Rivera mural. He had studied that mural for hours when he had taken up painting. *I have to get back to that*, he thought, scratching an itch on his arm.

"Look," he said, and sat across from Willie. "I built Nugget up and, well, I'm getting calls from people, smart people, about… fuzzy numbers in the prospectus. And other questions."

Willie shrugged. "Well, there're problems with the company, sure, any company. Maybe the information in the prospectus isn't perfect, but no deal's perfect. You of all people know that. Some of my partners are coming by. Stick around. See how tough it gets around here. I don't need to tell you, it's all about the rankings."

Nick thought about it: the damn rankings. All firms on the Street were measured by the dollars of the investment banking deals they transact. The big firms—Merrill Lynch, Morgan Stanley, firms like that—underwrote huge offerings. The top few firms received more underwritings. Catch-22: the more stock an underwriter sold, the more stock it received to sell. You had to be big to get big, or not survive.

Being a middle-tier firm, Spence Trask had to get more deals to underwrite so it could move up to the top-tier. Also, the partners—bloodsuckers, Willie called them—were never satisfied. After putting up the money so the firm could operate, the partners always wanted a return. How much? More, always more. Firms like Spence Trask made most of their money on underwriting stocks and bonds. If a company wanted to sell its stock to the public, it would go to an underwriter and have an Initial Public Offering (IPO). If an already public company wanted to raise money by selling additional shares, again they would arrange to have stock issued to the public, in a secondary offering. Brokerage firms also lent money; secured debt financing was often the biggest source of revenue. Secured debt income occurred when a brokerage firm lent money to customers for buying or selling stocks. The firm charged customers interest for the borrowed funds.

He's worried about Nugget, Nick decided, watching Willie fidget with a gold letter opener. About now he'd usually curse someone out, or throw an ashtray across the room, or fire a secretary. But Wild was keeping cool. *Probably his Valium's kicking in.*

Willie said, "Look, we need to do this Nugget. Our banking deals've dried up, and this is a big one. You know Malcolm Miller?"

"Sure." Everybody knew Miller. A billionaire, Miller had made money the new fashioned way, merging his company with a dot-com, then selling his shares before the dot-com burned through its money and crashed and burned. Now he stalked the Street looking for deals.

"Miller'll put money with us, and we need it, but he's underwhelmed by our underwriting calendar. I told him we'd get Nugget out, like yesterday. After that there's a bunch'a oil deals we can do."

A short, older man walked into Willie's office. His dyed brown hair had a slight red tint and he wore a three thousand dollar suit. "Hello, I'm Al Zucker. Who're you?" he asked Nick. Then to Willie, "When's the meeting? I gotta get back to L.A."

"Okay, Big Al. It'll start soon. Nick, say hello to our biggest partner. Nick here works for Nugget Petroleum."

"That's the company we're underwriting?" Al asked.

"Well, yes. I sent you the prospectus," Willie said.

"You did? I been busy. But I don't mind tellin you, I hate oil companies. I bought oils in the '70s, heavy. All I know's that they went down. I don't like stocks that go down. I should take my money outa this damn place and make more movies. I'll tell you, I'm afraid of this business. The IRS is all over me, all the time. This business has the SEC, the IRS, the state regulators. Everybody's always picking on me. Not even worth it makin money, you gotta fight those guys."

Willie chewed on his lip. "We're underwriting that company. I've already committed."

"Committed? What'm I, chopped liver? Remember the oils? Last time we did one I had a hernia."

"But, Al—"

"Yeah, *oils*." Al scrunched up his face. "I had to put more money here on the last oil company; then the deal didn't work."

"But—"

"Ah, shit. Not oils," Al said.

"Oil troubles are all in the past," Willie said. "Oils are hot again. Nugget'll work, big."

"Let's finish, I wanta go home, but first I gotta go to Sun Valley. Place is growin like crazy. We oughta all get outta this stupid business and put our money in land up there and sit and watch the sunset and take it easy, and who the hell knows how long you're gonna live, hell, my ulcer acts up the minute I get to a big city. I gotta go to New York next week and God my stomach hurts now but just wait'll I talk to those bastards about re-financing my buildings. They don't wanta hear nothin about occupancy problems but how much up front I can pay for new financing—Hi, Malcolm."

Another man walked in briskly, striding like an athlete. With short-cropped hair, Malcolm Miller looked around and smiled as he was introduced. His cold eyes contrasted with his friendly, big-teethed smile.

Willie said, "Okay, you guys, let's talk about Nugget. True, there're some *oversights* in the prospectus. It's nothing we can't fix. Sure don't want to cancel the deal."

"Should forget that dog," Al said. "What gave me the hernia."

"C'mon, Al. You can't get a hernia from a stock going down," Willie said.

"Who says? You? Where'd you get your doctor's license?"

Willie's eyes narrowed. "Well, unless our analyst finds somethin, and she hasn't made noises that she has, we're going with it. Also a bunch of us, you guys are invited too, Malcolm's going, we're motor-cycling through to the southern tip of Mexico, and I wanta get this deal out before we go. That gives us a couple of weeks."

"We need the money. It's a do," Miller said. "Next?"

"I don't have all day," Al said. "Whatever. Gave me a hernia, I'm sure."

"Is there anything that the company wants to add? What do you say?" Willie asked Nick.

All eyes fixed on him.

Careful, he thought. *Hell with careful, I have to be honest.* "I told you before, Willie. I went to Argentina and those wells are being policed for no reason I can think of other—"

"Policed? What you mean?" Al said.

Putting his hands up, Willie said, "Now, Al, don't worry. Nick and I covered this and straightened it out. There's just some problem with rebels down there."

"Rebels?" Al said, wide-eyed.

"Nothing major," Willie said.

Nick did not speak.

"Next," Malcolm Miller said.

"Rebels?" Al said.

"This one's getting done. Next," Malcolm said.

***

A pattern of large red roses covered the couch Nick sat on. Judy's office looked frenzied. On top of computers were stacks of papers; stuffed into and spilling out of her desk drawers, more papers, prospectuses, legal documents. On the wall hung a framed certificate: MASTER OF BUSINESS ADMINISTRATION, HONORS AWARD, STANFORD UNIVERSITY.

Judy Hart was Spence Trask's oil analyst. Her job was to approve the stocks and bonds the firm underwrote, and after the offering she'd usually issue a buy recommendation that would go out to the Spence Trask brokers, individual and institutional investors, the Internet, and the media. This would spur sales in the aftermarket, hopefully boosting the price of the securities. Hopefully for customers of Spence Trask, and Nugget.

Looking around the office, Nick waited for Judy and wondered what she knew about Nugget. *Really* knew. He'd known her for years, one of the old breed: honest, smart, a straight-shooter. He wondered if he could use her to take Nugget down.

She came into the office, her mouth tight, her short hair askew. Throwing folders, tablets, documents, and a purse on the desk, she looked at her watch and said, "Sorry, Nick, I just have a few minutes. I have another meeting and, frankly, haven't had time to dig into Nugget anymore."

"I just came from upstairs. They're saying they're bringing it right away." Nick smiled. "Willie and Malcolm are going away on their motorcycles."

Judy laughed. She took a tube out of her purse and applied lipstick heavily. "Just like two children, going off to play on their bikes. Leaving the damn work to us." She shrugged in resignation. Her red lips stood out against deep lines on her face. She gestured at the papers spread around her office and said, "It's not like Nugget's the only thing I have to worry about. Willie, all of them around here. Let's just do deals, they say."

She picked up some folders, threw them back onto the desk. "You should see some of the crap we, the whole Street's, bringing now. The prospectuses—I want to throw up after reading some of them. Damn deals. Companies are not makin money, maybe never will. Should be venture capital deals, but we do them to stay alive. You know what the smart money is doing with this crap? Throwing the prospectuses into a box, or storing them on their hard drives. They'll look at them again, maybe in a few years. When they can buy the stocks for a few pennies. And know what? I think they're right."

Judy's face had turned redder than her lipstick. "But I gotta help bring in these deals for underwriting. Am I going to say don't buy? It's just all so draining."

A secretary stood at the doorway, her glasses on the tip of her nose, and said, "You'll be late for your two o'clock."

"I gotta go."

Nick got up. "Uh, one other thing. Are you worried about what's going on down there in Argentina? The Invisible Hand and all?"

"Who is the Invisible Hand?"

"No big deal." He smiled. "A gang associated with Nugget and maybe tied up in money laundering."

Judy laughed. "Everything bothers me about that deal. I can't get any cooperation with them about projections on their Cordoba wells. I go to Willie and rage, and what does he say? 'You're the best, Judy. You can get it together. We need this deal.' Then he shows me a picture of his latest motorcycle and girlfriend, in that order, and asks me what I think. Think? The patients have taken over the asylum is what I think. What can I do? Not that it matters, Nick, but I need this job."

Nick nodded. He knew that Nugget was coming, with or without her. It would set them back time-wise if she refused to sign off on Nugget, and maybe it wouldn't be so hot, the Street questioning why she was fired over the deal. *It's coming*, he thought. *Book it. If Judy doesn't approve it, there'll be a new analyst here tomorrow, straight out of an MBA program. The Street wants the business.*

"Nothing surprises me about Argentina," Judy said. "And the last thing anyone around here wants me to do is to investigate any money laundering. You understand, don't you, Nick?"

Nick nodded. "Sure," he said, wiping sweat from under his lips.

***

"I have something to show you. You'll love it." Linda smiled, and her white teeth gleamed.

After leading Nick down a dark hallway, they walked into her kitchen. Several art works hung on a wall illuminated by bright lights. Linda led him to a large etching: a man in a tuxedo and a woman in a red dress, dancing on a huge boulder, the ocean crashing below.

"What do you think?" she asked.

He looked at it, feeling stunned.

"It's a Debra Walker, you know, she's the new rage. It was twenty-five thousand dollars. A lot, I know, but—are you all right? Nick?"

Inhaling the lilac smell of Linda's perfume and staring at the art work, he said, "I just remember, remember a time, it was long ago."

"Want a drink?"

"It was Julie and me, and we danced, we danced just like that, above the ocean. And we wore the same clothes."

"How interesting."

He'd sworn to stop thinking about Julie, but couldn't. "You remember what good dancers we were?" His thoughts raced, *Don't say anymore, damn it. Why not? Because it's mine, she is. But she's gone.*

The palms of his hands started sweating. "Julie and I, we once danced in the subway, in Paris. A short man, I guess a midget, played an accordion. People gathered, they watched us dance. Once, in Venice, we danced in San Marcos Square. You know how it drizzles there in the winter, and the square's deserted. But there was a crowd that night, and people took our picture as we danced. The violinist, the piano player, were dressed in formal wear, and they didn't know tangos but they knew all the old gypsy melodies and they had the same beat." Nick kept himself from crying. He looked at the reflection from the glass on the etching, he and Linda standing together. *I must look like a wimp to her*, he thought. *Nothing's working anymore.*

Linda put her hand on his arm.

He smelled at her, standing near. *Am I all right?* he wondered. *I always say yes.* "Probably I shouldn't talk about her, but I can't forget."

"How could you?"

His voice was thin. "Let's go."

Tears went down Linda's cheek. Nick held her. She looked at him, stopped crying, and laughed. "Oh, Nick. How did we get this way?"

"I don't know. The rules stayed the same but the game changed?"

***

Nick and Linda drove across the city to the Mission, a section of San Francisco once entirely populated by Latinos but now being gentrified, young professionals moving in and forcing out the working-class tenants, many of them elderly. Old people forced to live in Golden Gate Park, not something found in a slick tourist's brochure of the city. They held the dance in a building that had seen better days. Green paint faded on the walls. People were drinking and talking. Smoke traveled to the ceiling in the dimly lit, small room, a worn dance floor in the middle.

"Tango should be bottled and sold to people for depression," Linda said, laughing. Their plates had been emptied except for a few chicken bones and the leavings of potato salad and bread. The ice had melted in their drinks. Red lipstick circled the top of her glass.

On a small stage, a woman violinist and a piano player started playing a slow tango. Nick and Linda got up and melted into each other and the music. They continued, dancing a few more numbers. Then they danced a *milango*, moving quickly across the floor.

Back at the table, she drained the little left in her glass. Laughing and trying to catch her breath, she said, "I, I haven't had so much fun in—I don't know. Forever it seems."

"Me too."

"We should get out more."

"Yes." He took her hand. Usually he didn't, not in public. But none of their friends came here. The tango halls were far from the mansions in Pacific Heights, the formal dinners that venture capitalists and investment bankers gave, the charity balls that the rich sponsored in forty-room houses. That was all a distant memory.

He thought it was all so perfect: watching the dancers, the music light and sweet. *To hell with it*, he decided. *I can't take Nugget down, not after watching those Spence Trask vampires salivate at the prospect of bringing those garbage bonds. And who cares anyway? I got mine*. He envisioned the apartment he was about to buy, at the top of Nob Hill. It was in a glass and steel building that covered a city block, blue-uniformed doormen hustling to open car doors. Suddenly appearing in Nick's mind, Lenny's dark eyes, staring through him. His stomach knotted.

Holding Linda's warm hand, he said, "You know, all we've been through, the whole time there was—I do love you. I always have."

She smiled.

"And I always feel guilty, telling you that I love you."

"It's not easy for me either right now. But I love to hear it."

After a while, Linda said, "Maybe we should dance. It's getting late."

"Yes, it is."

They got up and joined the others on the floor. Lights twinkled, the music stayed light and gay, and they talked to others, laughed, and tried some new steps. They finished another bottle of Napa Valley Chardonnay. The hours flew by. It was a great night to be together.

***

In the tiny coffee shop in North Beach, magazines and newspapers were piled on top of the jukebox, on chairs, tables, and the counter where you picked up your cappuccino and biscotti and pannetone: *San Francisco Examiner, Poetry Flash, Poet's Journal, Literary Digest,* and *South Bay Express*, the Bay Area's major gay newspaper.

Red and blue lights blinked on front of the jukebox. Opera arias played over the din in the crowded room. Tables were packed next to each other, chairs drawn close together. Coffee cups being filled rattled in saucers. The ancient cash register rang *kachiing* every time somebody bought something. It was a place left behind in the rush to coffeehouse homogenization; no Peet's or Starbuck's or generic part of a coffeehouse chain, this place. Scruffy men had thick beards, wore tweed jackets and berets. Women in heavy sweaters and Birkenstocks sat talking, reading, sipping. *Lot of gray hair and gray beards here*, Nick thought. *About my age*. His black gym bag with sweat-soaked clothes spilling out was on the floor. *Well, do this deal, then hang out here like them. Paint, bullshit about stuff. Sounds pretty good.*

Picking up the *San Francisco Examiner*, he glanced through *Movies* (nothing looked that interesting), *Restaurants* (French? Italian?). He wasn't hungry. Just restless, he decided.

Flipping through the paper, he saw a small article.

"Examiner News Service. October 13. Cordoba, Argentina—Reports verify six killed and eighteen injured near this small city, located in the Pampas. Officials deny that Invisible Hand, a gang thought to be headquartered in Mexico City, was involved, and claim local bandits were solely responsible. The event was the latest in a series of incidents that have plagued Cordoba and the surrounding area. The region, once populated by over six thousand people, mostly native Indian land dwellers, has shrunk to about four hundred people."

Nick took a sip of cappuccino, bit on a croissant, picked up *Poetry Flash* from the next table, and read a couple of poems. Put aside the paper. *What the hell's going on down there?* Again he picked up *Poetry Flash*, tossed it down. *I know it's the Hand. Not my business. Yes, it is. But just pretend you don't know anything about this scam. But I do. Okay, I have to go down there; if nothing else, for due diligence. I'm still representing Nugget, aren't I? And they're still paying me. Okay, I'll go, but don't bullshit myself. I'm not going down there on a due diligence mission.*

Eight

Nick looked into the black night as he disembarked at the Buenos Aires airport. Linda's perfume was still on his fingers, on his clothes. Partly, he didn't want to be there. He told himself to forget it, that he had a job to do. He went to the rental car section.

The roads were bumpier than he had remembered them, but in the still night he found his way back to the fields near Cordoba. Yellow banners with Policia in bold print blocked the road that led to the well site. His car was a 1998 Peugeot with over a hundred thousand miles on the odometer. After parking behind a thick bush, he crawled on all fours to a fat cedar tree. He could hear the guards snoring in their small tents.

His left eye twitched. He tried not to listen to himself thinking, *Let's get the hell out of here, are you nuts*? He reached around and felt the derringer, in its holster hanging from his belt. His watch glowed red in the darkness: 2:13. Behind the tree, he waited.

At 3:05 his heart jumped when he felt a rumbling, the ground shaking. He wondered if he was hallucinating, then heard a whining as a truck geared down, the engine sounding smooth and syncopated as the truck reached the road leading to the well site. He saw the truck's long and wide cylindrical body, appearing as large as a jet plane. The truck was white with PETROL printed in large black letters.

His heart pounded. Policemen wearing tank top undershirts came out of the tents. After looking into the truck, they waved the driver on. With a whine of gears and the engine racing, the truck took off toward the site.

About a half hour later a similar truck came driving up. It slowed and stopped and then Nick heard "Vamos, vamos," after the policemen looked the driver over. They waved it through. The truck started down the road, the police returned to their tent.

Nick knew what they were up to, watching the truck kicking up dust. Crickets chirped and night birds twittered. Behind the tree, his teeth chattered. *They catch me, I'm dead.*

An hour passed and a couple more trucks went through the checkpoint and down the road. In the distance a slice of sunshine was cutting through the blackness.

Nick crawled back to the car. He released the brake, and pushed the car down the road for a distance before starting the engine. Breathing a sigh of blessed relief, he drove away, keeping the Peugeot's lights off.

The car groaned as it bounced over holes and kicked up dust. Finally, he reached a two-lane highway. Traffic was light. Dilapidated trucks with open backs carried workers in shabby clothes. They waved at him. Passing them, he smiled and waved back. His shirt was wet with sweat, and he shivered in the cold early-morning air.

After studying a map, Nick turned onto a narrow dirt road almost hidden by trees. After a few miles he saw a large empty plaza. It had the broken and abandoned remains of a cathedral. Names of saints were carved onto its walls. Rows of graves were off to the side.

A low orange sun was rising.

Arriving in a town consisting of a few shacks, he slowed down as he drove over a dusty street. Over a weather-beaten shack hung a dusty, unlit sign: Cerveza. *I need a beer, real bad*. He pulled up at the shack, wondering if anybody in this town knew anything about the wells.

Inside were some worn tables, about a dozen broken chairs; the paint was faded on the walls. Behind the bar was a calendar several years out of date. On the calendar was a picture of a young woman, her large breasts protruding from under a clinging, white tee shirt. Printed on the shirt: DOS Xs.

A large, swarthy man with a deeply pock-marked face stood behind a worn wood bar, wiping the bar with a torn white rag. A mirror with many cracks ran the length of the bar, reflecting the man's back. Nick ordered a beer in Spanish, then asked, "Habla Ingles?"

"Si. A leetle," the bartender said.

"Where is everybody?" Nick asked, looking around the empty room. "This is Cordoba, isn't it?"

Sighing, the bartender drooped his shoulders. "*Si*, this is Cordoba. The women are working in the fields. The men, at the wells or in jail."

"Yes, I was out at the wells. Don't know why they need so many police to guard a well site."

The bartender sighed. "They come and drink here, the policia. If a man looks at them crossways, to jail. Except ones like me. I am needed to serve them beer."

"They throw people in jail for nothing?"

"Or worse. But I am old and useless. And a coward."

"Como se llama?"

"*Soy* Manuel."

Nick took a swallow, thinking what a God-forsaken place it was. "Have you ever seen trucks, big ones, coming through here in the middle of the night?"

Manuel started washing the few glasses on the bar. "*Nada*. That is what I see," he said.

"Listen, you can tell me. Do I look like el policia?"

Manuel dried the inside of a glass. His eyes wandered toward the windows, as if expecting something. His mouth tightened. "You do not know what it has been here, Senor." Looking at the glass in his hand he said, "I know nada, Senor, nothing. That way I sleep in peace at night. Mi Ingles is very poor. Perdon."

Nick sipped the beer and thought it over. "Maybe I could help. I live in the States and know some, well, important people. If I hurt one of their money makers, it might set them back." The orange sun came burning through the window. He started thinking about the long, hot drive back to Buenos Aires. And who might be waiting for him there.

"Anything to hurt them."

"I'm not making any promises but... I'm seeing a Captain Pugliese in Buenos Aires. I'm trying to hunt down a group called the Invisible Hand, and anything you could tell me... maybe they are here?"

"They are here, those—worst animals a mother never had. You should be here when some of the Hand come, on their way to or from the wells. They get drunk crazy and laugh at us and then play soccer."

"Play...?"

"In the streets outside. They have prisoners, men I knew who grew up here with me, in Cordoba, who I knew, we were children, are tortured, suspected of... who knows. We see later their heads, hacked off."

"They what?"

"Senor, please. I speak the truth," Manuel said. "They kick the heads down the street, they laugh until tears come to their eyes, they fall down, they laugh."

Nick took a sip, and swallowed hard. "About the trucks?"

"Every night they run. Never one night are they not through our streets, shaking the ground as they go."

"How many?"

"Every night they wake us as they go. Maybe six, maybe seven."

More than Nick figured. "Anything else?" He drained the glass, and stood up.

Manuel's face was a tortured map of lines. "Nada. Mucho, but more and more of the same."

Nick stood there looking at Manuel. He felt sorry for the guy, but what could he do? "Thank you. I'll do what I can." Manuel nodded. Nick tossed down a few *dolares*, and left.

Back in the car, Nick felt a little woozy from drinking a beer at mid-day. *What are you getting into*? he asked himself. *Sure, I'd like to help that guy. They tried to murder me, but damn it, how will I eat if I do blow up Nugget? Which I can't do anyhow. But I could short the stock, take down Nugget and make money on the downside. Totally illegal, an insider with inside information.*

He slipped the key into the ignition switch. The beat-up Peugeot sputtered and coughed and finally caught. Driving down the road, dust flew from under the wheels and blew into the car's open windows. The car ran over deep holes and its springs bounced and groaned. Bright sunshine filled the sky. Nick noticed a black object, about the size of a small pumpkin, fixed atop a post on a barbed-wire fence. Birds pecked at the object, and a cloud of flies, mosquitoes, and yellow bees buzzed around.

Blinking the dust from his eyes, Nick looked closer. He saw a half-eaten ear, black hair, remains of eyes in sockets, lips grinning idiotically from the severed head.

He shivered, staring ahead at the road, then studying the rearview mirror, and driving faster, his palms sweating onto the steering wheel he held tightly. *What the hell am I doing here?* he asked himself again.

***

Manuel Ortiz stared at the back of the strange, thin *Americano* as he left the bar, got into the Peugeot and sped away down the street. Dust and stones kicked up from under the car's tires.

The heat and glare of the endless sun beat down upon the small, weathered shack housing the bar. A few peasant women sauntered by, carrying water jugs on their heads, and wearing bright blue or green skirts of woven cotton. Some wore sandals and others were barefoot, on their way to the brook that bubbled at the end of the village.

Maybe that gringo will destroy them, that Invisible Hand, Manuel thought. Warily he dried a few more glasses on the bar. *Don't think about it, you old fool. Do not think about yesterday, no, the day of the devil, the worst of the many days of the devil.*

Shivering, he could not forget, he would not. He had waited at the bar. He had stood there while the rays of the unforgiving sun turned a deep yellow and poured through the slats on the narrow windows in slices. Outside, the streets had been dusty as the rows of booted feet of the workers, coming home from the wells near Cordoba, trampled their way to the bar. Mud-splattered sombreros over slits of eyes; worn, frayed, heavy cotton shirts and gray, brown, and black pants; red and blue bandanas tied around necks; laughter, brown-stained teeth smiling; husky voices of the roughnecks, "Muy calienta esta dias, mucho trabajo para poco dinero, ricos gringos." Too much work, little money, hot days, rich and cruel gringos and their soldiers.

But where was Paco? Manuel had wondered as the front door opened and workers stomped in, tossing their oil-stained gloves on the table. Immediately the bar smelled of men, also the scent of oil and dirt and pipes. The odor of tar and grease mingled with the sweat-soaked stink of clothes.

"Un cerveza, Manuel, pronto, por favor, muy sediento," the workmen ordered. They grinned and laughed and talked as they sat on the broken and crooked chairs set up at the chunky tables.

"Si, si, ahora," Manuel answered from behind the bar. Glasses sat on the scarred counter, and he filled them to the rim with the heavy Tres Xs Mexican beer. The dark brown beer gleamed in the filled glasses. He set them on the table, the frost on the glasses feeling cool and wet on his fingers. More men walked in, their boots shaking the small shack. More man smell.

Manuel walked to the window and peered out, thinking *But where is Paco? With all of the troubles lately—stop it, stop it, old man. You worry like a woman. But I am like a woman.* He returned to the bar. *I raised him, my son, like a woman I was, Madre y Padre, both. After his mother died I became everything to him. Played soccer with him, out there, in those streets, dusty, narrow streets, I showed him how to kick the ball: foot grazing the top for forward-spin, the foot sliding across the ball for side-spin, yes, and do not forget to kick under the ball for under-spin, you must remember these things...*

He looked between the window slats to the street outside, now empty, almost always empty these days. *I don't like this trouble with the gringos—stop it, stop it, old woman.*

Nothing out there. Just the glint of a policeman's belt, one of the gringo-trained authorities, dragging along some poor wretch. More and more prisoners now. And all troubles traced back to the coming of those awful wells that pay us too little money.

Plants grew wildly on the sides of the dusty streets. Certain flowers glowed brilliant orange. Vines wrapped their tendrils around brooding cypress trees that bore large green cones. Green hairs and pinkish-white flowers bloomed on bushes surrounding the few dilapidated shacks that passed for houses. Just after the houses, the street became little more than a horse path. *So much beauty*, Manuel thought. *So much evil.*

"Manuel, mas cervezas," men at a table said, and not without respect. He had been in this village his whole life. Once, it was sleepy and the dusty road out there was thick with grass, and the trees all bloomed vibrant green. That was before, everything was traced to before.

Again he recalled Paco as he took the beer, still cold from the ice in the barrel, to the man-packed room. The beer had been delivered from heavy trucks with wobbly wheels driving in from a far-away city. Manuel remembered his son entering his teens, helping Paco with his books when the school was still here. Worrying about Paco becoming a man. Some had called him rebellious, but that was wrong. *Paco had a thirst and Paco was curious, and was not much for rules, or for the gringo and his guns. But the white-skinned men and their speeches about freedom. What freedom? Work all day at the stinking wells? Their wells. Their looks, the Norteamericanos, behind their eyes, their eyes that never really look at us, that only pass over us, their slaves, for an instant, with contempt.*

Clump! A heavy boot stepped into the tiny bar as the orange rays of the sun continued boring down. The buzzing of talk quieted, then vanished as a hard silence started with the other boot: Clump!

Authority stood there: black mustache on a brown face, made darker by the sun, a Latino with some faint Indian blood, *claro*, but not from around Cordoba. Already the face wore the look taught by the CIA schools far away in Virginia: a smile through clenched teeth. The policeman wore a starched and fresh uniform the color of shit, a shiny belt buckle, gold shining buttons on his shirt, heavy *pistolas* hanging from his thick black belt, black, thick-soled, polished shoes.

He motioned to Manuel. Shaking, Manuel followed him outside.

The prisoner sagged against the shack. Manuel studied at him, thinking, *Oh, Dios mio, Dios mio...*

He had trouble making him out. The prisoner's shirt was blood-soaked, teeth marks still festering on his chest and stomach; the policemen had big, wild dogs, which they let attack the prisoners, another game. His face was battered. *I don't want to recognize him, it can't be*, Manuel thought. The prisoner's left eye had been shattered, part of it dangling outside of its socket.

"Esta hombre was at the wells, along with some others. They know to stay away, we warned them. The others walk no longer. Sus madres son whores," the policeman said, looking at the prisoner, at Manuel, at the inside of the bar. Men stood at the window and looked out.

Manuel stared at the good eye of the prisoner.

The prisoner blinked, then blinked again.

Manuel's heart tore apart. The signal he and Paco had agreed on long ago if either of them were in trouble.

Don't cry old man, you silly woman, Manuel told himself as the world died around him. *You must be brave. Do your duty to Paco, as you agreed.*

"Do you know him?" the policeman asked.

Be a man, Manuel thought, his body trembling. "No."

"Are you sure?"

"No sabe."

"Si." He grabbed the prisoner by the neck and started walking him down the dusty street.

Manuel kept his mouth shut. He started after them, and then stopped. *You know what they do*, he thought. *First kill you and feed your body to the pigs, and make Paco watch. Then they will kill Paco. They do that to the parents.*

He watched the figures get smaller as they walked on and his heart curled up to die. Dusk was gathering. The small sparrows twittered furiously in the trees, the way they always did when the sun was disappearing. Manuel did not ever hear the birds again.

***

Nick woke up in a small hotel in an alley just blocks off of the Avenida Corrientas, and looked at his watch in disbelief: He had slept over fourteen hours. His clothes, dust-filled and still smelling of sweat, were scattered about the room.

He showered and shaved and walked out into the clear sun of Buenos Aires. The air felt brisk and cool. People busily walked along the sidewalks. Nick felt good to be back among the living, as he headed toward Café Tortoni. After a coffee and croissant, which were very good, about as good as one could get in Paris, he headed for one of his favorite *barrios*, the San Telmo district.

Once in that area, he walked briskly. There were townhouses built in the early 1800s. Rose and sand-colored, their paint fading under the constant Argentine sun, they had wide steps made of stone slabs, heavy wooden doors, and protruding eaves. As he strolled he heard, coming down from somewhere, a guitar playing sad and lonely music, a kind of Italian expatriate, lost, gypsy melody.

At the end of the block a couple was dancing high up on a balcony. She wore a red blouse and had long dark hair. He was tall and moved awkwardly. They laughed when he stumbled, then kissed.

Nick stopped and watched them, letting the sun warm his face. Linda's perfect-teethed smile went through his mind; Julie, looking at him under her thick eyebrows, appeared. He felt as if she were really there. *What the hell's the matter with me? Now I'm looking for ghosts.* Noticing his hands shaking, he wondered if it was going bad again. He told himself to calm down, take it easy. But things had been so simple once. Back then he had an office and went to make money every day. Now… He pushed the thoughts aside, and hailed a cab.

A short time later he walked down into the cavernous basement of the library at the *Universidad de Buenos Aires*. The many heavy tables scattered about the main reading room were almost empty. Lamps glowed dimly, and the musty smell of old books filled the air. He went to the microfilm machine. As he peered through its magnifying glass, the print on a reference card jumped to five times its real size.

He scrolled through oil logs and reserve reports and geological surveys, and wrote numbers on a yellow, legal-sized pad. After a while he reviewed his notes: "1952; yield of 800 barrels per day; reserves of 8.2 million barrels. 1956; yield of 780 per day; reserves of 7.5 million. 1963; yield of 920 per day; reserves of 7.4 million; 1972; yield of 840 a day; reserves of 6.3 million. 1999; yield of 910 a day; reserves of 4.1 million."

Studying the numbers, he knew he had the answer. He looked again and laughed, the only sound in the room.

He went over the numbers again and calculated that the trucks coming in held about a hundred fifty barrels each. Six or so of them a night, that was nine hundred barrels, easily enough to replace what was pumped out each day. Nine hundred barrels was about average for that deep a well. Eighteen thousand feet deep, it should have produced close to a thousand barrels a day.

But how can it still be producing that much? The pressure from underground diminishes over time and the amount of oil still left, it can't still be bringing up a thousand barrels a day, no way, he thought. He knew that the wells were producing from sand. Engineering-wise, geologists could evaluate how many acres were being drained, and come up with an estimated reserve. Engineers could justify their reserve numbers, and nobody would question the wells' production. *But with the type of sand near Cordoba, if I know anything about sands, and I do, there's bound to be a lot of water in the well hole. Fresh water shows up like oil on a log. Any engineering estimates could be way off.*

The more he thought about it, the surer he was: they were trucking oil in. He'd seen a similar scam before, but not on this scale. They were trucking oil in from somewhere, and depositing it into the wells. *Friends of Brett's or... who the hell knows?*

They were feeding that field, but he knew it takes a lot of oil to feed a field. It would take about a thousand barrels a day to produce that constant a reserve figure. Those wells were drilled long ago, in 1959. Normal decline curves would have brought their stated reserves way down by now. Those wells should have maybe only now about a million barrels in reserve. But published figures claimed much larger reserves.

In 1959, they estimated about 8.2 million barrels in reserves, and now they were showing about 4.1 million barrels. How could the wells have that much reserve when they had been producing a thousand barrels daily out of that hole? Wells don't last that long. Those wells had been used up long ago.

It's gotta be, they're feeding those wells for show. And probably feeding other wells also, anything around Cordoba. That's why they don't want anybody around. They can slant drill and connect wells under ground and do just about anything. How God damn big is this thing?

Nick thought that a scammer could drill into a neighbor's well and siphon oil away. But the neighbor would have to be in on the scam. All those guys that he met at the dinner in Houston were oilmen, from all over the world. Maybe all were in on it.

Nick thought about it, and threw his notes into the trash basket. *They're too big. I can't stop them. Besides, what do I care?*

He got up and went to the drinking fountain. He swallowed mouthfuls of water, the water feeling good and cold as he drank. He glanced up as he drank. His heart jumped. The man ducked down as Nick spotted him. Nick saw the wide-brimmed hat low on his forehead. *It's Hammer*, he thought. He heard his heart pounding. *Hammer couldn't have followed me from Houston. Did he pick me up in Cordoba? Does he know I went to the wells? He probably—slow down, think it through*, he told himself, shaking. *Probably he picked me up here, in Buenos Aires. Easy. Easy.* He breathed deeply. *Just cover yourself here.*

Taking out his cell phone, his hands trembled as he typed in Brett Well's number and waited as it rang.

"Hey, Nick. What's up?" Brett said.

"Just checking in," he said, trying to keep his voice steady. "I'm in Buenos Aires following up some of the people that bought Nugget before. And they asked questions I really couldn't answer, so I came to the library. There're things I couldn't find on the Internet."

"Yeah, good, Nick, thanks for calling. Stock's above fifty-four, a new high. How's it feel, being a rich man?"

"Good," Nick said, standing there shaking and looking around, wondering where the hell Hammer was.

"And we're just gettin started. Say, why don't you get back here to Houston, maybe next week. Just before the bonds come. Been telling some others about your work. They might need you."

"Sure. About the end of the week."

"Yeah, sounds good, pardner. You're a good man."

Nick hung up and walked out into the Buenos Aires night. Going back to his hotel, he kept to the brightest streets, glancing around for Hammer. *Ah, maybe it wasn't even Hammer*. The stock was up now, they were all happy, and for that they needed him. Feeling the derringer in its holster, he relaxed some. *Well, I can't go and lie down and throw a blanket over my head and hide.*

He took out his cell phone as he walked by the heavy stone townhouses near the center of town.

"Diga mi," a man answered.

"Captain Pugliese?"

"And who is wanting him?"

"Nick Larson, from—"

"Un momento."

"Pugliese. How may I help you?"

"I, I would like to speak with you. Nothing important but—"

"Senor, please. You call me, it is important. Si?"

"Si. Es muy importante."

"Tomorrow. Call me."

"It can't wait—I can't. Tonight. I'm leaving the city tomorrow, as early as I can."

"Why? Enjoy Buenos Aires."

"No. I can't explain. Not now. I'll meet you."

"Come to the station here?"

And have Hammer machinegun me before I walk in the door? "No, somewhere else. Tonight."

"Senor, this is the one night of the week I please my wife. She is good and patient and puts up with me, but one night a week—"

"Good, okay, I don't care where we meet. Just that if I'm being followed or think I might be, I'll let you know. I'll look at you, but won't talk. Okay?"

"Si. Muy bien."

"Splendid. Where?"

***

Nick opened the heavy, black hotel door and walked out into the Buenos Aires night. On the wide Avenida Florida, which was choked with cars, he signaled for a taxi. A dented yellow-and-black old cab came to a halt at the curb, its brakes screeching.

Getting into the back seat Nick said, "Regine's. You know it?"

The driver turned around, his young face pockmarked. "Comprendo muy poquito Ingles. Regine's? You go?"

"Yes."

They drove away. The bright lights from downtown got dimmer, then vanished as they entered a barrio in the far north side of the city. Down a deserted, cobblestone calle, the overhead street lights lit up the night. After Nick got out, he walked along a narrow path. Crickets chirped. A cat looked up, her eyes reflecting the bright moon. Passing through a wrought-iron gate, he heard the sounds of a violin and bandonion inside the old, stone house he was headed toward. The grass surrounding it smelled sweet in the heavy, dank night air.

Inside, there was loud music and dancers filling the small floor of the tango bar. Nick made his way through the crowd, looking for Pugliese. Shoes shuffled as the dancers moved to a brisk milanga. The music was too loud. He spotted Pugliese, sitting at a large, round table with others, his white shirt soaked through. Nick walked over. The others at the table smoked, and spoke Spanish rapidly, gesturing with their hands.

Nick said, "Buenos Noches."

Pugliese smiled, said, "Por favor," gesturing at the empty chair next to him. Pugliese's uncombed hair almost covered his ears.

Nick sat down.

"Bueno," he said. "My wife, she will be right back, I will introduce—"

"No, that's okay. I'm leaving. I just wanted to know, if I could bust the Hand, I mean, give you something to help maybe not destroy them, but hurt them, maybe seriously, could you use it?"

His eyes fixed on Nick. "What do you have?"

"Just right now a germ of an idea. But would you go after them?"

"Senor, I appreciate anything. Yes, it would be my pleasure and to my credit." He leaned closer. "When?"

Nick got up. "I'll let you know."

"Do you know how important smashing the Hand in any way is for me?"

"Will be in touch."

Nick headed for the waiting cab.

***

Driving back home, Nick kept looking over his shoulder. Once at the San Francisco airport he thought he spotted Hammer, but it wasn't him. Nick figured he was probably okay. The stock was still climbing, and if Nugget lost its chief spokesman, what would happen to its price? He drove down steep California Street.

Car lights shining into his rear-view mirror blinded Nick. He turned left, and the lights followed. He made a right into an alley, and the lights were still there, close. The other car passed Nick, swerved into his path, and forced him over. He slammed on the brakes just before smashing into the wall. The seatbelt kept him from flying through the front window. He watched a big man walk up to his car, lower his hat brim to just over his eyes, motion him to lower the window.

Nick thought it over, lowered the window. His knee hurt.

"Wanted to say hello," Hammer said.

Nick did not speak. Just shook.

"They say keep the stock up." Hammer took out a cell phone. "Or they'll call."

"Okay," Nick said. "I hear you."

"And stay away from Cordoba. Besides, only bar there closed down. Manuel sleeping next to his bastard son." Hammer peered into the car. "You remember Manuel?"

Nick nodded. "Okay. All right."

"Not worried about you. You are nothing."

Hammer went back to his car. The car burned rubber tearing out of the alley.

Nick's hand shook as he turned the key in the ignition switch. He drove to his office building, and after swerving into the garage and parking, held on to the derringer as he walked.

The black leather squealed as Nick slid into the chair behind his desk. Included in his mail was a large envelope. Opening the envelope he took out a prospectus: "Revised Debenture Offering, Nugget Petroleum." Skimming through the pages, in fine print near the end he read:

"... the Company has entered into a contract with Spence Trask, an investment banking firm, and Malcolm Miller, a private investor, to grant Spence Trask and Miller options to purchase 2,000,000 shares of common stock at the price of $40.00 per share. Said options are to have a life of five years from the date of the completion of the planned debenture offering. Any stock acquired through exercise of the option is to be unqualified for sale for a period of three years from the exercise of said options. If for any reason said bond offering is not competed within sixty days from the day of this addendum, said options will elapse. This transaction is subject to existing tax laws, and the Company is offering no tax or legal counsel regarding the consequences of transactions to those receiving the options. Furthermore, Malcolm Miller agrees to lend Spence Trask $25,000,000 to be repaid at the rate of a 10% override on all future investment banking fees derived from transactions involving the company and other parties."

Nick sat back, thinking, *So Spence Trask now is into the deep pockets of Malcolm Miller. Them hooking up with Nugget will start the wildest buying spree the oil patch's ever seen. They corner the world's oil, they'll dictate the price. Imagine the Hand dictating the worldwide oil price. Not pretty.*

Nick rubbed his aching knee gingerly. *What did he call me? Nothing?*

He got Willie on the phone and said, "I've got some questions about this Malcolm Miller deal. Certainly the people I've put into the stock will."

"Such as?" Willie asked.

"Come on, Willie. They want to know why Nugget's granting those options. Pretty juicy for Miller, I'd say."

Nick heard Willie breathing into the phone, as if just before one of his old Wild eruptions. But Willie calmed down. "We're, we're granting some other options, too. Just didn't announce them yet."

"Willie, hide it from the Street as much as you want, but I have to know what else you're giving away."

"No big deal, Larson."

"Then why didn't you announce these grants? Through a phone conference or something."

"I—"

"Let's get together tomorrow. I'll come down there."

"All right. Some of the board will be here, but that's okay."

Nick hung up and imagined Lenny Zellon yelling at him: Why are they giving the company away? Something wrong with that cockamamie outfit that they gotta give it away? Nick nodded his head, agreeing. *Brett was paying everybody off, but why?* Nick sighed. *Why do I care? I'm getting richer with every up-tick.*

Getting up, Nick turned off the computer. It faded to black and said, "Goodbye," as if it were his best friend. Nick wondered again, *What did Hammer call me? Nothing?*

***

From the seventieth floor, San Francisco looked as if it were in a painting: white buildings glowing in the sun, next to the blue ocean. Nick opened a heavy glass door with SPENCE TRASK INVESTMENT BANKERS stenciled in gold, and walked down the hall. He opened a couple of doors to find empty meeting rooms, then opened a third. It was filled with oil paintings, heavy mahogany furniture, and a long, dark oak desk that ran down the middle of the room. Thirty-something men and women sat at the desk and furiously scribbled. Their eyebrows knotted, their pens wrote on pads of yellow paper. Drawn faces showed an almost angry concentration.

Nick sat in the back.

Standing at the head of the table, Todd Pearson, a young man with disheveled blond hair said, "Okay, next item." He was the Director of Research at Spence Trask. Around him sat the edgy-sharp people of the institutional sales force. They sold stocks and bonds to the Fidelitys and Wellingtons and Vanguards of the world. The people in this room could move billions of dollars by lunchtime.

Todd flipped through the heavy paper on the chart stand. The stand shook. He stopped at "Nugget Petroleum: Sales, up 22%; Earnings, up 33%; Earnings per share $2.20; Revenue growth projected up 22% per year next 3 years."

"This," he said, "sums up most of the points. We're going to bring the bonds soon, in about a week, we hope."

A woman in a black suit, with many strands of white pearls around her neck said, "Why the hell're we waiting? I got orders almost for the whole deal myself already. I get calls every day about when are we bringing this."

"Our analyst hasn't given the okay. The prospectus has had some revisions that could be deemed material, and our attorneys have to approve—"

"Oh so what, Todd? Our attorneys never get off their ass and get anything done. And now that we have a hot deal, they're balking."

"Goes for me, too," a bow-tied man with gray hair grumbled. "It's all my customers talk about. When's the Nugget deal coming?"

"There's a whole process to go through," Todd said. "Sure, the bonds will sell. The numbers we're showing are being kept conservative. Also, Nugget'll soon announce more takeovers. But there are bases to be touched here. We want to bring Nugget, but bring it the right way. We need to keep our reputation for being honest."

"Yeah, and I got bills to pay, and I can't miss a trade," the woman said. "I'm not on salary, like you." Other brokers murmured, "We need this deal. We don't bring the bonds someone else will."

Todd flashed his boyish smile. "Okay, leave it with me. I'll get you a firm release date."

The brokers bustled out of the room. One said, "Yeah, but Judy's running the show and nothing'll get done. She's so damn... careful."

Nick wondered what was up with Judy. He went downstairs and into Willie Bornstein's office. Wild Willie towered over his desk, smiling tightly. Al Zucker, Malcolm Miller, and Judy Hart stood by the large window. And far below, the emerald-green waters of the bay sparkled in the early morning sunshine.

Willie said, "Hi, Nick. Just telling the guys here, we're increasing the size of the Nugget offering a hundred million. We got lucky. One of the salespeople, she caught a fifty million dollar order."

"Way to go," Malcolm Miller said. "Next."

"That'll help," Willie said. "We want it hot, up about four or five in the aftermarket. Come on, Judy. We're ready, get it through legal."

"I'm trying to get them to commit, Willie." Judy said. She walked away from the window. "They're trying to reconcile all of the inconsistencies. A few more days, that's all."

"Okay, here's the prospectus, just revised." Willie handed out the prospectuses.

On the glossy cover page, a large, black, oil derrick stood on spindly struts. Just below:

"Nugget Petroleum Debentures."

Nick turned to the first page:

"Nugget Petroleum is an exploration and development company engaged in four principal activities in the U.S. and Latin America: (1) the acquisition, production and sale of crude oil, condensate and natural gas; (2) the gathering, transmission and marketing of natural gas; (3) operating natural gas and oil properties for interest owners; (4) providing U.S. export services to facilitate trade in energy products."

Nick read more pages. *So, they buried the trouble with the peasants at their Argentine properties and other production problems, meaning their scamming, in small print in a "Latin Americal Miscellaneous" section. Everything's disclosed, but neatly worded to mislead. Lawyers can make anything look good. Okay, now what about disclaimers?* He flipped to the end.

"The information herein includes forward-looking statements based on assumptions that may prove not to have been accurate. The business activities of Nugget Petroleum, as usual to its industry, are subject to many risks both calculable and incalculable. Included in these risks are oil and gas prices, the need to develop replacement reserves, the reliability of reserve estimates, the feasibility of retracting reserves, environmental risks, drilling and operating risks, and the ability of the company to implement its business strategy."

Neatly done, Nick thought. *The reliability of reserve estimates. They covered themselves. If the reserves are found to be phony or wrong, it's the fault of the consulting company.*

Okay, so what else is new? He flipped to another section.

"This common stock warrant agreement shall evidence and disclose the understanding between Nugget Petroleum; Will Bornstein; Judy Hart; Spence, Trask, an investment banking firm. Vested Warrants may be exercised with three (3) years (the "Exercise Period"). The purchase price of the Warrant Shares is $40.00 per share subject to adjustment as provided in Section 15 hereof. The Company and the warrant receivers agree that… Will Bornstein, warrants for 50,000 shares, Judith Hart, warrants for 50,000 shares, Spence, Trask, 100,000 shares…"

Nick paused. He knew that it was not uncommon to give warrants to people involved in an underwriting. In this case the receivers could exercise the warrants at forty, with the stock now at about fifty-four. *They're all getting well. But that's a lot of warrants to grant for a deal that's in good shape. The Street will see it, probably let it pass. So Judy's getting all those warrants. She's up $750,000 already. They bought her off, just like everyone.*

As Judy finished reading, her face reddened and she stifled a smile, but it burst through. Nick asked, "You planning to put out a buy recommendation after the offering?"

"Probably," she said. "After all, with the consolidation occurring in the oils today, Nugget should turn out to be a major player."

"I thought you had reservations."

"Well, that's where I am now. Today."

Sure, bucks can buy away a lot of doubts. Nick almost said it. All eyes were on him. *Easy,* he told himself, *where are you going with this?*

"Do I think there're risks?" Judy said. "Yes. Would I put my grandmother's last dime in it? Definitely not. But as long as oil and gas prices stay strong, and why would they go any other way? Nugget should do well. With their takeovers, and if they hit something big in their exploration, Nugget should do really okay."

So it's all set up, Nick thought. *The syndicate department here at Spence Trask will over-allocate, sell about a hundred million more bonds than they're offering, and leave themselves short. When they buy back bonds in the after-market to cover, they'll drive up the price. The bankers, analysts, brokers will go out on the road painting a pretty picture. But nobody, it seems, except me has checked out the company, really. So what? I'm getting paid.*

Frowning, Al said, "So we're through here? Bring it. It goes up, people are happy, down, they're pissed. Willie how much longer? Is this a lifetime meeting?"

"Just a minute, Al. Look, Nick, a lot of people out there, they remember your picks in Europe in the old days. Keep working. This is the new big one."

Malcolm Miller stood up. "This is just the start of our deals in the oil patch. Brett's telling me he's lined up a bunch of little companies to merge into Nugget. Or take over some private companies and we'll take them public later."

"Do whatever, but I want a return," Al said. He had overdone the dye this morning, and his hair was shining almost a brilliant red. "It takes more money to live in L.A. than anyplace, even Paris. How come I get more out of leasing out a lousy sweatshop in Hong Kong than investing here? Here, Nick, keep in touch," he said, handing over his card.

"You know, with this much money," Judy said, "Nugget may be able to really build some value. Their plan to buy up little oil companies and with their management expertise make them more profitable could work."

Nick couldn't contain himself. "But they could also just do takeovers and become a giant company, in the hundreds of billions of market value, and the insiders sell their stock. Then if the reserves are questioned and the whole thing collapses, they'd blame the accountants."

They all stared at him. Then Al laughed and asked, "Why're you gettin crazy? We're talking about making money, Nick. You having a nervous breakdown or something?"

Willie laughed; they all laughed. *Watch it*, Nick told himself. *They're shooting real bullets out there*. He smiled, tried to laugh. "So, you're going out with a buy?" he asked Judy Hart.

"After the quiet period, yes. Maybe even a strong buy."

For thirty days after an underwriting, no research or opinions can emanate from the underwriters. After that, Spence Trask could give investors and the media their opinion, which in this case would be to buy Nugget, both the stock and bonds.

Nick decided it was all over. Nugget would go to the moon. Who was he to question?

Nine

"Hi."
"Hi. Long time no hear."
"Yes."
"Why?"
"Oh, been busy," Nick said.
"So have I. How about friends. Can we be friends?"
"No. I'd like to think… probably not."
"Well, if it's that or nothing, I think we could, can. Or try."
Nick didn't say anything.
"How about lunch. That's okay," Linda said.
"I don't—"
"Isabel, remember how much fun we had with Philip? And why should we pretend we haven't, both of us, been ignoring her." After awhile, Linda said, "Tomorrow, at her place. She's always asking about you."
"She has?"
"Yes. People do. Nick, what's happening to you?"
"It's business."
"Yes."
"And maybe not just business, but I keep ending up at the same place. And I don't feel good right now."
"I'm sorry. I—I think I know what you mean."
"Maybe. That doesn't make anything better. Well, maybe it does."
"Would that solve—"
"No." After awhile Nick asked, "What time?"
"Noon." Linda answered. "I'll tell her. She's so dear."
"She has been kind. Linda?"
"Yes?"

"How is he?"

"A little worse, Nick. It's okay, I'm used to it. He always seems to be getting a little worse."

Nick hung up and sat back in his leather chair. He looked at the computer screen: NUP, 57 1/4. *I'm rich*, he thought, sinking deeper into the chair. *It's all so absurd. I'm rich. Why don't I feel good?* He walked across the office, sat on a stool, picked up a paintbrush, and dipped its fine point into a small jar of yellow paint. Lightly, he painted a yellow slice of sunshine cutting through heavy, gray clouds, the brightness reflecting off of cobblestone streets below. His eyes stayed on the yellow liquid as it slid off the brush onto the white canvas.

Stacked up against the wall were a number of paintings in various stages of development.

I love this, always have, he thought. *What would life be like if I just painted?* He remembered that he did that once, but after a while—starting to run out of money, happening into people he once knew in the city, them looking at his paint-stained clothes, asking him where he was working, who he was seeing—he just felt so… lost. *But still, isn't hustling around trying to sell my paintings, and who cares if I wear paint-splattered clothes? Isn't that better than pimping for those crooks?*

The ringing of the phone interrupted him. He ignored it. It rang a few more times. Resignedly, he put down the brush, yellow paint on his fingers. *It's good*, he thought, *actually good. It would sell. Not for much, but enough. Could I make a living at it?* The phone became more terrifying with each ring. *Could I?*

He grabbed the receiver.

"Hey, Larson, those bonds, whad'ya think?" Lenny said.

"I, why are you asking? Something wrong?" Nick's heart thumped like crazy.

"Yeah, wrong. Like the company's a scam and like they're tied up into who knows what down there in Argentina, and you're in on it, and you're making toast out of all your friends. That kind of wrong."

Nick felt like he was shrinking, dizzy. "Lenny, I, everything I know—"

"Hahahaha, you jerk, can't even take a joke. I worry about you. Lighten up, you'll get a heart attack."

"You shouldn't—" Nick's voice shook.

"Yeah, yeah, shouldn't, couldn't. Hey, you never called me back about that short we was gonna do, you and I. Or me and you, I'm not sure, but grammar's important now. I'm datin an English teacher. Me, Lenny Zellon, can you imagine? English teacher. But what a pair of *gazamboes*, like two pyramids. What does she want with me? My money, my charm, my eight-inch dick, I wish, I should only be so lucky."

"Oh, the short," Nick said, the room stopping its spin. "I'm not ready, not yet. In fact, I, I've sort of shelved the idea." He could feel Lenny thinking. He could hear his heart pounding.

Lenny thought, then said, "Whatever. What else you been up to?"

"Not much. I'm having lunch with Isabel tomorrow. You remember, Philip's wife?"

"That old bag? That'll be pretty boring. I could buy you a couple teenagers, sisters, no less. Take them to that old witch Isabel and have a threesome. Do you some good. Sure she could use it too."

Nick could breathe again. "What did you think of Philip?"

"And my prize for answering that stupid fuckin question? A picture of your girlfriend's panties?"

Nick laughed. "Forget it, just curious." Speaking with Lenny was worth it. What Lenny did was bullshit all of the time. A walking, talking rumor mill, he couldn't help himself. You wanted to spread a rumor, hear a rumor, you call Lenny. Everybody knew that.

"The old man was okay, a regular guy," Lenny said. "Hell, we all managed some of his money. He didn't want to worry about his billions. All Philip wanted was to fuck girls. Liked 'em young, but old would do, what the hell. To tell the truth, he didn't care what age just so they had big tits. Or little tits. Very fair guy. And he tried to stay the hell away from Isabel. That woman doesn't have a brain, he'd say. So then he gets in with some Argentineans, back in the 1970s. They disappeared people. So what? I didn't know any of them. Bunch of crazy spics. Disappear 'em all for all I care. Philip gets sick. Prostrate cancer, maybe in his stomach, what the hell's the difference, when you're sick, you're sick. Takes all his money back from us, puts it into trust for Isabel, gives it to some stupid bank. Why all of a sudden he's protecting her? Guilt, I guess. What am I that I should know? A shrink? What am I, know all the answers? So Philip dies. And when you're dead, you're dead. All of a sudden the bank people're going to see her, kissing her ass. She doesn't know shit from Shinola. So she's got you to answer her stupid questions, and all she has to do is feed you lunch. She's lucky you're around. You won't rip her off, at least I don't think you will."

Don't think? Maybe I'd rip her off, and you? Is that what he means? He heard the click of the call-waiting indicator. "Got another one coming in, Lenny."

"Yeah, yeah, sure. Call me when your Pacific Heights honey can handle some *real* shlong."

Nick clicked over to the waiting call. He started sweating. *If only Lenny knew about Nugget, really.*

"Hey, Nick, Gunn."

"Ted. What's up?"

"You hear about Nugget and Triton?"

"No. What?"

"Well, word's that after they get the bonds out Nugget'll merge with Triton Oil. That this's just the start of Nugget's deals. It's flying, up another two this morning, to sixty. Want to buy for a short-term trade?"

"No, pass. If Nugget trades down the merger will never happen.

"Nugget's not going below fifty," Ted said. "The market says it goes higher, much higher."

Nick wondered if he should tell him the truth. Then figured for sure he'd end up laying on a street somewhere, hunted down by guys with guns and knives. No way. "Markets have short memories. Remember, you're only as good as your last trade. No stock's worth falling in love with."

"Yeah, whatever. You see Nugget going down, you're starting to lose it. Smart money says it's going nowhere but up." He paused, then said, "You know something I should know?"

Easy. Don't blow yourself up, not now. "No, I'm still a player in the stock." He recalled something and said, "But I remember when I went to Madrid and bought Spanish stocks, they said, why there? European stocks are so boring, they never do anything. But I was right. Sometimes you have to get ahead of the market, not follow."

"Can't live in the past, Larson."

Living in the past? I wish I could.

"No. But it has a way of repeating."

"What do you mean?"

"Just talking. Goodbye, Ted."

***

Linda watched Nick slip into a black double-breasted blazer to go with his black linen slacks. He was reflected in a three-way mirror. A tailor crouched and started marking for cuffs. In the middle of the store, escalators busily traveled up and down. She looked through Saks Fifth Avenue's large windows out at Union Square, with its stone benches, palm trees, grass, and sculptured bushes surrounding cement walkways.

Smiling at him, she said, "You look great."

After the tailor finished, they walked outside: bright sun, clear blue sky, the sidewalks packed with shoppers. Yellow taxis drove on the busy streets, up to hotel entrances. Tall concrete and steel buildings towered above them, partially blocking off the sun. People sat on benches, strolled, tossed peanuts to flocks of pigeons that devoured the nuts, a mass of black and white flapping feathers.

Linda took Nick's hand as they walked. At feeling his touch, her heart jumped and she tingled all over. *Don't know why he affects me this way*, she thought. *Am I being bad? Yes, Linda, you are.* She felt a frisson of excitement race up her spine.

They sat on a bench. She waited, knowing that he'd ask.

"How about dinner tonight? Dinner, and then we could go to my place?"

"No, After Isabel's—you know her lunches—food's out of the question. But your place? Now that would be nice." Her blood rushed: the day, the sun, Nick.

He looked toward the sky, let sunshine wash over him, and then said, "I'll wear the blazer to Houston. It's the right weight, always hot down there." A few moments later he asked, "Come to Houston with me?"

She thought about it. "I don't see how. You know."

"Thad?"

"What else?"

"Oh come on, Linda. A few days. He'll be all right."

But what if there's an emergency? Oh, he'll be okay. But still. "I just don't know. Not now."

Nick looked off to the pigeons feasting viciously on peanuts. His eyes narrowed to a squint. "So that's how it is? I have no rights at all? This, we're, I'm back at square one."

"Oh Nick." *I want to go*, she thought. *Damn it, I will then. I deserve it.* She got excited. The airplane, flying far away, down to Houston. She'd never been to Texas, never even thought about it, just knew that it was far away from here. And she'd be with him. "Oh, darling, it would be fun. Don't be cross; give me some time. I have to get used to the idea."

He laughed. "Okay, take your time. You'll like Texas. There's no place in the world that has barbeque like there."

***

The view from Isabel's penthouse apartment was like being in a helicopter over the Bay. To the left, the rust-colored Golden Gate

Bridge; to the right, the prison on Alcatraz Island. The low, squat building was right in the middle of the island, looking like a toy. Sailboats bobbed around in the brilliant blue water.

Nick and Linda stood on the penthouse deck, as he sized up his hostess. In her late seventies, and still very attractive, Isabel had obviously been a beauty in her youth. Her face had a map of lines that deepened when she smiled, which was all the time, and in the sun her scalp shone through her thinning gray hair.

"Philip thought you'd left town," she said, "gone to an island in the Caribbean. He called you a number of times. You never returned his calls."

"It wasn't a good time for me," Nick said. "I didn't return anyone's calls. I'm sorry, it was rude."

"Oh, I understand." She crinkled up her nose as she smiled.

Linda smiled. "Isabel's so forgiving."

"Well, some would call it a fault but… shall we eat?"

Crossing a heavy carpet, they went inside and sat down. In the center of the dining-room table was a silver vase of roses. The room was crowded, containing an armoire, a chest, a heavy side-table displaying photos of Isabel in her younger days, with thick, dark hair. Other pictures showed her husband Philip, a large man with a full mustache and sideburns grown to below his ears. A clock was in the corner, its pendulum ticking out the seconds.

Isabel rang a silver bell, and a withered, elderly waiter in a tuxedo entered with a tray of roasted lamb, miniature potatoes, and asparagus. He smiled, showing a few gold teeth. He served portions from the tray with an elegant certainty.

Taking a bite of pink and juicy lamb, Nick recalled when Philip had first paid him a visit years ago. Philip's eyes had darted from Nick, to the window, to some point over Nick's shoulder, then he said, "I'll wire you funds from Switzerland, a small bank in Basel. It'll be in francs; you'll have to convert it. Twenty million. Is that enough?" Nick had nodded, his heart pounding. Twenty very large to manage was serious money. "If my wife ever calls," Philip had said, his eyes searching the room, "hang up. She's a looker, but the damn woman knows nothing about money. Just how to spend it." Nick had laughed, and immediately liked Philip. And with twenty million coming his way, what was not to like?

Now as they ate, Isabel studied Nick. "I hear you're working for a company called Nugget Petroleum," she said. "I'd have thought you'd long ago retired."

"I took a few years off. Went back, missed the action."

"I see." Laughing a little, her forehead furrowing, she said, "Actually I have a problem. Well, maybe not a problem, but I need help." Her eyes stayed on him. "I don't know what to ask. You see, I have, well, own quite a few shares of Nugget Petroleum. Almost, maybe a million shares."

A million? He thought. Taking a bite of asparagus, he wondered how he could lie out of this. He tried to swallow, choked, coughed violently, then drank some water and smiled. "Sorry. Went down the wrong... now, about Nugget Petroleum?"

"Nick knows everything about that company," Linda said. "Don't you?"

"Yes. Everything."

"Oh, thank you. Could you advise me like you did with Philip, about money? I'm not so good with those things, but you know that."

He toyed with a potato. His appetite had disappeared. "Do you still have everything in trust?"

"I think so. Yes."

"What sort of trust do you have?"

"Revocable. No, no, irrevocable. Oh, I don't know." Isabel's face was a jumble of wrinkles, and her eyes almost crossed in confusion.

"Well, do you have the right to dissolve the trust? If so, then it's revocable."

"I guess I just simply don't know. Philip set it up and I just rely on people like you, who know and follow... oh, one thing. I must have somebody handle the stocks and things. Something about me being blind."

Nick laughed. "That simply refers to a person not being able to know which securities he holds. Not true in your case. But I seem to remember that your trust is irrevocable, and that it stipulated that the money manager has to be a nationally chartered bank or a registered investment advisor."

"Good. That's what you are."

"Yes, I am."

"We must talk about this then, soon." The lines relaxed in Isabel's face. She looked to the collection of photos. "You made him a small fortune. He liked you," she said.

"It's good to see him here," Linda said. "In pictures at least."

"Those are from our last time in Buenos Aires." A dreamy look washed over Isabel. "We loved it down there. You've been, haven't you?"

Nick said, "Once, we, Julie and I, went there and danced. I remember we were hot as hell the whole time because it was winter here, and we were dressed for the cold, and it was summer there."

They all laughed.

"I miss Julie," Isabel said. "She died—"

"Too young," Linda said.

Nick played with his fork, and thought about it.

Linda asked, "What exactly did Philip do?"

"Oh, he was in lots of things, that man. Importing, exporting, busy with banking. Would you like more wine?"

Nick drained the last of his glass. "Sure."

Nick thought, *That's the same answer Philip used to give me. This and that. Who cares now? She can get really hurt if it collapses.* Lenny's face appeared, and drifted away.

Isabel studied the rows of photos. "Oh, Philip loved to travel. He told me of places he went before me: Germany, Switzerland, France, Spain, he lived in all those. After Argentina, Spain was his favorite. He stayed there between the wars." She laughed. "Listen to me rattle on. Of course you're too young to know what it was to live in Europe then, before the Second World War."

"One of the few things I'm too young to know," Nick said.

"Then we were in Buenos Aires for years." Isabel sighed. "After Peron left, he said Argentina was never the same. So we came back to San Francisco. It's hard to beat this place, no?" She lifted the bell and shook it and the waiter appeared with more wine. They drank and sat silently.

"Nick, I wonder if—"

"Yes?"

"You could, well, this Nugget I own. Philip bought it years ago when he knew some people in Argentina, and I realize the company's probably changed a lot. I've told the people at the bank that I want to hold it, no matter what. The people at the bank, they're rather… I don't think they're that sharp. And, well, could you tell me what I should do with that stock? It just makes me, oh, I know I'm talking like a silly old woman, but it makes me nervous to put a lot of eggs in one basket, and Philip liked the company and I hate to sell it."

Nick's stomach tightened. *I can't get away from Nugget.*

"I told Isabel you made a lot of money with them," Linda said. "She didn't want to bother you, but I knew you wouldn't mind."

He took another sip of wine. The clock ticked. He urged himself to say something, anything. He took another sip, and realized that he could not, and felt frozen.

Glancing at her watch, Isabel said, "She should've been here already." Lines gathered on her face. "You know the investment banking firm, Spence Trask? Well, Judy Hart, the bank said I should speak with her and I invited her to come by. You know Judy Hart, don't you, Nick? She said she knows you. And she wants to show us something."

The doorbell rang. Sipping at his coffee, long gone cold, and starting at the half eaten cookie on the plate in front of him, Nick listened to Judy Hart come in, muttering to herself.

"Damn traffic. I knew I shouldn't drive through Chinatown. Isn't that always the case? Just one car holding everybody up." Frantically, she entered the dining room.

"Well, so nice to meet you, dear," Isabel said. She stood, and shook Judy's outstretched hand, introduced Linda, then went on. "You didn't miss very much, although it was a great piece of lamb. I saved you some. Join us, please. Oh, and some terrible coffee, you know my pot's broken and my girl hasn't bought a new one yet. I can't seem to find time to get it myself. Walking down Nob Hill is okay but up is really hard, and I'm afraid of the cable car, what if it slipped of the tracks, and can never find a cab.

Judy sat down. The waiter shuffled in, set a napkin, fork and knife, linen place mat in front of her. A plate with rare lamb followed.

After speaking of nothing in particular, Isabel said, "Nick was about to tell me about Nugget Petroleum."

"Yes," Judy said, looking at Nick. "Isabel wanted to know about Nugget, and I assured her it was okay. I'm glad you're here, since you know the Nugget story better than anyone."

"I wrote it," he said.

But there's something I want to show, just printed." She handed copies to everyone.

QUARTERLY MARKET OUTLOOK
Spence Trask Research Department

The winter/spring economic data appear decidedly robust. The fourth quarter data suggest GDP growth of 3 percent or even higher. There has been some concern about a spike-up of commodity prices, led mostly by oil prices; there have been mergers with the major oil companies, which are expected to continue. In our view, nothing changes our earlier forecasts: continued rapid growth, an increasing level of inflation, and a continued appreciation in the price of oil and growth stocks.

The big question is: how high will be the rise in consumer prices, or commodity prices, or interest rates? Our studies show that over the next six months there will be quite an increase; our model concludes that inflation could jump by four to six percent.

In Conclusion: We suggest an over-weighting of stocks in the oil and growth sector. Please contact your investment representative if you wish to receive our next report.

The Spence Trask investment research staff
Putting People First.

Not a mystery which people they put first, Nick thought.

"Well, well," Isabel said, "I don't know much, but all of this looks pretty good, I think. They say buy oil stocks. Isn't that good, Nick?"

"I—yes, it does look that way."

"In that case, perhaps Isabel should buy some Nugget bonds?" Judy said.

If she wants to end up sleeping in the streets, he thought. "Perhaps. Certainly she could consider it." He couldn't look Isabel in the eye.

"Good," Isabel said. "I'll speak to the bank. I'll go there tomorrow and talk about selling some of my CDs. They don't pay very much interest, you know. Well, that's a load off my shoulders and this has been a fine afternoon. And thank you, Nick."

"Sure," Nick said.

They chatted some more, Judy ate heartily, and Nick and Linda left.

Nick's stomach was in knots. They got into his car and started toward Linda's house. *Hell with her, she's just a stupid, old rich lady*, he told himself. *Yes, but I care and I'm betraying her. Stop it, just stop it. Nothing I can do.*

"You're being awfully quiet," Linda said as he drove.

After a while he said, "Just thinking."

"I'll go."

"Where?"

"Come on, Linda. Where? I don't have time for games."

"Don't snap at me."

"I didn't."

"Yes, you did."

He thought it over. "Sorry. Just got things on my mind."

"Okay, that's okay. I was talking about Houston. Next week. Do you still want me to go?"

He smiled. "Yes. Very much." He held her hand, and steered the car one-handed up the steep hill. Pacific Heights was alive with black and Mexican gardeners pushing lawnmowers, trimming bushes, clipping flowers. A group of school children, walking in neat rows and wearing navy blue uniforms, followed a gray-haired man wearing a red bow tie. "To Houston? You'll love it. We'll go to the River Oaks Club and dance. There's Hermann Park, of course we'll have to jog early in the morning as Houston's always hot as hell."

Nick froze. A crowd of people on Linda's porch surrounded something. Driving closer he could see the body of a man, his white shirt gleaming in the midday sun, an overturned wheelchair.

She put a hand to her mouth. "Oh God. Oh no." They scrambled out of the car, and Linda ran to Thad, crouched down and cradled his head in her arms. Blood from his cut head stained her white blouse.

A big, bulky, woman said, "He fell, told him not to try. Tried gettin outta that chair, I told him, he didn't want to listen. Tipped over, nothin I could do." The maid was shaking, looking at them with an ashy white face.

His eyes were closed, and white foam gathered at the corners of his mouth. His breathing was slight.

Linda said, "Thad, wake up, darling."

"Here it comes," someone said. All heads shifted toward a siren sound coming toward them quickly.

Stepping back, Nick started walking away from Linda, crouched over and holding Thad. *It's over*, he thought. *Forget Houston. Who am I kidding? What the hell am I doing mixed up with this?*

Walking to his car, past the curious eyes of strangers trying to see what was going on, past the white-smocked people jumping out of the ambulance, its bumpers gleaming in the sun, people carrying a stretcher and an oxygen mask, past laborers on the expensive lawns in Pacific Heights, Nick thought that he might really end up on the streets, maybe with a knife in his back. And that was okay. *If I do, I do. I won't have to lie anymore. Fuck that.* He also decided, opening his car door and getting in, that if he were going down, he might as well take some people with him.

Ten

Nick and the Dart stood on the packed trading floor of the Pacific Stock Exchange. It seemed football field in size; highly glossed pineboard floors; green, glaring computer screens; traders rushing about, carrying leather-bound order books. Like the others, Dart wore running shoes, the top buttons on his shirt unbuttoned, no tie, and a khaki jacket. From his lapel hung a badge with large red numbers: 506.

Nick stood there, affixed to his lapel, a visitor badge. "What's the latest?"

Dart shouted across the din of the screaming traders, "There's a rumor out about Nugget, after they take over a few companies, they're gonna cut down on oil production."

"Those takeovers done deals?"

"Between Nugget and Triton, I think so. Who the hell knows about the others? But look at the oil stocks—up every day. Anyhow, it's a good story and, look, traders grab it and run with it. We get paid to trade. I got three Porsches. Nugget crashes and burns, people lose money, I still got three Porsches."

"What if somebody—what if I shorted the oils?"

"You mean it? That'd be fucking suicide." He thought a moment. "Or damn right."

They didn't speak as traders rushed by, shouting. Yelling filled the air.

"You tellin me somethin?" Dart asked.

"No. Just getting a feel, you know?"

"Nobody just gets a feel. Okay. You know where I live."

Turning and walking off, Nick thought, _I can burn Nugget. Maybe. I don't know._

He went off of the trading floor and took out his cellular and made a call. "How is he?"

159

"Resting," Linda said. "The doctor just left. Everything all right?"

"Sort of."

"Maybe it'll all get straightened out in Houston."

He knew it wouldn't. His voice shook. "This will be goodbye for awhile. I—I'm going away."

"I…"

"I'm not even sure where."

"I'll miss you."

"You too. Greatly."

"Take care."

"I will."

Dread started creeping in as he hung up, resigned. He knew he couldn't stop anything anymore.

***

TapTapTap. The tree limbs tapped on the window, making sounds like drums in a jazz piece. It was early in the morning but Nick was already up, wearing jeans, long-sleeved, black, cotton jersey. He was barefooted, and sat on the couch next to the armoire. On his lap, the laptop computer, its screen glowing green. Outside, the wind blew the leaves on the trees. The wind blew harder, sounding like singing.

He hadn't shaved. The packed, black leather suitcase sat on the floor, by the front door. Hanging on the doorknob was a double-breasted blazer, the one he'd bought with Linda at Saks Fifth Avenue on a day that now seemed so long ago. Just a few shirts and pants were left in the closet along with some brown wooden hangers. In the corner, a thick, black-handled brush lay on an easel, its bristles wet with brown paint.

The phone rang. Nick jumped and picked it up. "Hi, this's Steffie. I met you with the Dart, that morning you got jumped. I work on the floor."

"Oh, yes, hello. Sorry, I can't talk but I was just ready to—"

"Just real quick, okay? Dart tells me you're getting ready to pull the plug on Nugget, that maybe there're problems and—should I sell? For me, my customers? I mean, I don't want to get stuck."

Nick said, "Nothing new, that I know of."

"What're you telling me? What about the other day when you told Dart maybe somebody should short Nugget?"

"I'm saying, Steffie, I didn't tell Dart that. We talked about shorting, that's all."

"Okay, okay. Don't forget that I'm here, too."

Click. Buzz.

Hanging up, Nick thought, *Dart put her up to calling me. They're trying to find out if something's happening.*

He looked at the yellow tablet with scribbled notes, on the couch.

"Nugget Petroleum: Specialist: John Herzog. Bluffs a lot, likes to do monster big trades. In partnership with incredibly deep pockets. Doesn't scare easily.

In weak hands: 986,000 shares from my Nugget Masters database. Also some of this stock might sell:

Deven Value Management, Westport Conn., 400,000 shares. Portfolio Manager, Joseph Grogin.

Topper Value Management, Boston, Mass., 170,000 shares. Analyst, Mark Barney.

Fidelity Investment Management, New York, N.Y., 250,000 shares, Portfolio Manager, Lisa Allen.

Koga Natural Resources Fund, Boston, Mass., 600,000 shares, Portfolio Manager, Shirley Schuss."

There were about half a dozen more names on the list, all figured as being weak holders.

Nick picked up a pen, dropped it down, ran fingers through his hair. *The Nugget Master group isn't enough stock,* he thought. He thought about John Herzog, the specialist on the New York Exchange trading Nugget. Every order had to go through him. He had serious money backing him. *He's the guy I have to scare. Not easy to do.* Nick was sweating under his arms. Herzog had to buy and sell Nugget to make a fair market, had to show his bid and ask price. The quote could be for a thousand shares, five hundred shares, ten thousand shares. *The problem is he doesn't have to show his size. If he wants to buy ten thousand shares—maybe he'll buy only a thousand, then drop his bids as stock's offered to him, hold off and try to buy stock lower.*

He kicked it around, and called Ted Gunn.

"Yeah. Hold on," Ted said. After a while he came back. "Sorry. I'm jammed here, the opening and all."

"Look, what would you say if—?"

"Gotta—I'll be right back." Again Nick was put on hold. Then, "Sorry, Nick. What'cha got?"

"How's Nugget?"

"Strong. The bonds're oversubscribed about three times. Lot of people won't get filled. Don't think I can do you any good, but you want me to call in some favors?"

Nick looked at the screen: NUP 60—60 1/2. The stock was strong. He was having trouble breathing.

"Look, Ted, maybe about a million shares of Nugget sold, in twenty to fifty thousand share lots; maybe also some big pieces. Let me know if you see these blocks coming through. And if you hear any new buzz about the stock."

"You think those blocks'll drop it?"

"Perhaps."

"What're you smokin? Nugget's going nowhere but up."

"Maybe, we'll see."

"Oh. Okay. Nick, you think there's more after this?"

"Could be."

"But—"

"Get back to me."

He hung up and thought, *Maybe I'll catch some of these guys right and they'll sell. If not, go on to the next pond. Problem is, there are only a few ponds. Well, the goal now is to get some sell orders in, have Herzog fade with his bid, then find more sellers and keep pounding the stock, dropping it lower. I gotta take a chance here. If Herzog think there's just a light seller out there, he'll just keep his bid high and the stock won't drop.*

Nick called Joseph Grogin, the fund manager. Grogin came on the line right away.

Speaking fast, in an ersatz Southern accent, Nick said, "Mr. Grogin, this is the Shark. Ahh'm on the Nugget message board. I uncovered damn Nugget as a money-laundering fraud and one that—"

"Who are you? What message boards? I don't read 'em."

"Well, you sure should. Nugget's a scam and only pumped up because an international drug cartel, money launderer named the Invisible Hand is cleanin money through it."

"Whoa. Hold on there."

"Jest so sick and tired of seein this company cheat and lie—"

"How did you get my name?"

"Big Action."

"Who the hell are they?"

"An Internet research company. List all the big holders. Look, check out the bond prospectuses in detail. You take out Nugget's Argentinean wells, hell, that pup doesn't pump enough oil to fill your car tank."

"Why are you doing this?"

"Damn company's dirty. Murdered people down in Argentina, people that ahh really care about."

"Yeah. You're a short."

"Hell I am. Go check out Shark on the message boards."

"I think you're a short."

"See if there isn't a net loss, you carve out Nugget's sales of leases—to insiders, I might add—and their phony Argentinean wells. How come the damn company has hardly depleted their wells? They're pumpin oil back into their wells in Argentina. Check out the production logs. Ahh sure have."

"You're a short."

"You got a fiduciary interest. You sure better check it out."

"... wasting my time."

Click. Then the buzzing of the dead line.

Nick's shirt was soaked under the armpits. Staring at the receiver in his hand, he thought, *I don't know. I don't think so. Does Grogin sell? Maybe. Keep going.*

He made another call.

"Lisa Allen."

"Hi, Lisa. Like to speak with you about Nugget Petroleum. It's a fraud and I can prove it and about to collapse. Any time."

"Who is this?"

"I'm on the message boards as the Shark. I know all about Nugget, and am trying to help investors so they don't get caught holding—"

Click. The buzzing of the dead line.

She's not selling, Nick thought. *But you never know. She may think about it and check it out and dump the stock. You just never know. Could use my own name, these people'll listen to me. But it'll get back to the Hand right away.* And Nick couldn't finish the job very well with a knife in his belly.

He made another call, to the analyst at Topper Value Management.

"Mr. Barney, you don't know me but on the Street and all the websites I'm known as the Shark. I'm calling to alert you about Nugget Petroleum."

"What about it?"

"The company's a fraud. They're about to sell bonds that'll cover up their operating losses, but without taking over other companies, it won't be covered up for long. If you check their reserves you'll see that—"

"I have."

"You have?"

"Yes. I've been uneasy about that company for some time."

"I'd say sell, Mr. Barney. The word will get out, and this is my first call and when I'm through—"

"Call me Mark. Look, let's have lunch."

"Gotta hop. Get your orders in soon, like now."

Nick hung up. He didn't know; sometimes people will tell you anything. But still, the guy sounded like he knew what he was talking about. Nick thought he'd sell.

Nick called the people from the Nugget Masters list. After he finished he still didn't know. Some of them said they'd sell, some hung up, some didn't indicate any direction. *They're not all selling like I expected*, he thought. *I was sure I knew this game, but maybe not. Or I'm not that good anymore.*

The phone rang, and Nick grabbed it. In one breath Ted Gunn said, "About half a million shares went off, in a few pieces. But look at the stock."

On the screen: NUP, 61 1/2, up 1. *So much for me scaring Herzog.*

"More sell orders are comin in, and it's around the specialist's looking for stock. He's short."

Meaning Herzog had sold stock short, and now he wants to buy stock to cover his short position. Nick wondered just what would it take to beat this stock down. "Thanks. Look, is anyone out there shorting this thing?"

"You crazy, Nick? No. They'd get eaten alive."

"Shorts could make money. The stock could drop. You let the institutions get a whiff that there's trouble, you get some very smart people knowing that all's not kosher, and all bets're off; the stock gets hit. We better not forget the institutions run these markets, and any bad news, they're gone. If the institutions don't buy those half-million-share blocks, who will? The specialist can't forever, not by himself. The market's all perception. There were stocks selling at thirty times earnings in 1970; a year later, down to two or three times earnings. Stocks can collapse, do collapse."

"C'mon, Nick, the Nugget people're smart. They know the oil game. Who can beat 'em?"

"All it takes is one guy, knowing how it all works and having good information."

The only sound on the line was Ted Gunn's raspy breathing. "You tellin me something?"

Plant the seed, Nick, go ahead. "Sort of. And it could be done."
"Yeah."

Nick returned the phone to its cradle. He knew when he did his best thinking: jogging and working out. So he donned sweat pants and running shoes and drove to Crissy Field, a large grass area fronting the bay. There was the smell of salty air. Seagulls flew over the water and walked on the beach; the blue, endless sky, the orange girders of the Golden Gate Bridge. People jogged and ran across the sand and pebble track.

He started in, running toward the bridge. Water crashed into the rocks just below, sending salty spray into the air. Rocks were submerged, then reappeared as the water receded. People fished on piers.

There's got to be a quicker way than nickel and diming that stock down, Nick thought. *I don't have that kind of time. They'll be planting dynamite in my car before I've dropped the stock an eighth.* He picked up the pace.

Breathing hard, sweat fogging his sunglasses although the day was cold. It was almost always cold at some point in the day in San Francisco. Nick kept running faster. He ruminated that he didn't have much money to fight Nugget with: only about five grand in the bank, and the Nugget stock options were worthless until they vested, about a year away. *Hell with it. I'll just go somewhere, get a job. Am I running away again? Yes, but the hell with it. I speak enough Spanish to get by. Maybe in Buenos Aires I can—*

He slowed down, and thought about Buenos Aires. And thought it was time to play that card. He thought about Pugliese. Was he just talking, like people do? Figured he'd soon find out. He remembered standing in the men's room in Houston, standing at the latrine and listening. "Rosas has names listed as stockholders. My friend, there are people that have been dead for years, maybe not born, listed as Nugget stockholders." *Rosas is the key to the Hand, and the stockholders list, and God knows what else. Maybe, just maybe.* He made himself keep jogging. To not stop, not until he'd finished the three miles. He speeded up.

Running under the orange Golden Gate Bridge, framed by the blue sky, then turning around toward his starting point, sweat poured down him. White seagulls perched on rocks watched him closely. The sun shone bright and warm. Strollers went by in sweat bottoms, and sweatshirts, and latex jogging outfits.

His heart pounding, breathing hard, Nick finished. He sat on a board left on the beach. Boats sailed offshore, bobbing in the fierce waves. After wiping sweat from his face, he reset his sunglasses. He took out his cell phone and made a call. After a few rings a man answered and said "Si. Diga mi."

"Captain Pugliese. Nick Larson."

"Senor. It is the middle of the night."

"Sorry. It's important."

"And? How may I help you? I am awake, my wife is now awake, and if we talk long enough, mis ninos will also be awake."

"Perdon… but there is a man, a Ronaldo Rosas, who is linked to the Hand."

"Yes?"

"The Hand holds about thirty percent of Nugget's stock, all in nominee names. The stock is physically held in a bank in Uruguay."

"Entonces—"

"So Rosas is a Nugget board member, and a member of the Hand. You can find him. He works at the Argentinean Foreign Ministry. Just bring him in, Captain. Tell him you know the Hand owns a slug of the stock, is involved with Nugget. Get him to tell you anything, just a whisper of a connection. That's all I need."

"I will try, but I think I will get very little."

"It doesn't matter. Just do that, trust me."

***

Nick strolled through North Beach. He was tired of thinking. He hopped a cab and went to the gym, did some yoga, lifted some weights, and looked at himself in the mirror. He went to the café, and had a cappuccino. He wondered if Pugliese cared, or if he was just another blow-hard. No, Pugliese could get famous busting the Hand. Or dead. He stopped thinking and went home.

In the middle of the night the phone rang. Nick jumped and grabbed it. "Hello."

"Si, El Capitan aqui."

Through his apartment window the moon hung low over the city, glowing brightly.

"How'd it go? Did you find—"

"Si. We found your Senor Rosas, we brought him in and asked him questions. Many, many questions. We threatened, we bribed…"

"And?"

"Nada. This man, Rosas, nothing. Yes, I think he tied up in many things, not good things, but before we could question…"

"Yes, yes."

"His attorney, Pepe Santano, very powerful, know everybody in the government, very expensive. He represented the Hand in Federal Court. Si, Rosas is guilty of very bad things, I'm sure. How else could Rosas afford him?"

"Nothing?"

"A waste. Next time we question him, there will be more attorneys around. And I am afraid. My bosses, they will stop me maybe after one more time. Things, people are very strange here in Argentina, Senor. Business is bad. For money they will do anything. I am sorry. It is not safe. I have a wife and children. I have many children."

Nick's mind raced. "Your report, the one that you file. It is for public record, is that not so?"

"Si."

"And the parties at the interview. You and Rosas and the lawyer Santano, the record shows all of you are present."

"But of course. We must record everything. We are a democratic society."

Nick thought it over. "Thanks, Pugliese. Maybe it'll be enough. I hope."

"Yes?"

"Well, facts often are... fillers. And this about the stock market, which is to a great deal, perception."

"I do not understand."

"No. I don't expect anyone would. But I have to convince some that I know what I'm talking about. And maybe I'll get lucky."

After hanging up, Nick looked out of the window into the cold, bright night. At the corner of the street, the tall spires of Trinity Church could be seen in contrast with the sky. He recalled the church was modeled after the Cathedral of Notre Dame. *It's been too long since I've been there,* he thought. *Paris. Europe.*

He picked up the phone, then put it down. *I'm not calling her. The past is dead, let it alone.*

He got dressed and headed for his office.

***

He got to his office and thought it over and it was obvious. He had to go on the attack. Nugget was not coming down, not without a fight. He would have to execute a strike globally, from South America to Europe. He could not go back. The computers glowed as he made a call to Europe.

A woman with a German accent said, "Trudy Schlanger."

"Nick Larson," he replied. "How is everything in Zurich?"

"Fine, fine, Mr. Larson."

"I may want to do something."

"Yes. Gut. How may I help you, bitte?"

"My short. You said that I could get protection on a hundred thousand shares of Nugget Petroleum?"

"Oh, easily."

"Could I, can I do the short in a joint account with someone else, a Lenny Zellon, and the margin money will come from him?"

"That will not be a problem, Mr. Larson."

"Well, get me protection then."

"A hundred thousand shares?"

"Yes."

"Can you hold?"

"Yes."

Listening to the silence on the line, Nick looked through the window to the lights in the Transamerica Building.

I'll miss this place, he thought. *But once I get started, I have to run. All the paperwork will be kept at the bank, no trails. Every ten points down on Nugget is a million for me, less Lenny's cut. If I mess up and the stock climbs, I'm dead. I can't pay my losses and Lenny will be stuck and I'll have to grow a beard and hide. But if I'm right, I take this stock down fifty points. I'll make five million, and Bret'll never find me if I have that kind of money. And I'll keep my gun handy.*

A click on the line, then, "Mr. Larson, I have your stock protected. Now, on the joint account, you have to maintain a forty percent equity. The interest rate will be fourteen percent. I am sure this is satisfactory?"

That's a stiff equity requirement, Nick thought. *The stock goes up a little, they'll call me for money, which I don't have. Ah, what the hell.* "Okay. Where's the stock?"

"Just a moment, please."

His stomach tightened. He knew that this was illegal. He had inside information, was an insider, and wasn't allowed to trade on that. Everybody knew that.

"Sixty three and a quarter."

He thought about it, that nobody would ever know. It was all set up. He was doing it all in a numbered account. Unless there are drugs or fraud involved, no Swiss bank opens an account to investigators. He started sweating. *Using inside information's real wrong. Ah, who cares? Look how crooked the Nugget guys are.* Another voice said, *But so what, I'm not them.*

"Sir? Mr. Larson?"
But it's illegal.
"Mr. Larson?"
But nobody'll know.
"Mr. Larson?"
But I know. He bit his fingernail.
"Are you all right?"
Am I all right? No. "Yes, just thinking." *Am I all right? Five million down the tubes because I'm a damn wimp. I could use that money.*
"If you'd like to call back?"
But I can't make money that *way. Brett would, everybody else would. I can't. Fuck it.* "No, that's okay. I changed my mind."
"Think it over?"
"No. Sorry I took up so much of your time."
"Is it the interest rate? I am sure that—"
"No, it's not that. Thanks for your help. Have a nice day."

***

Standing in the early morning blackness, under the towering glass and steel buildings in the San Francisco financial district, Nick watched something zooming down steep California Street. As it got closer the something metamorphosed into a short, wiry guy wearing a helmet. He passed Grant Avenue, racing toward the financial district. Finally, Lenny Zellon, in jeans and a heavy wool sweater with a Diesel logo, roller-bladed up to the curb, grinning at Nick.

He removed the helmet, his bald spot gleaming with sweat. "New routine," Lenny said, "exercise, exercise. Can't get old, you know what I mean? Look at me, over forty, well, over fifty, but who's counting? Do I look it? My clothes—gotta dress like the kids. You know what the average age on the Street is? About twelve."

"Well, it's only natural to grow older."

"Only natural, only natural, what are you, preachin some kind'a bullshit honesty? I'm scared. What about my sex life? What there is of it. Women got problems, they don't get wet? Big deal. They ever gonna know what it's like to not get it up?" Lenny sat at the curb and started removing the rollerblades. "I've had shots, shots right into my dick, hurt like hell. A bee sting, the doctor said, just inject this rifle-sized needle into the head of your dick. So that didn't work. I tried DHEA, the wonder drug: nothin. I tried vitamins, minerals, went to a yoga guru. Fuckin nuts, he was. Wanted me to eat plants or fuck cows or some damn thing. Young guy, says I should come to class, yoga cures all. So this kid's standin up in front of us in this smelly room, havin us bend this way and that, torture. I'd rather read *Playboy*. He's young, sure he gets hard anytime he wants. But, hell with everybody, now I got this Viagra, like bein reborn, better'n a cure for cancer." He looked at Nick, as if seeing him for the first time. "Say, what the hell're you doin here?"

"We need to talk," Nick said.

"Sure, come on up."

Lenny carried the blades over his shoulder, and they went to his office. He snapped on the lights. The office lit up, showing chrome chairs, a heavy black desk, computers and TV sets. Outside, stars twinkled in the early morning.

After sitting at his desk, Lenny flipped the switch on the computer with the giant screen. Letters glowed in white against a green background: "Virus Check." He typed on the keyboard, and after a moment, in large white letters: "Market News: Gold, Oil hit new Highs."

"Texas oil cowboys takin over the damn world," Lenny said. "Bunch'a damn yahoos." He clicked the remote control, and a thirty-something guy with a big-teethed smile appeared on the screen. "…and the reason for the continuing market advance—"

"What the hell's he know?" Lenny shouted. "Right out of Harvard MBA. Big deal. When the market goes down he'll come up with some stupid cockamamie reason why. Who cares what you think? You know shit."

The talking head went on, "…leading the market is the continuing strength in the oil and gas stocks. The recent rash of proposed mergers—"

"So oil's strong. Tell me something I don't know, like the color of your grandmother's panties." Lenny clicked the remote and white numbers scrolled across the screen: …COL 54 3/4, GM 55 1/8, IBM 84, NUP 64 1/4 … He stood up, sat down. "Damn Nugget's flying again." Looking at his watch, he said, "Damn, two hours until that Wasp piece of ass blonde's on."

He clicked again, and a large woman appeared on the screen, fat face, several chins, black mole on her cheek. Speaking while keeping a frozen smile she said, "And the stock market rose again this morning, the oil companies, the gold mining shares…"

Standing up, sitting down, Lenny said, "I can't believe this. She's fat, and I'm gettin turned on just watching her talk. What a blow job with those lips."

He could be institutionalized, Nick thought. *But then, so could we all.*

The phone rang. Staring at the screen, Lenny said, "Man, I wish they'd lower that camera. Bet her legs're crossed up high. Get a squirrel shot." The phone rang again. He picked it up. "Zellon. Yeah. Yeah. Okay, put me down. A hundred thousand more." He hung up. "Circled more Nugget bonds on the offering. Woman over at Merrill doing me a favor. Won't fuck me, so that'll have to do. She's married. So? He can watch, can't he? Probably an MBA."

Nick held his breath, then said, "You know, Lenny, I'm hearing stories. Real bizarre and strange stories."

Staring at the TV, Lenny said, "Like what? Damn, I wanta fuck her. It's not that I just *would*, like do her a favor, not that she's got two chins and big fat tits and I just would, I mean, you know, put a bag over her face and give her a grudge fuck. No, I mean I want to!"

"Nugget Petroleum," Nick said.

"Yeah, so what. It's goin to the moon, takin over the world, blah, blah, blah. Tell me somethin new."

"Can you keep a secret, Lenny?"

"You know me."

"I know you, and you *can't* keep a secret. But on this, wait awhile before shooting off your mouth. Give it a few days."

"C'mon, Larson. Just because I bullshit with people all the time—"

"You blab with everyone, Lenny. They call from New York, Paris, Berlin, Omaha, everywhere. That's okay. Talk. Just wait."

"Okay. What d'ya got? You're about to bore me, and I can't stand—"

"You know Nugget? That everybody has on his buy list? It's a short."

Lenny stared at Nick. As the information sunk in, the color drained from his face. "Short? Short? Why'd you put me in that mother-fucking ass-hole licking stock! You come to me, Lenny, you say, buy this shit! I buy this scumbag mother-fucking shit. Then you say, hey, Lenny, go in a deal with me to short stock. I wondered about it, but I said to myself, hey, Lenny, you're being paranoid. Larson wouldn't screw you. But you screwed me. What would you short else but this garbage, the only stock you know? What else you selling? Cancer?"

"Lenny."

"What? I got 732,500 shares of that garbage that you put me into. Now I'm long, because of you."

"It *was* Nugget I was going to short. But I can't because, you know, I'm a control person and the law—"

Lenny's face threatened to explode, his face as red as the muleta a matador waves in front of a bull. "The *law*? What am I, a boy scout? Regulations? Here's my regulation," he said, grabbing his crotch. "Short this, you lying bastard."

Nick wiped sweat off his forehead.

Lenny said, "You're looking for stock, that's it. You're like everyone else. You want to get me to sell. You got a buyer and you want my stock and you owe somebody a favor, so you're here, early in the morning, before coffee or doughnuts or bagels or what the hell do you and Miss Pacific Heights eat in the morning, tea and crumpets or some shit, hustling me out of my stock. Giving me a short story, like I'm a child. Fuck you, Larson, and the horse you rode in on."

"I—"

"And how about all those bonds? Should I cancel my orders? Do you know what those cock-sucking sister-brother fucking underwriters will do if I cancel my orders? The Street'll know I backed out of the deal in eight nano-seconds. Don't you think they'll wonder why? Don't you think everybody watches me? I'm Zellon, you mother-fucking, cock-sucking whore of a friend that I trusted and now you're like everybody else. No, worse, you slut."

Nick wiped sweat from under his chin. Lenny sunk deep into his chair, his eyes quiet.

Nick figured that Lenny's wrath had ebbed. He said, "Look, you've made how much in Nugget?"

Lenny inhaled, his eyes wandering to the computer screen.

"Seven-hundred thousand plus shares times about what, thirty points?" Nick said. "Lenny, you've made over twenty million dollars in that stock. How have I betrayed you?"

"True, that's right. But not enough, Nick. You know that. Never enough."

"I know. But twenty million, come on, Lenny. How have I betrayed you?"

Lenny watched the screen. "Gotta watch everybody. Three wives, yeah, as soon as they got their greedy fingers into my money, they were gone. My son, probably he's about twenty now. Don't even know where he is. Ten years, over, I haven't seen him."

"I didn't know you have a son."

"Yeah. Threw the ball with him, everything. Then, I don't know, his mother left and..." A tear started down Lenny's face. His face scrunched up, he clicked the remote furiously, faces appearing on the screen, vanishing, other faces appearing. He wiped the tear away and sat up, his eyes turning hard. "And—what are you doing, Larson, makin a human being out of me? Why're we talkin about that? Or you still tryin to get my stock?" His face started turning red.

"It's a short, Lenny. Check it out and you'll find about half a million shares traded yesterday. That was my block, some fund managers I got out early. How could I be betraying you?"

After thinking it over, Lenny said, "What'ya got?"

"This is one of those conversations you never had."

"What'ya got?"

"I'm serious, Lenny. Could be life and death."

"You're not even here. Not me either. I'm hosin a movie starlet in Hollywood. That'll be the day. Talk to me."

"A South American money-laundering drug criminal gang with ties to the Nugget board; proposed takeovers that're based on phony reserve estimates; real, real bad guys. Need more?"

Standing up, clicking off the TV, sitting down, Lenny said, "No."

"Good. I have people that'll use stock. Otherwise, do anything you want."

"Puts?"

"They're okay," Nick said.

He had figured that's what Lenny would do: buy options to *put* the stock to the seller at the current price. If Nugget tumbled, the put would go up in value. Plus, the leverage was fantastic. Lenny could control hundreds of thousands of shares of Nugget for just a little cash.

Lenny clicked on the TV, and a thin woman appeared. "Look at that," he said. "Like to have those matchstick legs around me." He punched some numbers on the phone. After a few rings, a man said, "Trading."

"This's Zellon. Account one-oh-three-four."

"Yes, Mr. Zellon."

"In my account, sell Nugget Petroleum, all the shares. Then buy five hundred Nugget Petroleum 60 puts, for March. All at the market."

Lenny bought a put that had a short maturity date, just a few months. Lenny had bought the right to sell Nugget at sixty dollars, through the third Thursday in March. If the stock went down, say to fifty, Lenny could put the stock to the seller at sixty, making ten points. Because there were only a few months on the option, it sold at a cheap premium, or price. But Lenny bought Nick's story: the stock was going down—now.

"Yes. And your limit, Mr.—"

"Limit? Can you hear?" Lenny said. "At the market, there's no limit. Your wife got a limit? If I wanted a limit, I'd give you a limit. Buy the damn things. Are they bought? What am I holding here, my dick or my phone?" He clicked the remote; another face appeared on the TV screen.

"Yes, sir. Right away."

In a few moments: "Mr. Zellon, you're filled, at twelve and a half."

"Good. Now, buy me a thousand more, at the market."

"Yes, Mr. Zellon. I am buying one thousand, that is one - zero - zero—"

"Yeah, yeah. I know how many zeros are in a thousand. You think I'm stupid? Then how come I got hundreds'a millions ta' trade? So, what're you, an MBA? Yeah, an MBA queen that dances around the office. Buy 'em already. Hey, I'm tired of holdin the phone, call me back." Lenny slammed the receiver into its cradle.

Nick got up and started for the door.

"Say, where're you going?" Lenny said.

"Away."

"How the hell can I call you?"

"Forget it, you can't," Nick said. "Where I'm going, nobody can."

Eleven

Nick watched San Francisco grow smaller as he stood on the deck of a long and wide ferryboat as it made its way over the choppy, blue waters. A few children ran on the deck, their mothers following. He thought that if he had children they would be about their age. He would've made a good father, he decided.

The white boat spewed steam into the air. Bright scarlet lettering on its side spelled out RED FLEET. Sunshine reflected sharply off the waters. Salty water from the bay sprayed into the boat, smelling like raw oysters.

Nearing Sausalito, a community made up of houses covering hills, just across from San Francisco, the boat slowed. Seagulls flew over the boat, in the clear blue sky.

Nick walked to the front of the ferry. The houses covering the hills looked tiny in the distance. He thought they looked like small suspicious eyes, all watching for him. *And maybe they'll get me, but they got to catch me first.*

The boat approached the shore. He waved to a middle-aged woman standing on the shore. She wore a gray and white, plaid, linen suit, black pumps: casual and expensive, it was very Marin County. She waved back, smiling with big teeth, her smile showing under huge sunglasses, her too-perfect black hair piled high. Just another Marin housewife.

Nick took out his cell phone and typed some numbers. After a few rings he asked for Brett Wells. "Oh, yeah, hi," Brett said. "We were just talking 'bout you. How's it going?"

"The stock's acting well," Nick said. "In fact, I'm on my way to see a big hedge fund right now. She's always good for half a million shares."

Brett laughed. "Well, c'mon see us. How 'bout tomorrow?"

Nick's gut tightened. He liked Brett. *Too late for that now.*

"No, I can't. Too much to do here."

"Okay. Next week, after the bond deal?"

He thought it over. "I'll be there."

"A hell of a time, pardner. Aren't you glad you hooked up with us? A hell of a time."

You should have left me destitute, Nick thought. "Yes. One hell of a time. Goodbye, Brett."

The boat docked, and he went to meet the smiling woman with very large teeth.

About an hour later Nick was back on board, watching as the boat pulled away from the dock. The Sausalito shops, trees, and a small parking lot surrounded by hedges and grass shrunk as the ferry picked up speed. He waved. The woman behind the sunglasses waved back. Soon, Sausalito was far behind.

He reached into his pocket and took out a slim, black wallet with Passport embossed in gold. He opened it and looked at his picture, with the name James Underwood underneath. He could go anywhere in the world and not leave a trace. Nobody was out on the deck. All the benches were painted white. Rows and rows of benches, and nobody there. He sat down. The sea air blew; gulls circled overhead. The choppy ocean sent sheets of spray into the boat. San Francisco with its steel and glass buildings shrouded in gray from a light fog grew larger and larger as the ferry moved closer to the dock.

It's time, he told himself. *Not just yet. Yes, right now. There is no reason to wait. I don't want to. It's time.*

After staring at his cell phone as if it were a snake, he made a call. A woman answered, "Steffie here."

"This is Nick Larson. How's it going?"

"Hey, where you been? I've called your office—"

"I'm away, for a while. The Nugget bonds still look good?"

"Sizzling is what they are. Haven't come yet and they're up about five points in the after-market. Everybody wants—"

"Funny, Steffie. I'm hearing that some very very smart money is shorting the bonds, *and* the stock. In size. Do the same, that's if you want to make money. Also tell the Dart. Now you owe me. Gotta run, Steffie, and tell the Dart hello and also goodbye."

"Hey, hey, wait! What the hell you mean?"

"Simple. Check Nugget's put volume the last couple days. Three times the usual level. Somebody's buying, and the offer doesn't climb much. Don't you wonder why? It's because the public isn't buying puts.

There's just one big buyer out there, and the put sellers don't see the stock going lower. And I turned him on to what's happening. Like I'm trying to do with you, if you would just put down your comic book for a moment and listen."

Silence on the line. Nick figured she was checking this information on a computer. "You see that big block a few days ago?" he said.

"The sell? About seven hundred—"

"Seven hundred thirty two thousand five hundred shares. The seller's a friend of mine. There'll be more. Do yourself a favor. Sell it."

"The hottest stock—"

"Who has the handle here? The buyer or seller? Wake up, Steffie. Stop smoking that joint and listen." Nick was asking her who she thought had the handle of the axe, the access to *real* information. "Yeah, well, forget about this call, but next week, next month, when it's too late, for you anyhow, don't you think it'll eat at you? Why were there sellers out there, isolated, but size sellers? You'll look back, and kick yourself. Where's the stock now?"

"Sixty two, off about two points. Just a correction."

"That's what they said in 1929."

Steffie's breathing into the phone became irregular. "Okay, right. So, what'ya got?"

"The prospectus has flat out lies of exploration prospects. A board member named Ronaldo Rosas has been hauled in for questioning by the Buenos Aires police about his ties to a drug mob. Also, dead people are listed as major holders of the stock, to hide that criminals really own it. I'd say criminal investigations, SEC crackdowns, maybe jail time. What do *you* think that'll do to the stock?"

"Do many people know about this?"

"Not yet. But when I drop a few million shares on the specialist, a lot'll know. You think he won't make noise? And I got some other tricks."

"Are you sure?"

"Why would I waste my time?"

"Why are you telling me this?"

"Because I like the way you do your hair."

"But—"

"Go to Brett Wells. He's so high on this stock he'll never see it coming. Butch Byrd's more suspicious, ex-Army man and all."

"But—"

"Go to Brett Wells. He's not as smart as he thinks. Goodbye, Steffie. Remember, we never had this conversation."

"But—"
He hung up.

***

Steffie pressed the "End" button on her cell phone, her hand shaking. She stood watching the traders shouting at each other, barking out orders, tearing up executed order slips and throwing them on the floor. Paper covered the shiny, polished, yellow pine boards. *I'm gonna shit right here, gotta cut out drinking that damn coffee*, she thought. *God I need a cup now, I need a joint, man, I gotta pee. Okay, okay, later. Should I short Nugget? If Nick's gonna start people selling—who knows if they will, but he says so. Is he lying? Buying and getting me to sell so he can buy cheaper? Or is he really short and wanting to drop the stock? But why would he lie? I lie sometimes, sometimes a lot. But Nick's old. Why would an old fart lie? They're gonna die soon. I gotta believe sometimes, don't I?*

Wiping sweat off her face, she told herself, *Okay, this could be the chance of a lifetime. I gotta pee—no, gotta beat the other sellers. Where do I go? Call, call now. No. Yes.*

She pressed numbers on her cell phone.

"Brett Wells," he said.

"Mr. Wells, this is Steffie Healey. I'm a trader on the P-Coast."

"Well, sure am glad to make your—hell, call me Brett. Everybody does."

"Okay, Brett. The reason I'm calling: I have a seller of Nugget Petroleum, in real size, and I figured I'd check with you first."

"Well, glad you did."

"Are you a buyer?"

"Could be. How many?"

Christ, I gotta pee, Steffie thought, squeezing her knees together. *Think, think. I mortgage my house, put up all my stock, sell my cars. Hate to do that but it's just steel and rubber, I need money, real money. Max out my credit line by lying to the bank, they never check, dumb bastards, I can scrape together, oh shit, say it, say it.* "Half a million shares."

"Half a million?"

Oh shit, what have I done? I hope he doesn't take it. Say the stock's not for sale, the seller changed his mind. Say no. "Yes." Silence. Silence. "You interested?"

Brett took a deep breath. "Yeah, hell, I'll buy it if the price's right. Go down a half from the last trade, and it's a deal."

"I may be able to get it off, down a quarter." *God, I can't see. I'm going blind, going to faint.*

"No, a half."

"Okay. Just wait."

She looked across the room at men and women scurrying around in khaki jackets, prices racing across computer screens. *I want to fuck somebody, she thought. I never want to come here again. I want money.*

Steffie spoke into her phone: "You're filled. The hedge fund said it was a lousy price but you're done. You bought five hundred thousand shares of Nugget Petroleum at fifty nine and a half."

"Good."

She pressed End and took off across the floor. *I'm about to wet my pants. Damn, I've done it. I actually shorted half a million shares of stock. Nugget goes up, I'm screwed royal. I believe I heard Nick right. Would he lie? I pray to the ever-living God that he didn't. I promise, God, no bullshit this time. I'll be good, really, really good.*

***

After speaking with Steffie, Nick strolled off the ferry and sat on a bench at Pier 54. Water pounded up against the dock, sprayed him. He opened his laptop and waited until he saw NUP 500,000 ... 59 ?. He figured that was Steffie's trade. He thought about it, then took out the card given to him recently and called Los Angeles.

In L.A., about an hour's plane ride from San Francisco, Al Zucker walked out of a multi-storied high-rise apartment building, to his black Rolls Royce, sitting on the circular driveway. Carefully manicured bushes surrounded the apartment building, and palm trees fronted the driveway. Cars zipped by on wide Wilshire Boulevard, driving into busy Century City.

He strode fast, anticipating a hell of a full day. The early morning Los Angeles air smelled sweet and fresh, like just-mowed grass. His cell phone rang impatiently in the pocket of his cashmere jacket. One of his many assistants informed him that his latest movie returned thirty-five million over its first weekend. That was good news. His assistant also reported he had signed an actress that Al was interested in.

"Never did get a good look at her," Al said. "She's got some tits on her. How's her ass?" He opened the door of the Rolls and got in.

"Surgically corrected, about perfect. And, she can act."

"Act? My dog can act. Nobody pays to see anybody act anytime.

Tits and ass what's they want. Some kinda plot—hey, hold on." Al switched to call waiting. "Hello?"

"Al, Al Zucker? This is Nick Larson."

"Who?"

"I work for Nugget. Met you in San Francisco, with Willie."

"Oh, yes. Look, I can't talk. I got a guy holding and this movie's more important than all the damn stock deals."

"I think you'll want to talk with me. You don't like Federal lawsuits, do you? You don't like the SEC, the IRS coming around and—"

"Biting my ass." Big Al's heart started to pound. The sweet air of L.A. was gone. *Who the hell is this weirdo?* he wondered. *I hate the stock market.* "Hold on." As he got rid of the other call he pictured the actress in a tight black skirt. *Love a good ass*, he thought. *She's got a great ass. What does this guy want from me? I don't even remember him. What does everybody want from me?* Again he imagined her ass in a black skirt.

"Look, Larson, is it Larson? Call Willie, Willie Bornstein. He runs Spence Trask there for me."

"I know all about Wild Willie. Known him for years."

"So? What's the problem? You call him and tell him—"

"It'll be a waste of time. He won't want to hear about it."

"So. He knows what he's doing. I think. Gotta go, Nick. Is it Nick?"

"It's Nick. Al, Spence Trask is about to unload eighty million dollars of Nugget bonds, bonds of a bad company on an unsuspecting public. In Buenos Aires they just hauled in a member of Nugget's board. He's tied to a drug ring. A lot of Nugget stock's held in nominee name by a bank in Uruguay for people who are either dead or never born. A drug ring, called the Invisible Hand in case you're interested, is the real holder of the stock."

Al's heart was pounding so hard he almost couldn't hear. Cars rushed by on the freeway; the bright L.A. sun shone fiercely. He wanted to lie down. In vain, he tried to remember that great ass in a black dress, couldn't. He concentrated, trying to listen.

"Wait until the SEC finds out, they will because I'll tell them that the producing wells in Argentina have had almost no depletion in a few decades. Wait until the FBI checks the records of certain trucking companies that shows how oil was *delivered* to wells that were supposed to be pumping. Can you imagine the front page of *Time* magazine? The fraud of the century? It's not just eighty million dollars. Spence Trask could be assessed punitive damages that could run to about three times that. Now I don't know about you, but a two hundred and forty million dollar hit would give me heartburn at least..."

Al was dizzy. The cars he watched speeding by seemed to be driving sideways. Al thought, *I hate that fucking stock market. The hell is that crazy Willie doing to me? I want out, out, what do I need this for? I got movies, I got women, beautiful fucking women with pussies...* "Hey, look, Nick, is it Nick? I'll take care of it, talk to Willie."

"Better make it quick, Al. You're the major partner. They'll be lined up with subpoenas and come to your house; they'll ask your doorman where you are. A lot of time in courtrooms. You like courtrooms, Al, you like spending time there? Sure, you take care of it." Nobody said anything. "Nice talking to you," Nick said.

Al sat in his Rolls Royce after the voice clicked off. The walnut trim on the dashboard and armrests gleamed in the L.A. sun. His stubby fingers viciously punched out numbers on the tiny cell phone. He got Willie on the line. Willie did not even get a chance to ask how he was. "Cancel that deal, that shit, that deal," Al said.

"But look Al, we've already—"

"Already, hell with already. Cancel that deal."

"Al, I, I've staked my reputation, promised people bonds. It's hot, I tell you. I can't just—"

"Fuck your reputation."

"Al, let's get in touch with Nick Larson. You remember him? We'll have a conference call."

"Larson?"

"Yes. You met him in my office."

"Larson? He knows about Nugget?"

"Everything. He works for them. He got the story out about the company. He made them."

"I can trust him? Larson?"

"Trust him?" Willie laughed. "Yes, you can. Look, tell me where you'll be in an hour and I'll set up a call right now."

Al watched the cars driving by on their way to and from Century City. Sweat covered the leather-covered steering wheel as he gripped it. Damn oil stocks. A hernia before? This time I'll get a heart attack. "Cancel the deal."

After a moment Willie said, "I can't do that, Al. It's my reputation. If I have to I'll walk, and take the deal with me. Maybe Deutsche Bank across the street will do it."

"Walk. The deal's history."

"But my reputation."

"Walk. Leave your five million a year guarantee, country club, bonuses. Leave, like I need this? I'll fire you, bigshot. Like Deutsche Bank is waiting. Do what the fuck you want, but the deal will not happen." A great ass in a tight black dress reappeared in his mind. Al looked at the passing cars. Traffic was building up, and he had to get going.

"But people—"

"Fuck your reputation."

***

Nick looked at his face, reflected in the mirror in the airport men's room. His face had the beginnings of a beard; his eyes had dark circles under them. He washed up and went out to the waiting area and sat. Through glass windows he saw planes taxiing in the bright sunshine. He smelled popcorn being popped nearby, at a stand that had a red umbrella opened above it. Travelers walked about with carry-on bags. Everything looked normal and ordinary, but Nick felt lost.

He took out his cell phone then thought, *Just put it back. Do I call? Why am I calling? I don't care why I'm calling, I want to speak with her. Just forget her. Why don't you be tough? I don't know, I'm just not.*

Viciously he typed in her number.

It rang and then, "This is Linda Thackery speaking, and I'm not here right now to take your call. So would you please leave your name, number, and a brief message, and I will get back to you as soon as I—" Linda interrupted the recording, "Hello? Hello?"

"Linda, this is Nick."

"Hold on, until the tape stops."

He was so glad to hear her.

She said, "I've been so worried. Are you all right?"

"Sort of. Yes."

"Where are you?"

"I—I'm about to take off." Outside the airport window, the nose of a jumbo jet gleamed in the sun.

"I miss you."

"I'm having trouble staying away. I miss you, too. Should, could we meet?" *How could we meet, it's impossible. I'm getting desperate,* Nick thought. *I don't care. I do, but I don't.* "I'll let you know where."

"I can't, Nick, you know that. You saw what happened."

Over the intercom a woman's voice announced, "Senor y Senoras. Air France Flight number nine-o-two to Paris will board in thirty minutes at gate six."

"I gotta go."

Linda sobbed, stopped. "I love you."

Nick got suddenly cold. *It's over. I don't know if I can take this again, but here it is.* It was hard to speak. "I love you, too."

"Goodbye."

"Goodbye."

Keep going, he told himself, *you can do it. I can do it.*

He started toward the departure gate. *I want to go home. There isn't any home anymore, not for a long time.* He shivered.

***

Ted Gunn's hair looked like it hadn't been combed for days. As always when under pressure, he closed himself off by staring at the computer screen. His necktie was hanging untied. He hollered at a trader a few seats down, a dark-eyed twenty-something young woman. "Hey, Anna, you buy me that hundred thousand Nugget yet?"

She wore a severe black suit that matched her hair and eyes. "C'mon, Gunn. You gave me the order a nano-second ago."

Smiling, but his eyes cold, Ted said, "Look, Anna, you like it here? You like nice things? Please, please, find me some stock."

His eyes stayed riveted on the screen, the phone receiver resting on his shoulder. His bowling-ball-sized-belly hung between blue suspenders that he hooked his thumbs around and pulled, lost in thought. The phone rang. "Gunn here."

"This is Nick."

"Yeah."

Anna said, "Hey, Gunn! You bought a hundred thousand Nugget at fifty-two. Happy?"

"Anna, you're the best. Sorry, Nick. What's up?"

"Couldn't help hearing, after all, you're both screaming. You buying Nugget?"

"Stock's down to fifty-two for God's sake. I got customers, my firm, everybody wants in here."

"You like it?"

"Love it. True, there are some sellers around, hot hedge-fund flippers. But all the oils're soft. After they recover Nugget'll make new highs."

"Whatever," Nick said. "As long as it's not your money."

Ted Gunn looked around the trading room. A guy in a white shirt at the water cooler joked with the other guys in white shirts about golf and women and money, the things of real importance; traders yelled into phones. Investment bankers were easily distinguishable because they wore suits and ties. Women in white blouses, skirts, everyone seemed to be moving in slow motion as what Nick said sunk in. "What the hell d'ya mean?"

"Call Pattie Levin at Barney. Tell her Nugget's a fraud and to get out. She's made plenty. Tell her I said for her to give you the order. You still take orders, don't you, Ted?"

"Funny you should ask, that's how I make a living. But what—"

"Call a woman named Isabel, I'll e-mail you her number. Tell her I said to sell. Take her order, too. Do this like now. The bond deal's going to be called off. There's some real size about to be sold. The company is very, very dirty."

"Okay. Okay. Where're you?"

"Funny. Everybody asks me that. There're a few more people, I'll e-mail their names. Goodbye, Ted."

"But what if they won't sell?"

"They'll get fried—tell them I said that. So what? It's not their money. But get Isabel out first."

Ted heard over the phone, "Now boarding, Flight 223." He thought that this was going to be a very good day. "Okay, Nick. I'm on it."

***

"As I said, Mr. Larson?" the woman asked.

"Yes, Nick Larson."

He listened to the woman on his cell phone as he sat in a row of black leather seats in the crowded Charles DeGaulle Airport, outside of Paris. His black suitcase was on an adjacent bench. The man next to him wore a gray hat, and blew out a stream of cigarette smoke. It certainly wasn't California, where smoking indoors at airports is pretty much forbidden. The smoke drifted over people rushing past.

"Yes, you do come very highly recommended," the woman said. "But we at Suisse Credit, we manage over, let's see, in American dollars, over four-hundred billion. And, well, we don't take tips. We're long-term investors."

"Tell that to your customers," he said, "not to me. You guys jump in and out of stocks just like everyone else."

"Yes. Well, we have been known to take a flyer every now and again."

"I'm sure you have." *Keep it going*, he thought, *smoke and mirrors*. He needed to make it seem that the story was coming in from all over the globe. He needed the right people, and the woman he was speaking with was wired into trillions.

Sweating, stroking his three-day beard, he said, "This's more than rumor. All I ask is you keep my name out of it. Who knows where it'll lead with a Nugget board member being hauled in for questioning? And the bond offering, it's history."

"Yes, all right, Mr. Larson. And if I find out that this is so?"

Nick picked up his suitcase, walked past a sign saying Sortie and started down the corridor. "I'd say, first sell Nugget, which could start a run on the other oils. Nobody knows how it'll play out, so sell all your oils, then put some shorts in. When these companies crash, they'll pump as much oil as they can to raise money; that'll increase supply. That should drop the price of crude, and it'll go back into the high teens. After that, oil stocks could go even lower."

She thought it over. "Yes. And where can I reach you?"

"What for?"

"If our board members wish to confirm—"

"Look, can you pull the trigger, or not?"

"I can. And I will. You're sure of this?"

"Why the hell would I cross you?" he asked. "I'm in enough trouble, already."

***

Early in the morning, Nick woke to the steady beat of rain on the roof. *It sounds so pleasant,* he thought. *It often rains in Paris, and it's so clean and fresh afterwards. More than any other city. I'm being foolish, it's just rain. No, it's not. It's a different sort of rain. Come on, spare me. I don't care, I love Paris. Early Hemingway, James Joyce and publishing* Ulysses, *Beckett's production of* Waiting for Godot, *cappuccinos at the Café de Paris, strolling through the Louvre and no end to the Impressionists. The only city where being alone makes you feel so alone, but you almost don't mind, it's okay.*

He looked over to an easel in the corner, holding his just finished painting: a man and woman walking on a stone street in a moonlit French village. He studied the painting and stretched out on the bed. Raindrops were splattering on the small, square windows.

The room contained very little: a stiff bed, an ancient armoire, a small table with a telephone, a few chairs, and a *toilette*. After awhile he got up and looked out of the window. Down below were the black-tar roofs topping the small houses and shops dotting the Left Bank. The several gabled buildings of *l 'Universite de la Sorbonne* glistened in the strengthening sunlight. The thin, steady drizzle kept making tiny puddles in the middle of the narrow cobblestone street.

Nick dressed carefully in a denim shirt, black jeans, black boots, and descended a narrow flight of stairs and out the front door. Walking on a narrow side street, he smelled garlic, onions, and roasting chickens coming from the marketplace. At the corner, vegetables and fruit were piled high on a stand; oranges covered another farmer's stand. Walking down the Boulevard St. Michel, he passed buildings of the Sorbonne. Down an alleyway was a cafe. A cat scampered across the entrance. Opening the door, Nick smelled just-ground coffee.

Behind a low, wood counter stood a wiry man with a mustache. Traces of coffee-grinds streaked his white T-shirt. Behind him was a cappuccino machine and rows of bread.

"Bonjour," he said.

"Bonjour," Nick said. "Un croissant et un cappuccino s'il vous plait."

"Oui."

The machine hissed as it steamed milk. The man poured the milk into coffee that was in a paper cup, put on a lid, and placed it into a bag with a croissant.

Nick paid and went back to his room.

Standing at the window, he watched an orange sun rise over the city. The rain slowed, drops barely disturbing the deep puddles on the pavement. A woman came out of a house, shook a rug, then went back inside.

Peeling the layers of the croissant, Nick ate it while watching the rain. He removed the lid from the container and sipped the cappuccino. The heavy aroma of coffee filled his nose. *Come on, it's time,* he thought. *I don't want to. I've never squealed to the authorities. They're the enemy. But I've got to. Don't have a choice.*

The phone sitting on the table was from a distant past, a circular dial that clicked as it was turned. As he dialed, his fingers felt like ice. He shivered. *Nick, the rat*, he thought. He kept dialing.

The phone rang a few times, then a woman cheerily said, "Securities Exchange Commission."

His voice trembled as he said, "Yes. Paul Braxton, please."

"Surely. I'll connect you, sir."

A few moments later a young, peppy voice said, "Braxton."

"Yes. This is—I'm a money-manager, and I've dug up some facts about Nugget Petroleum. In fact, they're more facts than you'll ever need to stop a giant fraud from continuing, and I can document—"

"I—sorry, sir, but I'm late for a meeting. I'll have my assistant take down your number, and I'll get back—"

"Well, you won't, and you'll be really blowing it. And you'll miss catching the biggest scam since the savings & loan fiasco. You remember that one, don't you? Cost the taxpayers a quick twenty billion. SEC regulators like you built their careers on it."

There was a dead silence.

Good, Nick thought. *He's probably taking me seriously.*

"Nugget's calling off their bond offering. Haven't announced it yet. This story breaks here in Europe, and I'll see that it does. I know how to work the media and people learn that you had this info and didn't investigate—which, again, I'll see everyone knows the ugly facts, including the company being a money-laundering scheme. Instead of being a hero, you'll be pushing papers maybe in, I don't know, Alaska?"

"Hey look, this is—what did you say your name is?"

"I didn't. Doesn't matter. And I'll give you another minute—"

"Okay, okay. Go on."

Hearing a click, Nick thought he'd better hurry. They were tracing the call.

"Check with a Captain Pugliese in Buenos Aires and ask about his questioning a man named Ronaldo Rosas recently. Then find out who the *real* owners are of so much stock held in nominee name in a bank in Uruguay."

He took a sip of the cappuccino. It wasn't warm anymore. He'd get more. "I know you guys've got thin budgets and can't investigate every call that comes in, but here I've done your work for you."

"Yes. Thank you, but—"

"You got it all?" Nick had very little time left.

"Yes. But how do you figure in all this?"

"Oh, me? Something I do in between holes when I play golf."

"But—"

"Goodbye, Braxton. Good hunting."

Nick hung up. Orange sunlight streamed in through the windows, and the rain had stopped. He called New York City and asked for the number of the New York Stock Exchange, the enforcement division. Feeling like a coward and snitch the whole time.

He looked at the canvases stacked in the corner and thought, *Well, there's still painting. Maybe that's all there is.*

"And in Washington, D.C.," he told the operator, "I need the number of the Federal Bureau of Investigation. I think the main number will do."

***

Brett picked up the receiver as soon as his secretary said, "Mr. Wells, line two, please."

He was so rushed he hadn't even taken off his suit coat. Papers and memos and prospectuses covered his desk.
"MERGER AGREEMENT, Sunbelt Resources.
INITIAL PUBLIC OFFERING, Southwest Properties.
ACKNOWLEDGMENT OF SALE, Indonesian Petroleum."

Damn, he thought, *no end to the paperwork needed to do anything anymore today.* Still reading, he put the phone to his ear and said his name.

"Hello, Mr. Wells, this is Leslie Houton?" The young woman spoke in a heavy southern drawl, with a rising inflection, as if her statements were questions.

"Yes?" Brett asked vacantly, signing his name to an agreement to buy or sell a company or oil field or building. *Money's just rolling in. Damn fool phone call only takes up my time, which I got little enough of these days*, he thought.

"I'm with the SEC, in Washington, D.C.? And would like to get together with you this afternoon? About two o'clock. Will that work?"

Feeling a chill start up his back, Brett put down the pen and looked up from the pile of papers. "You're with the—why sure, sure, Miss, who? What's your name?"

"Houton. Leslie Houton."

He turned on the computer, his hand shaking. "I'd sure like to get with you, but ah'll tell ya, Ms. Houton, I got a meeting scheduled for after lunch and, well, what's it all about?" He was getting a headache.

"We can get into that then. I mean, what it's about. How about three, is that better?"

"Why, how about my public relations director? Will she do? Then maybe you and I..." Brett started thinking, *Damn, this is nothin I* caan't handle. Just some silly-ass little piss-ant outa law school tryin to be tough. Hell, she doesn't know tough. "Listen, how about makin it tomorrow and we'll have lunch? There's a restaurant just opened down the freeway. We'll go over everything you got, and have a coupla bottles of wine, some lobster. You like lobster?"

"No, Mr. Wells. Fact is, I can't eat fish; it makes me sick? And let's make it three o'clock today, because I'll be there at three anyhow, and I'll have a search warrant to go over your books?"

"But, now, just wait there a minute."

"No, I don't have a minute. And have your CFO there also, please, with the company filings over the last two years, and the details of Nugget's income statements before your last five takeovers. Just give us the records, my team can crunch the numbers."

Brett's head throbbed. "Yes, but—"

"And, also, we'd like to see your stockholder records. Especially those detailing the accounts set up with the Banco de Uruguay?"

Brett studied the computer screen:

NUGGET PETROLEUM, Most Active: 47 3/8, DOWN 3 1/2, 8,521,931 shares. Rumors regarding an SEC investigation; questions about their impending bond offering.

"I'm sure you know the rules on foreigners owning more than five percent of a domestic stock?"

Brett rubbed his forehead and closed his eyes. "Yes, no problems far's I know. I'll be ready. Three's good."

"Fine." She hung up.

He looked at the screen: DABNEY OIL, 46 7/8, DOWN 4.

Thing's dropping like a stone, he thought. He felt like throwing up. Starting toward the bathroom, he froze when the phone began ringing. He rushed back and grabbed the receiver and said, "Brett Wells."

"Mr. Wells, is this a good time?" The man had a slight Spanish accent.

Now, who the fuck's this? "Good a time as any."

"My name is Jorge Gonzalez, sir. I am with the Federal Bureau of Investigation."

His heart pounding in his ears, Brett could hardly hear. "Why, sure, hello there. Always have time for any kind of help I can give to the fine people at the Bureau. You know, we always contribute to your Christmas drive—"

"Yes, sir, and I want to thank you. But the reason I called, well, every now and then we cooperate with agencies even though we technically don't have jurisdiction. And Interpol, you know, the international criminal investigators, why, they're sending some agents here from Buenos Aires. There are a few questions about one of your directors, a certain gentleman named Ronaldo Rosas. It seems that Mr. Rosas has been taken into custody, and is giving information, very much information about Nugget Petroleum."

Looking again at the screen, Brett froze:

NUGGET PETROLEUM, Most Active, 28,253,431 shares. Down 5, 45 7/8 last. Probe widens to include CEO, Brett Wells, other board members. Butch Byrd agrees to assist in investigations, which include money laundering and racketeering. Foreign bank records subpoenaed.

He read it again. "I'll help any way I can."

"Good. Our men are on their way. Also let me assure you that we appreciate you assistance. Sometimes there are matters that come up that seem remote and strange. Hopefully, this is one of them and we are sorry if this causes any inconvenience."

***

The frantic knocking on the door startled Butch Byrd. *At this early in the morning?* he wondered. His watch showed 1:32. He got out of bed, snapped off the TV, and went to the front door of his Buenos Aires apartment. Through the peephole he saw a huge man wearing a brown camel hair coat and a wide-brimmed fedora.

"Oh, it's just Hammer," Butch said.

Hammer walked into the living room. His eyes greedily took in the red broadloom rugs, belle époque furniture; a sterling silver lamp atop an inlaid stand; heavy wooden chairs; an antique table with lion's claw legs; a writing desk next to a steel safe.

"And," Butch asked, "Where is Brett?"

"He not—come," Hammer said.

"Look, Hammer, it's late. Hell, if Brett wants to talk—" He noticed the bulge under Hammer's coat and a chill ran through him. "He's not coming, is he, Hammer? You—you're here for me."

"Wells says you talk too much. Everybody says you talk too much. That you decide to kill people but they don't die."

"Okay, okay. I messed up with Larson. But I made up for it, ask Brett. I told Pugliese a bunch'a crap. Brett told me what the Hand wanted me to say."

Butch looked into Hammer's dead eyes. He couldn't breathe. "I don't want to die," he said. "I'll take care of you, Hammer, you'll be rich, live in style. What do they pay you? I say rich, Hammer, look!" He took out his wallet and held out a stack of bills.

Hammer didn't look at the money. He started walking toward Butch.

"Oh, my God," Butch said, the room closing in on him. He smelled the night air from Hammer's coat. Keys rattled as he took them out of his pocket. "Look, Hammer." He ran toward the safe. A flick of a key, and the door opened. Inside were gold bars neatly stacked, piles of jewelry, currency.

"Hammer, whatever you—" As the knife tore into him, Butch felt no pain, just a numbness a dull throbbing near his belly. Heavy, gooey blood spurted out of him. *Damn mess*, he thought. *Rug's an antique. How can I ever get damn thing restored?*

"Hammer," Butch said. His voice sounded distant, as if it were coming from the bottom of a well. He felt the knife tear through him again, at the middle of his chest. He felt something inside of him rip. He started throwing up blood.

He wondered where Hammer was as he slid onto his knees. With his face on the floor, he tasted his own blood. *Stuff's thicker, much thicker than I imagined,* he thought. *He'll leave, I'll have someone in to clean.*

Butch started getting up, then felt a pain in his back, another tear. More blood spurted out of his mouth. He tried to speak but no sound came out. *I'll rest now, jest for a moment,* he thought, sliding onto the carpet.

As he lay there the light got dim, dimmer, then almost gone. He watched Hammer. Blood was smeared on his coat. The long-bladed knife lay on the carpet next to him. Hammer's face was red, and his eyes were small and hard. Butch watched him, sitting in front of the opened safe, trying on ring after ring. He wondered which ones Hammer would choose. He wanted to get up and assist, but he couldn't move. Then the lights went out.

Twelve

Dart stood wearing his khaki trader's jacket on the floor of the P-Coast. His rodent-like eyes watched one of the computer screens that surrounded the trading floor. The numbers of the stocks were almost all in red, meaning the prices were going down. He saw Steffie across the room, munching an apple while she watched a screen. She was smiling and bantering with other traders.

He walked over to her and asked, "Damn. What the hell're you so happy about?"

"Ah, what's money if you're not happy? I mean inner fulfillment." Steffie tossed the apple core into the trash.

And I'm rich, rich as Bill Gates, she wanted to scream. But she swallowed her words. Dart was one of her best friends, but nobody, nobody there ever told anybody what they were up to. Steffie was in bliss since she had shorted that huge piece of Nugget Petroleum months ago. She had told Dart about it, but he thought Nick was wrong, and hadn't shorted. Steffie had covered the short, and with the trade had made enough money to buy a small South American country.

Dart said, "You're talkin crazy, and grinning for weeks now. Liked you better when you were depressed. How much did you make in that trade?"

Steffie laughed. She always laughed now. Life was *so* okay. "Not enough," she said. Dart walked off. Feeling restless, a little bored, she wondered, *What's up with that old dog Nugget?* She made her way through the crowd of traders, and typed on a computer keyboard.

Up came "NUP, News." She pressed *Send*, and saw letters against a blue background: "HOT NEWS. Nugget Petroleum, Most active, up 2, last 9 1/8. Reorganization planned by Brett Wells. Brett Wells announced today that Nugget Petroleum plans to split and then spin off its exploration and development divisions. The exploration division will be majority owned by Brett Wells, CEO, and members of the

Nugget Petroleum board, and be named Nugget Exploration. Nugget's shareholders will receive one share of Exploration stock for each one hundred shares of Nugget Petroleum owned. A new class of security, Nugget Development Ltd., will then comprise the development division. Shareholders of Nugget will be granted options to purchase new Exploration shares, at a price to be determined. Brett Wells, soon to be confined to Bayshore Prison for a six-month stay, said he is 'confident this move will restore investor favor to this fine company.'"

You know, maybe it will work, Steffie thought. *Who knows? Who cares? You know what? Maybe I care.*

She typed some more keys: "NUP, Current News.

Washington, D.C. Honored today, Colonel Butch Byrd, Army hero of Desert Storm, and a consultant to the Army on the Afghanistan war on terrorism. He was supposed to be one of the five most important figures of Desert Storm. He spent months in Afghanistan, directing logistics in that mountainous region and hunting suspected terrorists. In private life, Colonel Byrd became involved in many business endeavors, most recently as a board member of Nugget Petroleum. He was found dead last month in his home in the El Telmo District of Buenos Aires. Police have ruled his death a suicide. Byrd was reportedly despondent over personal matters."

Her heart pounding, Steffie thought, *Nugget's gotta be a buy. All the bad news is out. Wells is taking pieces of the company, which means it's worth something, a lot probably. Damn, I made all that money, don't want to risk it. Do I? Do I have to? Gotta pee; but not sure I gotta. I was gonna leave, never get caught fucking with this crazy stock shit ever again. But Nugget: it's gotta be a buy.*

She stood up and raced over to the khaki-wearing crowd trading Nugget. "Any sellers?" she asked. Chattering erupted from the crowd. Like frenzied sharks, all of their dead eyes turned toward her.

"I got a hundred to sell, a hundred-thousand," a man said.

A woman said, "I'll sell two hundred seventy-five."

"What's your appetite?" another man, the size of a small house, asked.

"Size," Steffie said. "Show me size."

They all had their books out, their pens and pencils ready.

"Five hundred thousand," another man said.

"Last price?" she asked.

They all nodded.

"Done. You're done, you're all done," Steffie said.

Her legs shook as she walked off, thinking, that's it. *I've gone long eight hundred seventy-five thousand shares of that shit.* Her stomach hurt. *They're damn fools for selling.* The room spun. *It's going back up, isn't it? Isn't it? Oh sweet God, I'll be good, I promise. I know I forgot you—a lot, in fact—don't even think of you most of the time. Didn't go to church last time like I promised. But I will now; I'll even give money, anything.* Steffie decided: this time if she hit, she'd give her life to the church, become a nun or some such thing. And never, never, ever trade the stock market, or anything else, ever again.

***

Nick drove down the Champs Elysees in a black, four-door, Citroen sedan. Its wheels sprayed water as they ran through puddles. A typical Parisian winter day: cold and gray and damp. There were few people out, and as they meandered along the sidewalks he could see their breath when they exhaled. The cafes were packed. The Eiffel Tower appeared in the distance like a child's toy, a heavy, black, spidery jumble standing in silhouette against the dark day.

He looked at himself in the rear-view mirror. His beard was trimmed, and he noticed that the gray hairs now outnumbered the black. He thought that it couldn't be happening, that he was getting old. *Yes, well, maybe I am. It happens.*

With one hand he cocked the black beret on his head just right. Pushing down the gas pedal, he watched the speedometer climbing to 80, 85, 90. There were few cars on the outskirts of the city. A beat-up red Renault drove on the other side of the street, one of its headlights gone; a shiny new BMW sedan roared past, its lights illuminating the pavement and the trees on the sidewalks with brightness.

Nick watched each car warily, half expecting a rifle to appear out of a window.

Continuing to drive away from the city, he passed an old townhouse with cracked and decaying walls. Then, an empty field, a dilapidated barn leaning heavily to one side, another open field, deep furrows running its entire length. Now, nothing but the open road, his headlights cutting through the darkness, the lines in the middle of the road turning white from the car's headlights.

He leaned back, pushed down on the accelerator and took the car to over 130. *I'm finally free,* he thought, looking out into the emptiness. *Free. No problems with Linda anymore. No Butch Byrd or Brett Wells, or guys with long knives coming after me.*

Smiling, looking at himself in the rearview mirror, he decided that he was happy. *So this is what it feels like. How great. No responsibilities. A few bucks in my pocket; no one knows where I am. I answer to no one.*

Again he checked the mirror. It was hard to keep smiling. *Never was that good at bullshitting myself. Not for long. No, I'm not happy, whatever that means, happy. I'm lonely. No, you're free. I'm not free; I miss her. I miss… I miss* jogging, *of all things. I miss running by the ocean.*

He imagined waves lapping up to the bench by the jogging path, and gulls overhead, flapping their wings and diving to the water. The images filled him, and the French countryside vanished and he smiled. Then loneliness reappeared as the trees by the side of the road in Paris reappeared. He reasoned that he couldn't leave Paris, not now. Not when… *what about my painting? I'm just about to break through. I sold two, for a thousand dollars each. I could make it as a painter. And the teachers here are great, but, but, I want to go back.* He thought some more. *You what? What? I miss the market. I liked taking Nugget from nowhere to sixty. Wonder what they're all doing now?*

The speedometer was at 160. *I miss Linda. But Thad, what about Thad? I don't care about Thad.*

The thought of her ate into him and would not let go. He found a fork in the road, turned, and started back to Paris. Outside the city, as soon as he could get a signal, he called her on the cell phone. He heard, "This is Linda and Thad Thackery. We will be out of town until March fourth. Please leave a message and—" Nick hung up. *That's three weeks,* he thought. *She won't be back for three weeks. Where the hell is she?*

The Citroen purred now as it ran at a steady pace. He wondered where everyone was, and that empty feeling started in his gut. *Where's the way home?*

He got to his room and packed up, then drove to the airport and booked a flight to San Francisco, leaving early the next morning. He'd sleep at the airport, on a bench. What the hell, he was done with Paris anyway, for now. All they had was first class, twenty-three hundred bucks. *So what*, he figured, *they might shoot me as I get off the plane. Might as well enjoy it.*

***

Nick flipped the light switch back in his apartment in San Francisco. In the living room, the mahogany armoire with its gold-leaf carvings shined in the light. The tree outside his window had grown over the months, its limbs playing taptaptap on the window.

The window was slightly ajar. *Did I leave it open?* he wondered. *Did someone break in? Oh, hell, probably not.* Nick looked around, then walked in and dropped his bag.

The apartment smelled musty. He opened the window, and the cold air rushed in. It felt good. He walked through the bathroom, the bedroom closet and kitchen. There was no one there. He pushed down the red messages button on the phone.

A man's voice said, "Yes. Mr. Larson? Sorry I missed you. I am Gustav Atshuler, and I head up the management arm of Deutsche Bank, out of Hamburg. Well, we wish to expand our U.S. operation, and want to speak with you about spearheading it for us? We have about three hundred billion under management now, that is, globally. We want to establish a beachhead in the States. Nothing major, maybe raise fifteen or twenty billion or so. Quite frankly, we've heard good things about you. Call me? Four-oh-one-five-six-nine-two, in Hamburg, Germany. A-t-s-h-u-l-e-r."

Nick played it again, thinking, *What? Someone wants to hire me? For big bucks? Me? Why?*

He clicked on to the next message, and a woman said, "Mr. Larson? This is Nancy Rosen at UCB Switzerland; you know, the old Union Bank of Switzerland? We knew of your Nugget Petroleum call, saw the company collapse after that, believe me we have our sources..." She went on and on about how smart he was, and ended with a job offer, including a salary in the millions.

He thought about all that money. But something else was on his mind. *I can't,* he thought, *go back to corporate. Raise money for someone else to manage and go to meetings and schmooze out on the golf course. Hell, I don't even play golf. I paint. And I jog. And I want to go home but there's no home to go to. Just this.*

Looking at the trees shaking in the wind, he figured it would to rain tomorrow. In San Francisco you could always tell rain's coming because the wind kicked up at night. He was glad to be back.

He checked another message. Brett's voice filled the room. "Hey, Larson, look, all's okay with me. With you, I mean. You were right about us, yeah, we fucked up, should'a played it straight, could'a stayed out of trouble but that's all past, live and learn, I say. Give me a call, would'ya? Not my fault those damn fools that invested out there couldn't figure it out. You did. Don't worry, the Hand and damn Butch Byrd messed everything up. Look, make it soon 'cause I gotta go away. Who gives a shit. Short stay in prison may be just what'ah need."

Think I need to see him. Can I trust him? He slid open a drawer in the armoire and placed the derringer there, secure in its holster.

He played another message.

"Where the fuck're you? This is Zellon. Hey, hot shot, Zellon. What're you doin? Hosin Linda while her old man lays there like he just had a lobotomy or something? Hey, look, seriously, I ain't got all day. Call me. Zellon. Nice call on Nugget. Guess I owe you a cup of coffee; you can leave the tip. Hey, Larson, guess who I'm fuckin now? Ah, what do you care? You got Miss Pacific Heights Queen who would not even deign to talk to a guy like me. I care? I care? I can buy and sell her, and half the other phony bastards screwing each other in secret in Pacific Heights. That goes for Nob Hill too. Nick, call me, let's do lunch, like they say in L.A. We'll go to Tadich's. You like Tadich's. Hey, dead Philip's wife Isabel called me about Nugget after you told Ted to have her sell. I told her I did, she should too. Don't know what the hell… no, hell no, she's not who I'm screwing. Or is it whom? Why am I wasting my breath, I gotta go. Call me. Zellon. This is final, my last to you, hello and now goodbye."

Nick laughed. He played the message again and laughed some more. Then he went downstairs, brought up his paintings and bags and sat on the couch. *No message from her. Ah, the hell with it. Just leave her alone. But I can't. I have to. But I can't.*

He called her. The phone rang a few times before a recording said, "You have dialed a number that is not in service. If you are not sure of the number please check with your operator and dial the number again. Thank you for using Pacific Bell."

He tried again: same message.

He called dialed information and gave Linda's name. "No, sorry," he was told, "nothing for that listing in San Francisco. Do you want me to try Marin?"

He walked over to the window. The street outside was deserted. A few wisps of fog drifted by. *Damn, I'd almost rather have bullets than* this. *Where the hell is she?*

***

Waves pounded onto black rocks, then broke up and washed away, white and foamy. Nick watched a woman jogging toward him on the path. He wondered if she was Linda. The wind jostled her short hair as she ran. He thought Linda had lost weight. *Why am I so excited about her?* he wondered. He didn't know, didn't care.

He stood there in black shorts and running shoes, as she got closer. *No, that's not her. If it were, I'd apologize for all the times I left.* The memory of Linda's lilac perfume mingled with the smell of the ocean. *If she were only here.*

He imagined that she'd say, "Oh Nick." He'd kiss her, then they'd watch the ocean crash into the rocks. Her hair and the band around her forehead would be sweaty from running. "You, you have a goatee," she'd say. "I sort of like it."

"Sort of?" he'd ask.

"I'll get used to it," she'd say, laughing.

And then he'd say, "I had a beard but shaved it off. I didn't want a full beard. I grew it back and shaped it into a goatee when I left Paris. I like Paris, but it seemed so lonely this time..."

He wondered why this time Paris was different. Looking at the ocean, he thought, *If she were here, we'd start to jog.*

Nick started running with an imaginary Linda. First, the hard part, running as the wind blew in across the bay. Soon, he thought, *Man, this running's harder than I remembered.* He kicked up stones and sticks as he ran.

Above and a little ahead were the black supporting girders of the Golden Gate Bridge. In the water a girl in a surfboat, her hair blowing in the wind, held on to the white sail, which was filled with air. The surfer hung on to her boom, struggling to keep the board balanced. More wind surfers were off in the distance. Nick remembered Linda and he planned to learn that. The dark blue water of the bay contrasted with the lighter blue of the overhead sky.

Nick ran faster. Turning under the bridge, he started back to the Marina, back to the tiny coffee houses on the narrow streets by the water. *Well, I can still run*, he thought. *And I'll see her soon, won't I?*

He got home. He cleaned up and started a painting. It didn't work. He got up and decided to walk up and down Nob Hill. Passing Isabel's apartment building, he figured, what the hell, might as well stop by. The doorman smiled, and sent him up on the elevator.

"Now, look here. What a surprise this is," Isabel said, smiling and opening the door. Lines spread wildly across her face to the corners of her mouth. Through the large windows behind her, the blue waters in the bay gleamed in the orange afternoon sun.

"How about staying for lunch?" She led Nick into the dining room. Even more pictures of Philip Morgan sat atop a table.

"No, thanks. Just came by to see how you're doing. When I left it wasn't the best of times."

"No. No, it wasn't. And I didn't know what to do. Why, I called and called you and then when that nice Mister… Pistol? What was his name?"

Nick laughed. "Gunn. Ted Gunn."

"Yes, that was it. After he called and told me to sell those shares of Nugget I have, why, then I called some of Philip's old people."

"Lenny Zellon."

"Yes. And, oh, I was so *perturbed* when you left word for me to sell that stock. I hate to be told that something I have is not good. But by then you were… I didn't know where. And nobody else did either."

Isabel sat down and took a sip of wine. Philip's pictures stared on silently. "I thought maybe something had happened to you. Then I worried. You shouldn't just leave like that. People *care* about you, don't you see?"

Nick wondered, *Where is she*? The room felt empty.

"And then, after what happened to that Nugget Petroleum, and those awful people, why, I had no idea what they were up to. That you saved me from losing money—now I don't mind a small loss, mind you, everyone knows that there's risk, at least that's what I'm told, but something like that—why, it would've been a lot! And I am so grateful."

"Good," he said. "And… what's new?"

"Like what?"

"Oh, you know. Anything with, let's say Thad and… Linda, for instance," Nick said.

"Poor man." Isabel shifted in her chair. "And Linda. Why, she seems not at all like her old self."

"They, they're still here?"

"Oh, yes. Linda found a full-time care place for Thad. She did her homework, poor thing, to find him the best place she could. In Arizona, I think."

"Where, where in Arizona?" Nick asked, picking his fingernail.

"Oh, I don't know. Arizona. It's all the same, isn't it? Would you care to stay for lunch?"

"I—thanks, but I have still a lot to do."

"Of course. They're leaving soon."

"Where are they now?"

"She's at a hotel, and he's at the hospital, now that they've sold the house. Got a good price, too. He's not doing well, poor man. She looks a fright. I have lamb."

"Thank you, but I have—"

"Poor man."

"What hospital is he—"

"Oh Nick. I so appreciate... I could have lost a lot of money."

"Yes. Okay. In the city?"

"What, dear boy?"

"The hospital. Is it in the city?"

"No, somewhere... No."

"Where? Where's the hospital?"

"Somewhere, Marin or Oakland or... I don't know. They all have such strange names outside of San Francisco, dear boy. Besides, what's the difference?"

***

There was not a cloud in the sky as Nick rushed down California Street. In the financial district, along the bank buildings, the sidewalks were packed. The spring tourist season was just underway. A group of people in front of the restaurant wore badges: "Jack Fenster, Denton, Texas; Sally Rinds, Omaha, Nebraska; Patty Emken, Falls River, South Dakota."

Tadich's was embossed in gold script on the front window. He squeezed through them to the old, heavy door of the restaurant. He opened the door and pushed through the crowd inside. The smell of fried fish and alcohol was heavy in the air. Conversation and laughter roared through the room. A heavy, highly polished bar ran from one end of the room to the other. Ted Gunn sat on a stool, lifting his glass and drinking and laughing. On both sides of him traders all leaned toward each other, gesticulating while they talked.

Nick saw Steffie and Lenny at a table near the window. The mid-day sun shone in and reflected off of her sunglasses. On the plate in front of her was a bit of fish and some French fries. She was drinking a beer. The leavings of lettuce and shrimp salad were left on Lenny's plate.

"I'm hungry, sorry I'm late," Nick said, pulling a chair out at their table and sitting down. He ripped a hunk of bread off a small loaf, buttered it and took a bite.

A gray-haired waitress walked over, carrying a green, plastic-covered menu and a glass of water. "About time, Nick," she said, setting down the glass and handing him a menu. "They were getting worried."

"Thanks, Emma," he said. "You have chowder today?"

"The sun's up, isn't it? Tadich's has chowder every day."

"I gotta go," Steffie said.

"In a minute," Lenny said.

"The chowder. And a mineral water."

Emma walked off. Nick took another hunk of bread. "Sorry," he said, chewing viciously. "I got to painting and forgot the time, and forgot to charge my cell phone, and couldn't call—"

"Yeah, yeah," Lenny said. "Big painter now. Guy comes back from Europe, biggest name on the Street, and all he does is paint. Big man until the SEC catches up. I'm sure they'd like to know about your little European sojourn." His rat eyes turned back to Steffie. "How about it?"

"Nick can be as late as he wants. No big deal. Not as far as I'm concerned," she said. "How about it?" she said, returning Lenny's gaze. "If you were the only man left in the whole wide world, I'd still say no. I'd rather be gay. No question. Or I could abstain from sex forever. Does that answer—"

"Oh, you're duckin me," Lenny said. "Come on, we'll go rollerblading. That's what you young hard-bodies with no brains like to do, isn't it? Whatever. Or we can go to the gym, and afterwards we'll go to a health food bar. You like health food, don't you? You ever have sex in a health food store? I'll buy you a health food store. Look, if you're bothered about our age difference. Thirty years isn't that big a deal, not for me."

Steffie got up, flashed Lenny a look expressing that she regarded him as little more than a loathsome maggot. "Before I'd go out with you, Zellon, I'd stick needles in my eyes." She started walking off, turned and said, "Nick, in case I haven't told you, you're the man," then disappeared into the crowd at the front door.

Lenny put his face up to Nick's. "See? She's crazy about me. Know why? You know, Larson? Size. That's it, it's all true. Freud just couldn't figure it out." He held up his hands, palms facing each other at about shoulder width. "Chicks dig the long ball, and that's me. Zellon."

Nick chewed on a hunk of bread.

The crowd had gotten thicker and the buzz of conversation louder. Ted Gunn walked over from the bar, with a little man wearing a bowtie. "Hey you guys," Ted said, "this's Brad Gilbreath from the Montgomery Conference over at the Fairmont." They all shook hands and introduced themselves.

Emma put a bowl of chowder in front of Nick. He started eating; it was hot. "How's the conference going?" he asked.

"Packed," Ted said. "The market's hot again, and the attendance is the biggest—"

"I heard of you," Gilbreath said to Nick. "You're the one who blew the whistle on Nugget."

Nick kept eating his soup.

"That's him," Lenny said. "And now the hot-shot is... what do you do, Nick?"

He kept eating. "I paint, and I'm not sure what else."

"Well, nice to meet you all," Gilbreath said, and left.

Ted Gunn sat down. "Nice guy. He runs about a few billion in Dallas. Every couple months or so he gives me trades to do, maybe two, three hundred thousand shares. Don't know where he gets his ideas, and don't care. I just trade 'em." Ted slurred words, his eyes half closed. "Sons'a bitches come and go, but I'm still here. 'Til they carry me out."

A waiter came by and placed a fresh drink in front of Ted. He put his finger in, stirred, took a sip. "Hey, you hear about Willie Bornstein?"

"No," Nick said.

Ted smiled, looking like a Cheshire cat with many chins. "After the Nugget bonds were pulled, Willie looked like on his way out. Then Malcolm Miller came in, and saved the company. Malcolm goes out and finds the deals, then feeds the stock to his friends. Everybody's gettin well. They're sayin he'll take over Spence, Trask, sell it to a bank, but who knows?" Ted took a swallow. "I just trade 'em." He dropped a fifty-dollar bill on the table, drained the glass, said, "Trade stocks, and keep running faster than these kids we keep hiring."

Nick kept eating.

"But before long they'll replace us, all the traders, with machines. They'll have computers match the bid, asked prices twenty-four hours a day. We won't be market makers any more, buying and selling for our own account. We'll hire computer nerds and pay them peanuts to set up and monitor the systems. The machines'll make money for the partners, and the traders'll be unemployed."

Ted stood up. "Sons of bitches, if they had their way, we'd all make the minimum wage. See that jerk over there?" He pointed to a man a few tables away. He was reading a magazine that had a picture of a computer on its cover. "He runs a few billion. Used to trade with me. Hell, now he does it all with a couple computers plus a few damn, part-time consultants. His record's lousy, but he spends his time marketing and the money keeps pourin in."

Ted was unsteady on his feet, and he stood there as if he had nowhere to go. "Ah, the hell with it. I just trade 'em. I got an early day. See you guys." He walked off and was swallowed up by the crowd, like vanishing into thin air.

The crowd had gotten even thicker. There were stacks of dirty dishes on the tables; glasses with melting ice, slices of lime, a lot of the glasses lipstick-stained.

Nick finished and wiped his lips. Through the window he saw a cable car making its way up California Street; another coming down. Many of the tourists at the front door mistakenly wore short-sleeve shirts, as visitors often do. Although the sun was bright, the air was cold; tall buildings blocked sunlight in places in the financial district.

"Guy's scared shitless he'll be out of a job," Lenny said. "Street just changes. There's always a way to make money."

A big man wearing a hat with its brim just over his eyes walked by the window. Nick's heart was pounding. Before he knew it, he had taken out his derringer; its barrel glistened in the sunlight.

Lenny's face turned white.

The man walked on and was swallowed up by the crowd outside.

That was him, Nick thought. *Hammer, I'm sure.*

Lenny sat erect as Nick slipped the derringer back into its holster. *Was that really Hammer? It was. Maybe not. I don't know.*

"Hey," Lenny said, "what the hell you doing with that thing? What is this? War against the Taliban breaking out here in fucking Tadich's, for Christ's sake?"

"Look, I just thought—"

Lenny got up. "Yeah, yeah. Get a grip. Guns? Where're you coming from? Thought I had problems, but guns?" He gave Nick a look, walked off.

Maybe I am going crazy, Nick thought. Through the window, the sun pouring in, he watched Lenny walk down the street. *How come I can't pull myself together? I got bills to pay, why can't I go make some money?* His fingers had red and blue paint splotched on them. On the top of his hands were more paint splotches.

I'm not going back to that corporate meat grinder. I'm finally breaking through. I'm not giving painting up again.

He paid the bill, wondering if he was losing it again.

***

The heavy beating sound of the huge blade swooshing above made the helicopter cabin shake. Below, in the gray Gulf of Mexico, just off of New Orleans, the water gathered into large waves, then broke, leaving trails of white foam. Nick felt dizzy looking down from the helicopter. A giant platform ship floated in the middle of the endless sea. The people scurrying about on its deck looked like ants. A black oilrig, about the size of a tall office building, was in the center of the ship.

Leaning across to Nick, Brett Wells said, "My people, hell, they're the best damn geological team west of the Mississippi, they say this well they're drillin'll pay out at about fifteen million cubic feet'a gas a day. Great bid'ness. Get richer every day."

Nick thought he looked older. Brett's hair was unkempt, and he had a slight double chin. His hairline had receded quite a bit.

The helicopter descended steadily, and the drilling ship got larger. The pilot opened the cabin door and turned to face Brett. The lenses of his gold-framed sunglasses reflected the noonday sun. Smiling with large teeth, he said, "Better get ready, Mr. Wells."

Brett nodded, turned again to Nick. "This'll put us back in the hunt. Hell, no tellin how many zones down there we can drill. Yeah, I gotta go do this damn prison thing. Caan't get out of it. But soon's I do my time, I'll have three, maybe four ships here, dependin on the damn bankers. Sons of bitches. They love me now that I got good prospects again. And some money backin me."

Staring at him through the red glare of the sun, Nick said, "I think I saw Hammer. I'm concerned, Brett. You told me not to worry."

"Damn Butch Byrd." Brett's eyes narrowed into slits. "He's the one put out the hit on you. And you were makin us rich, but the Hand went along with him. I had to give him up, well, truth be known, the son-of-a-bitch was gettin too big, at least in his own mind. I told the Hand, well, I'm not proud of this, him or me's way I saw it, I told the Hand it was Butch's idea to hire you. Non'a this for you to worry over. They don't even know you blew up the company, they're plenty busy with other things. Besides, hell, I'd like to use you again. I told them you're plenty okay. But you never know what they're thinking."

The cabin was stuffy. "Anyhow," Brett said, a smile playing over his face, "you were supposed to be taken out in the library, in Buenos Aires. Hammer couldn't get it done, then you called me, I made a few calls, got wind of it. Why you lookin so worried? You're still here."

The helicopter shook as it descended. Nick felt nauseated.

"Soon's I get settled in a cell—E-mail, faxes, caan't think of anything ah caan't do behind bars. It's one of those low security prisons. Great. Ahh'I work on my golf game. 'Bout time I had a break."

The helicopter dropped slowly toward a giant "X" on the ship deck. The sun, wind, chopping motion of the helicopter, the height, all made Nick dizzy. He sweated. Below him, men in ankle-length, blue slickers stood on the deck. The slickers and their hoods blew about from the helicopter's propellers.

Brett shouted above the noise, "Anyhow, keep in touch. I'll be back on top again. All this stuff? No big thing."

"Yes. Sure," Nick said. *It's no big thing,* he thought. *Just my life.*

With a thud, the helicopter set down. Its doors were opened; heavy, salty sea air poured into the cabin; brilliant sunshine; the noise of seagulls. Brett got up and hopped into the crowd of blue slickers that quickly surrounded him.

***

While in the shower, Nick heard the ringing of his cell phone. No one called him anymore. He figured it was probably a cold-caller: *Sir, are you happy with your long-distance carrier? Would you try Sprint? No obligation; only a dime a minute, anywhere, anytime, no fooling. And we'll give you fifty-thousand bonus mile on any airline of your choosing.*

He decided he was just getting grumpy. Not sleeping much does that.

After toweling off, he tossed on a pair of jeans, button-down-collared white shirt, and a pair of Doc Martens. He'd found them in Paris, most comfortable boots he'd ever worn. Of course now they were are all over San Francisco. Or Houston, or New York, or just go on the Internet. He thought about the global economy, and how it makes everything available everywhere. He thought he was missing out, that something had been misplaced. He wondered why he was so restless. *Don't sell some paintings soon I can't pay my mortgage,* he thought. *Have to go corporate. I won't, I just won't. Okay, stiff upper lip and all that.* Coagulated paint was under his fingernails, on his hands. Paintings were stacked next to the armoire in the living room. He pondered the usual dinner question: go get take-out or cook something? *I don't want to go out, see anybody. Ahh, I'm not hungry; I'll have yogurt.*

He pressed down a button on his cell phone. "You have one new message. First new message, sent today, at 7:35 P.M.: "Hi, Nick, Linda.

I'm... we're at the airport, San Francisco. The plane's been delayed for about an hour. I... I thought I'd give you a call. I don't know what you're doing, I didn't call, what with Thad being... he's, well, I can fill you in. I'm at the United ticket counter, that's United domestic. Maybe you can make it... if you can?"

If I can, if I can make it to you? I'd crawl there on all fours if I had to.

After playing the message again, he frantically threw on a black jacket. He rushed out of the door, slamming it behind him. A moment later he came back and grabbed the car keys; they jangled as he stuffed them into his pocket. Halfway out of the door, he returned and strapped on the derringer.

Racing down 101 South, almost no cars on the road, he watched the lights of the city recede behind him in the mirror. Just before the San Jose exit he saw the distant lights of the San Francisco International Airport, and headed straight toward them. After parking, he raced up the escalator and followed a sign, *Departures*. As he rushed to the United counter, he spotted Linda. Thad sat in his wheelchair, looking at nothing.

She'd lost weight. She had lines on her face that he hadn't seen before. He picked his way through gray-haired travelers with gaily-sparkling eyes; airline captains and flight attendants in blue uniforms, with winged pins on their lapels; young couples, the parents worn-out with the exhaustion of traveling with children.

She smiled and waved, seeing him. His heart pounding, he rushed up and pulled her close. He felt the heat in her body. When he tried kissing her, she nudged him back.

"Not here, darling," she said, looking around.

"Okay. I was just so happy."

"I understand. There'll be plenty of time. You see, I found a place where Thad can live. I'll stay with him and I'm free on the weekends "

"So, just that, that's all I get?" Everybody except Linda had disappeared in the airport.

She smiled, an obligatory, proper smile, as one would to a waiter. *Fuck your proper smile,* he thought. *Fuck everything. I need you.* "I need you. Don't go."

She studied him. "How could I not go? It's Thad. Don't you see?"

Nick couldn't see, see Thad or anything else, just Linda's face; her perfect teeth now as she smiled. "Why didn't you call before?"

"I knew, I knew it would be like this. I didn't know what to do. I can't leave him. Still, I want you, but... I couldn't call."

Nick noticed a janitor in a white uniform emptying trash; a woman carrying a baby; a young soldier, hurrying by with frightened eyes, wearing dress greens. *No, she couldn't call*, Nick thought. *She's as confused as I…*

He looked at Thad, and felt terribly cold and alone. *What am I doing here?* he wondered. *Because I love her, that's it. But so what? How did we all get this way?*

An announcement was made: "For those passengers traveling on United flight eight-oh-nine to Albuquerque, we will begin boarding momentarily. First to board will be those who need assistance and first class…"

"I have to go." She started weeping, and grasped the handles of the wheelchair. "Oh, Nick. We're not going far. You can fly there in a few hours." She wiped tears away. "We have it good, don't we? Isn't it okay?"

Nick took her hand. It was hot, like fire, like his. "I, I don't know what's okay."

"I really, really have to go."

"I'll miss you."

"We'll talk about it. Isn't that what friends are for? We can be friends, can't we?"

Nick nodded yes, at the same time thinking, *No, we can't. But I see it, I love her, doesn't that change anything? No, it doesn't. A bitch, but it's over, no, love changes nothing, not here.* He kept nodding, not even knowing he was continuing. "Yes. Friends. Sure, we can be friends."

She kissed him lightly on the lips. "Come soon, please." Then she wheeled Thad off. Just before entering the boarding area, she turned and waved.

He made himself stand there and wave back. She smiled, then disappeared. He turned sharply and started walking. *This all sucks*, he thought, passing the magazine shops, the luggage shops, the hot dog stands in the airport. *We can't be friends, worse, we can't be lovers. Is this how it ends? I guess so. Keep walking, one foot after the other. Put on your dark glasses. Inside? Yes, better put them on. Don't want to be seen walking through the airport like this, not with all these tears.*

MAX ISAACMAN is an investment advisor and was a columnist at the *San Francisco Examiner* and other publications. Among his appearances are CBS MarketWatch and Bloomberg, and his published investment books include *How to Be an Index Investor* and *The Nasdaq Investor*.